"I don't expect you to marry me just because we had sex. I don't expect any kind of commitment."

Caroline's words brought Zach up short. "You *should* expect a commitment!" he shouted at her. "A woman like you should demand nothing less from a man after what he did—what I just did—to you."

She stared at him, blinking. He knew he wasn't making a lot of sense, but he couldn't help plunging on.

"You *deserve* a man who can stand by you. You deserve—" Dear Lord, she deserved the best of everything, and he had nothing to offer her, not even a future. There were no words to explain what he had to do, or how deeply he felt his loss.

"What you're trying to say," she whispered, "is that you're not that man and never can be."

"Right." The one word broke his heart.

Dear Reader,

Welcome to a new year of reading here at Silhouette Intimate Moments. As always, we've got six top-notch books for you, starting with Sharon Sala's *Shades of a Desperado*. This Intimate Moments Extra title is a compelling tale of a love that would not die, and the lovers—a desperado and his lady of the night—who are reincarnated in twentieth-century guise to complete the circle begun so many years ago. Theirs is a tale you won't soon forget.

In *Angel's Child*, Kathryn Jensen creates a hero whose heavenly mission brings him face-to-face with the all-too-earthly feelings he harbors for the heroine. Suzanne Brockmann brings her TALL, DARK AND DANGEROUS miniseries to a close with *Frisco's Kid*, the tale of a man who thinks he has no future, and the woman and child who transform his life. Welcome Kayla Daniels to the line with *Wanted: Mom and Me*, and join an on-the-run mother and child as they find safety—and a renewed sense of family—in the person of one very sexy sheriff. Ingrid Weaver is back with *On the Way to a Wedding...* You won't want to miss a single pulse-pounding page as lawman Nick Strada fakes his own death—then has to take beautiful Lauren Abbot on the run with him. Finally, welcome Cheryl Biggs, whose *The Return of the Cowboy* captures the feel of the West and all the passion you could want.

Enjoy them all—then come back next month for even more of the most exciting romance reading around...only in Silhouette Intimate Moments.

Happy New Year!

Leslie Wainger
Senior Editor and Editorial Coordinator

Please address questions and book requests to:
Silhouette Reader Service
U.S.: 3010 Walden Ave., P.O. Box 1325, Buffalo, NY 14269
Canadian: P.O. Box 609, Fort Erie, Ont. L2A 5X3

ANGEL'S CHILD

KATHRYN JENSEN

Published by Silhouette Books

America's Publisher of Contemporary Romance

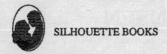

SILHOUETTE BOOKS

ISBN 0-373-07758-0

ANGEL'S CHILD

Printed in U.S.A.

KATHRYN JENSEN

has written many novels for young readers as well as for adults. She speed walks, works out with weights and enjoys ballroom dancing for exercise, stress reduction and pleasure. Her children are now grown. She lives in Maryland with her husband, Bill, and her writing companion, Sunny, a lovable terrier-mix adopted from a shelter.

Having worked as a hospital switchboard operator, department store sales associate, bank clerk and elementary school teacher, she now splits her days between writing her own books and teaching fiction writing at two local colleges and through a correspondence course. She enjoys helping new writers get a start, and speaks "at the drop of a hat" at writers' conferences, libraries and schools across the country.

To Mallory Kelly Jensen, born October 3, 1995—
the most beautiful angel I know.

Chapter 1

The August sun beat mercilessly down on Zane Dawson's muscled shoulders and back. All around him, other men, stripped to the waist, their bodies glistening, cursed the blazing orange sphere overhead and wiped trails of sweat from sunburnt faces with sinewy forearms.

Temperatures rarely rose so high in Connecticut, even at the peak of summer. But thermometers in Hartford had rocketed to over 100 degrees for the eighth day in a row, breaking all records, and a man didn't stop putting up a building the size of the E.P. Madison Commercial Towers just because of a heat wave.

Zane rolled up the blueprints he'd been checking and blinked droplets of perspiration out of his eyes, to more clearly observe his job site. *His,* he thought automatically, much as a medieval duke would have surveyed a village within his domain. He took his job personally.

"Don't look like no engineer I ever seen," a gruff voice taunted from behind him.

Zane laughed and poked the neon yellow construction helmet back from his forehead. He spun around to face Matt Trainer, his job foreman. "A shirt and tie may be my usual uniform, but losing the fancy duds makes a hell of a lot of sense on a day like this."

The older man nodded, grinning. "Worst heat I've known since that job I did down in Washington, D.C., 'bout fifteen years ago. Same as this—humidity so thick you could cut it like a damn birthday cake. That's on top of it bein' 110 degrees in the shade."

"And I'll bet you didn't see much shade, either," Zane added, thinking of some of his own experiences with uncooperative weather conditions at construction sites.

Starting in his teenage years, Zane had scrambled along scaffolding, welded girders and balanced on I-beams through driving rain, freezing blasts of wind and scorching heat. He'd labored alongside tough, good men who knew their jobs and the dangers that went with them.

Under the apt tutelage of veterans like Matt, he'd learned to cuss with exuberance and signal the passing of a pretty woman to his mates with a low, appreciative whistle. He'd hung out after hours at local bars, sharing cold beers and spicy stories of hot dates, more male fantasy than fact. He'd had a fine time growing up with the guys, enjoying their easy camaraderie...but then he'd wanted more.

Zane had enrolled in night classes at the local community college in Manchester, then transferred to the University of Connecticut, in nearby Storrs, where he'd eventually earned his engineering degree. These days, he was one of the youngest, most-in-demand construction engineers on the East Coast, working with top New England architects. Zane credited his early job-site experience for his ability to predict problems and deal with them effectively.

His professional status also gave him some nice perks. With a larger income, he could afford to drive a white BMW convertible with buff leather seats as soft as warm butter. He could treat an attractive woman to a meal at the best restaurant in Hartford or a lusty weekend on Cape Cod. He liked his new life, he liked his job—and, most of all, he liked that he was only thirty years old and had a long, long time to enjoy both of them.

"Hey, Zane," Matt said, nudging him with an elbow, "you listenin', boy? I said, don't you think we should haul up that generator about now? It's almost quittin' time."

Zane blinked, refocusing on the older man's face. Matt had been the foreman on the first construction job he'd had, the summer of his junior year of high school, and he'd treated him like a son ever since. The fact Zane now had a degree and was his boss made no difference in their relationship. And, although the man was in his mid-fifties, he was wiry, strong, and had more savvy about putting up a building than anyone Zane knew.

"Sure." He looked beyond Matt toward the crane operator, who seemed to be waiting for his signal. "Take her up, Sid!"

Suspending the most valuable pieces of their portable equipment aboveground was one way crews discouraged looting at construction sites. They still lost considerable building materials to after-hours theft, but replacing a generator could cost thousands of dollars and days of valuable time.

Zane listened absently while Matt chattered on about his family. He was more concerned with the details of shutting down the site for the night than keeping up on family news. Shading his eyes, he watched the enormous steel box that weighed close to a ton soar effortlessly into the air at the end of a massive chain. He cupped wide hands around his mouth. "Swing her over that way!"

The operator didn't seem to hear him.

Zane removed his helmet and waved it over his head. "Over there, Sid! By the backhoe!"

At last the man signaled that he understood. He threw the appropriate levers to maneuver the metal dinosaur. Slowly, with a grinding roar, the crane swung the dangling generator above the work site in a semicircular path.

Satisfied that everything was under control, Zane reached for his shirt and used it to mop up the sweat beading on his face and trapped in the clipped blond hairs on his head.

"Guess I'm just about at my wit's end with that boy," Matt finished, looking at Zane as if he expected a response.

Zane stared blankly at him.

"You didn't hear a word I said, did you?" Matt asked, his irritated expression easing into a smile. "Good boy, you *should* concentrate on your work."

"I'm sorry, what's this about your son, Matt?"

"Just that my boy, the youngest one, Tony... he's got himself mixed up with a bad crowd. Ever since school got out in June, he's been hanging around these boys, some of 'em are doing drugs, and I suspect at least one is selling. There has been a rash of break-ins and car thefts in our neighborhood. I can't prove anything, but I'd swear that gang has something to do with 'em. Tony's a good boy, but he's just got too much time on his hands, and there's another whole month before school starts up again.''

"Sounds like he needs a job, something labor intensive to drain off a little of that adolescent energy.''

"That's just the trouble,'' Matt said with a sigh, "there's nothing much around for kids like him. Most stores and businesses 'round here hire college kids for the summer, and the fast-food joints have all the help they need.''

Zane nodded, studying the familiar pattern of dents and scratches in his helmet as he turned it thoughtfully in his hands. "Well, you're the foreman, but if you want my opinion, I believe we could use at least one more apprentice on this job. We never have enough time to set up properly in the morning or to break down quick enough at the end of the day. One more pair of hands would sure make things easier on all of us.''

Matt's face lit up. "I was hopin' you'd say that. Thanks, thanks a lot.''

Zane slapped his old friend on the back. "No problem. Hey!'' He laughed. "I'm just glad *I* don't have kids to mess up my life the way they do every father's.''

"You wouldn't say that if you had 'em,'' Matt said, suddenly serious, a quiet but proud gleam in his steely eyes, "There's no way to explain how important a man's children become to him.''

"I don't know about that. A bunch of rug rats can cramp a guy's style, if you know what I mean.'' Zane winked roguishly at the older man, and gave him a playful shove.

Even as his hand rebounded off Matt's shoulder, Zane sensed that the sun's glare had suddenly been blocked.

"Heads up!'' someone shouted.

"Zane! Matt!'' another man bellowed.

He immediately looked around for the cause of the alarm. Matt had been thrown off balance while they'd been horsing around, and he was stumbling backward, a surprised but amused look on his face. No harm there.

Then another motion, from somewhere above caught Zane's attention. He shaded his eyes with his helmet and looked straight up.

For a fraction of a second, the dark shape over his head failed to register as being anything in particular. Metallic colored, beginnings of rust, squarish, solid . . .

Then Zane knew, with cold certainty, that it was the generator. And its hulking form seemed to be swelling, growing larger. His heart hammered in his chest. The sweat on his brow turned chill.

It's not getting bigger, his brain telegraphed him urgently, *it's falling!*

A ton of steel . . . falling on top of him . . . but he couldn't make his feet move . . . and his body felt like an iron pilaster, immovably sunk in a cement foundation. The chain had snapped, and the generator was plummeting, and there was nowhere to go and no time to go in and . . .

Then Zane knew he was going to die.

The light in the nursery looked golden that day. It glimmered off the water of Long Island Sound, through the window hung with dainty ruffled curtains, and flung itself gaily, like an impish playmate across the pastel-print sheets of the baby's crib. Caroline North stood with her hand resting on the crib's railing, looking down at the spot where her baby's head had lain, so sweetly, so softly, nestled amidst pink and blue balloons on linens she'd picked out herself.

A tear slid down her cheek, followed by another and another. The weight in her chest felt as if it were a lead anchor, pulling her down, down, down into the black crevice that had swallowed her up nearly a year before. Her three-month-old son, Jimmy, had fallen asleep one night. The next morning she'd been unable to wake him.

She recalled the doctor's words, intended to comfort her. "It's not your fault, Mrs. North. It's no one's fault. Sudden Infant Death Syndrome is a catch-all medical term that's not really definable. We understand only that something caused Jimmy's heart to stop beating in the middle of the night. He died painlessly, if that's any comfort to either of you."

Then her husband's words, minutes later when they were alone with their grief . . . "Not your fault, my ass. Didn't I tell you he seemed restless? Didn't I tell you to check on him?" Rob's anger stained his voice an ugly color, condemning her to guilt others said she shouldn't feel.

But Caroline *had* checked on Jimmy. She remembered lovingly stroking the soft, pale fuzz on his little head and covering him loosely with his blanket, and he'd been fine. But Rob seemed to need someone to blame for his son's death, and she was the only one available.

"Caroline?" a voice came from the kitchen.

She didn't answer, couldn't choke out a single word over the tears clogging her throat.

Suzanne Godfrey poked her head through the nursery door. "Oh God, what are you doing in here?" she whispered.

"Just...just remembering." Caroline pressed her fingertips over her eyes, hard, to stop them from burning. It didn't do any good.

"Oh, honey." Suzanne dashed across the room and brought her into the reassuring circle of her arms. "Don't do this to yourself. Come on, let's get you out of here."

Weeping copiously, Caroline allowed her friend and business partner to gently lead her out of the nursery and into the kitchen. Suzanne sat her down at the small, oak table, set a box of tissues on the table in front of her and put the teakettle on to boil.

"I'm making us both some tea," she stated in a firm voice that also said, *You will drink it and pull yourself together, and everything will be all right.*

Caroline reached for a tissue and blew her nose, then willed away the piercing ache in her heart. "I had to go in. I heard a sound, like a baby's cry, and I had to look at his crib to convince myself he wasn't really there."

"It's been a whole year, honey. Jimmy's gone."

"I know...I know." Caroline sighed.

"Look, it's your day off. The shop doesn't need you. Hell, it practically runs itself most of the time. Denise is tending the cash register right now." Denise McDaniel was the high school girl who came in on Fridays and weekends to help them at the Silver Whale, the gift shop they'd bought and ran together. Located on Water Street in Mystic, Connecticut, it catered to thousands of tourists who flocked all summer long to the New England town to visit the famous Mystic Seaport, a restored version of an eighteenth century whaling town.

"What's your point?" Caroline asked, between sniffles.

"The point is, on your day off you should be outside enjoying the beautiful weather. Go to the beach and take a long swim. Buy a ticket for a boat ride with the tourists. Order a pint of those fried clams you love. Get back into living again!"

Caroline shook her head.

"Why not?"

"I don't feel as if . . ." How could she explain what was tearing at her heart, without sounding as if she were looking for pity? "I don't deserve to be happy or—"

"You don't deserve happiness ever?" Suzanne broke in, sitting down across from her. "Is that it? You *let* your baby die—as if there was any way you could have prevented it—so now you have to pay for it the rest of your life? What a warped view of life!"

"Of course I don't think that," Caroline objected. "It's just too soon to forget."

Suzanne pulled her chair around to face Caroline's. She clamped her hands over the knees of Caroline's blue jeans. "Listen to me. You'll *never* forget. No one expects you to. But you should open yourself up to meeting people who can bring some joy into your life again."

"If you mean men, no thanks."

"They're not all insensitive jerks like Rob."

The teakettle began whistling violently. Caroline launched herself out of her chair, glad to have a reason to move. "I'm sure there are some nice men in the world," she admitted. "But have you ever thought that those are the ones I might want to avoid?"

Suzanne stared at her. "Now you've totally lost me."

"If I meet someone I really like and he likes me, he might expect me to marry him."

"Now that would really be horrible," she said with a wry twist to her lips.

"And he might want a family."

"So?"

Caroline lifted the teakettle off of the burner. "I'm *not* going to have another child. I can't risk the same thing happening again. It would kill me," she finished woodenly.

Suzanne nodded slowly. "I understand how you must feel. But does the doctor say it's likely?"

"No promises, one way or the other." Suddenly Caroline felt drained by the mere thought, compelled to sit down again. She collapsed back into her chair, leaving Suzanne to pour steaming water over tea bags in two mugs.

"So, maybe just date casually, have a good time. And if sex rears its ugly head," Suzanne said dryly, "there are ways of not getting pregnant these days."

"I know, but what if something goes wrong? Or what if I fall hopelessly in love and then I can't give this man the family he wants? He'd leave me just like Rob."

"Nobody will leave you 'just like Rob.' He's a cruel, selfish, twisted little man."

Caroline started trembling, first in her toes, the shivers traveling up through her limbs until her entire body was shaking uncontrollably. "But I really believed he cared about me. I thought we'd be together forever."

"Well, *I* never liked him," Suzanne said abruptly, dunking the tea bags fiercely. "But we won't go into *that*. The point is, you deserve someone much better than Rob could ever have been for you. But if you don't ever leave the shop or this apartment, you'll never find him."

Caroline looked on sadly as Suzanne finally quit drowning the paper pouches of apple-cinnamon herbs and brought the two fragrant mugs to the table. She longed to feel whole again, to be able to laugh and go dancing, take long walks on the beach while holding hands with someone special, do all of the other things she loved to do. But enjoying the company of other people seemed impossible as long as she carried the terrible pain in her heart that hadn't left her since Jimmy died.

They sat, drinking their tea in companionable silence. Eventually Caroline felt a thin ray of light slip into her heart. The darkest spells lasted less time these days, but they always came back. She smiled dimly at Suzanne across the table.

Suzanne said softly, "Every time I introduce you to a nice man, you panic and find ways to avoid seeing him when he asks you out. One of these days, you'll have to learn to trust again."

"I guess. But I don't know how. Sometimes I think I'll never get over Rob's defection." She concentrated on taking measured breaths, and gradually found she could control the trembling.

"How can I trust another man to stay with me and be strong enough to love me through tragedy as well as the good times?"

"He's out there, you have to believe he is," Suzanne said. "I didn't think I'd ever find a man who understood me, with all my crazy moods. But along came Ralph, and the three years we've been married have been the happiest of my life."

Caroline smiled, genuinely pleased for her friend. Suzanne and she had met in high school and knew each other better than their own families did. Suzanne had gone through some rough times, too, but quiet, intelligent Ralph Godfrey had come along and Suzanne had never looked back.

"I know he makes you happy. He's a good man," Caroline murmured.

"And yours is out there somewhere, honey. You just have to let him find you."

Caroline took one last deep, soul-cleansing breath. "Well, about all I can manage right now is lunch. How about we hit the Captain's Table and splurge on a double order of fried clams with french fries."

Suzanne threw back her head and laughed as she stood up. "Add a side of coleslaw—and I'll swear I'm in heaven."

Before Zane could actually see anything, he could feel his surroundings. It was as if every inch of his skin had been exposed and was being caressed by the softest breeze. The heat of the construction site seemed to have evaporated into the air, leaving only the fresh, coolness of a forest glade. He tried to remember what had happened just before the sudden darkness. He recalled the generator, only a few feet above his head, closing fast.

"Oh God," he groaned, "I *am* dead."

But he couldn't tell where, exactly, being dead had landed him. There was no light at all to help him see anything around him. If there was a heaven or a hell, how could he tell which he was in? Maybe being dead was just a nothingness, an endless nothingness.

How depressing, he thought. Immediately he was assaulted by a wave of regret for all the time he'd wasted and all the things he'd left undone...and dreams he'd had as a kid and sworn he'd never give up...dreams that would never be realized now.

"Aw, hell . . ."

"No," a voice stated, "that's not where you are."

Zane blinked once, and a soft gray light filtered through the darkness. He blinked twice more, and the light grew stronger. Concentrating on the action, he squeezed his eyes shut then opened them wide—and the light intensified, but there was still nothing but the light—no people, no objects, no trees, not even clouds.

"Where . . . am I?" he asked hesitantly.

"We don't need to label places here," the voice said. "But if it makes you more comfortable you can think of this as one area of Heaven, since that was the word in your mind."

He laughed uneasily. "Whew, thought maybe . . . well, you know."

"Yes, we know. You didn't always follow the path of goodness, did you?"

"Guess not," Zane admitted with a nervous laugh. He couldn't help picturing the women who'd come into, and just as quickly left, his life. There was an embarrassingly long list. But heck, he'd never lied or intentionally set out to hurt any of them. They'd had a good time, too. A damn good time, if he recalled correctly.

"Be that as it may," the voice said, as if the entity behind it had read his mind, "you are here and you need to do your part."

"My part?"

"Yes, you see, you are—since you need labels—an Angel of the Third Tier."

"Me, an angel?"

"It's either that or—"

"Never mind, consider me your man . . . I mean, angel," Zane amended quickly. "So what does the third-tier business mean?"

"It means you're just starting out. You must serve in the third tier before you can rise to the second."

"Like being an apprentice welder."

"A what?"

"Never mind," Zane said. "Go on. I shouldn't keep interrupting."

"We understand, you're curious. After you've served as both a third-tier and second-tier angel, you move on to first tier. And after that you are fully and eternally accepted into Grace."

"And that's good, right?"

"It's the best."

"So, I should go for it," Zane said thoughtfully. "What if a person doesn't make it? I mean what if I screw u—I mean *mess up* somehow?"

"That would be very unfortunate," the voice said, with a tragic overtone.

"Oh." Zane felt a chill slither through his soul, like a serpent cutting through shallow water at the edge of a brackish pond. Then another question occurred to him. "Who are you?"

The source of light seemed to thicken and sway before his eyes. "I am many things. The Zoroastrians of many millennia ago called me the Archangel Meher, the Angel of Mercy and Light. I comfort the soul and bring peace to those who have suffered or been wronged."

"I see," he said, not at all sure that he did. "So, what do I have to do, to do my part?"

"Look down there," the voice directed.

The endless flow of pure white light that had covered everything around him, seemed to thin in one small area. Zane peered into wisps of mist. A figure moved haltingly across his line of vision. A woman. A slender, dark-haired woman of about his age—thirty, give or take a year or two. There was something familiar about her, although he was sure he'd never met her before.

She stopped beside a piece of furniture, and it took him a moment to recognize it as a baby's crib. Resting one palm delicately on the rail, she peered down into it—and began to weep. Her grief pierced through him, as if he were feeling the pain tormenting her.

"Why's she so upset?" Zane asked.

"Her baby died."

Zane nodded. Yes, he could feel her loss. "That's terrible."

"For her, it seems so . . . certainly," the voice allowed without emotion.

The ache in Zane's heart intensified as he witnessed the young woman overtaken by helpless sobs. "Isn't there someone to be with her at a time like this?"

"It's been over a year. She's having trouble recovering from the loss of her child." The voice paused, as if wanting to give Zane more time to absorb the tragic scene before him. "Her husband blamed her for their son's death. He left her a month after it happened."

Zane involuntarily flinched. "The bastard," he muttered, then remembered who he was talking to. "Sorry."

"It's all right. Your reaction is appropriate, if poorly worded."

"Tell me," Zane began hesitantly, "what will happen to her? I mean, she won't become so desperate that she'll ... you know, try to commit suicide or anything, will she?"

The longer he looked at her, the more appealing she seemed to him. Her dark brown hair framed her face in soft chin-length waves. Her eyes, although blurred with tears, were the color of rich coffee before milk is added. She was petite, maybe a little too thin to be healthy, and he wondered if she'd lost a lot of weight in the past year, mourning her son. Somehow he knew it had been a boy.

"Her life is in the balance right now. You see, Zachariah, there are certain directions a mortal's life may take, depending upon his or her destiny. Ultimately it's the choices a person makes for him or herself that determine the course of that person's life."

Zane only half heard what the Archangel had said. He hadn't gotten past the name. "Zachariah? You called me Zachariah."

"Yes. That is your name now."

Another change to get used to. What a shame. He'd really liked his name. He sighed. "Okay, so far I know I'm dead. I'm a rookie angel and my name is Zachariah. So what does that woman have to do with me?"

"Why, she is your assignment, of course."

"My assignment," he repeated. He had a feeling in his gut, or at least where his gut used to be, that this afterlife stuff was going to be even more complicated than his time as a mortal. "You mean, I'm like her guardian angel?"

"There you are. You're catching on fast." Was it his imagination or did Meher sound just a little sarcastic?

"But...but what can I possibly do for a woman who has lost her child and husband? What sort of comfort can *I* give her?"

The voice assumed a musical quality, as if it were chuckling up a scale of notes. "Oh, you can do quite a lot for her. You see, she's destined to remarry, very happily. And she will bear another child. This will be no ordinary baby, though. It will grow to become a very important person. As an adult, it shall alter the course of human history in a most positive way."

"Like find a cure for cancer, or stop a war, or invent a way of feeding starving nations?" He had started rattling off the list as a joke, but by the time he finished the sentence he realized he was on the right track.

"Yes," Meher said, "something like that."

Zachariah scratched his nose, still trying to figure out his own role in this new life, if he could call it that.

"So, what you're saying is, it's my job to sort of hold her hand until Mr. Right comes along."

"Oh, no, no, no…your job is much more important than that."

"It is?"

"Yes," the Archangel assured him. "You see, Caroline North is a very strong-willed young woman. She's been so terribly hurt by the loss of her baby and her husband, she's vowed to never marry again, or have children. Your job is to see to it that she meets and accepts the man who will father her child."

Zachariah frowned at the image of the distraught mother, even now shaking with harsh sobs as another woman entered the room and pulled her away from the empty crib. "I don't know. Sounds like a pretty tall order to me."

"If it were easy, she wouldn't need a guardian angel. Now would she?" the voice prodded, a little less gently.

"No," he agreed reluctantly. "I guess not." He thought for a second. "So who is this guy? I mean, I should know who to look for so I don't make a mistake and steer her wrong."

"He is the perfect man for Caroline North," the voice stated placidly. "He will be the one man who will care for her and their child, no matter what difficulties lie ahead for them. He will love her more deeply than any other man could. His love for her will be infinite and unchanging."

"But how will I recognize him?" Zachariah persisted.

"You will know him," came the answer, and he sensed that was all the help he'd get.

Chapter 2

Caroline followed Suzanne out of the apartment complex and down Main Street. They walked toward the little drawbridge that split the old New England town, lifting on a set schedule each day, to let sailboats drift lazily down the Mystic River and into Long Island Sound, or enter the river to dock for a while and allow passengers ashore.

This time of year, the parade of gaily spinnakered boats, large and small, was at its peak. They sometimes lined up an hour or more before opening time. When the old, iron bridge finally raised to the jarring clang of bells and a show of flashing red lights, all traffic along Route 1 came to a dead stop for a full twenty minutes. Locals knew to take the inland highway or back roads if they were in a hurry to get anywhere. Tourists sat and roasted in their cars.

The two women walked, arm in arm, heading east along Main Street, passing familiar shops owned by friends and neighbors. Caroline knew that, as trustworthy as their high school helper was, Denise shouldn't be left alone in the Silver Whale for more than a couple of hours. So she didn't waste time trying to argue Suzanne out of lunch.

"Where do you want to eat?" Suzanne asked.

"Anywhere. The Captain's Table is fine, I don't care," Caroline murmured. She'd succeeded in stopping the tears, but a persistent pressure filled her chest. Her heart felt, quite literally, as if it were breaking. But she knew that couldn't be true; for it had already shattered into so many pieces it couldn't possibly break into finer chips.

"How about the Fisherman's Den for a change?" There were a half dozen hole-in-the-wall seafood shops that catered to tourists. If you steered clear of the specials and ordered a la carte, choosing only that day's catch, the food was excellent.

"Fine," Caroline said.

They took a table near the back of the room, closest to the kitchen, and let the tourists have the window seats. Caroline felt something brush her shoulder and scooted her chair in to make room for whoever was trying to get past her.

"Is something wrong with your chair?" Suzanne asked.

"No, I was just making room for—" Caroline glanced over her shoulder, but all she saw was the rough plank wall, a brightly dyed fishing net and pretty blown-glass floats tacked to it. "Oh, I thought someone was squeezing behind me."

Suzanne shrugged. "I didn't see anyone." She reached for two menus propped between the ketchup bottle and napkin vendor, and handed one to Caroline. "I'm having second thoughts about the clams. Those broiled haddock platters at the next table look scrumptious. Here, we'd better order right away. You may have the day off, but I have to get back to the shop."

Caroline flipped open the sturdy, plastic-encased menu. "Maybe we should do this another day."

"No," Suzanne said firmly. "You have to eat. I'm going to sit right here and make sure you do."

Caroline sighed. The specials, as always, tempted her, but she knew better. There was nothing worse than too-old fish, fried up to disguise its age. She snapped the menu closed. "I'll just have that broiled halibut, with a side of steamed broccoli."

"Sounds good to me." Suzanne raised a hand and signaled the waitress that they were ready to order. "I'm having a small lobster. They're so cheap this time of year, it's a sin to pass them up."

Caroline looked around the room, feeling strangely drawn to study the faces of the other diners.

"What?" Suzanne asked, following her glance with a curious smile.

"Noth—" Caroline frowned. But there was *something*. "I feel as if someone's watching me."

"Maybe that cute guy clearing the dishes off of that table over there," Suzanne giggled, nudging her with an elbow.

"I didn't say *flirting* with me. Someone is staring at me. I can feel it."

Suzanne ran her tongue back and forth across her lips. "Listen, honey, maybe everything that's happened to you is too much for one person to deal with. I've been thinking for the past month or so... maybe you should see a professional. Depression is a serious illness. If you—"

"I'm not feeling depressed, now," Caroline assured her. "This is different. It's as if my skin is prickling all over. Half an hour ago, when we left the apartment, I felt numb. Now I'm... tingling, picking up these weird vibrations, like when you know someone's staring at you."

It was true. The ache in the middle of her chest had dulled to a steady pressure, then to no more than a gentle reminder of her pain. And her awareness of people and motions around her had somehow sharpened. It was almost like focusing a camera before taking a shot. One second, the room you saw through the viewer was blurry, a mosaic of shapes that meant nothing. A twist of the lens, and things seemed to take on form and sort themselves out.

Suzanne's gaze swept the dining room. "Well, I'm glad you're feeling better, but I don't see anyone staring at you now."

Most of the diners seemed to be families with young children. A few locals on their lunch breaks sat at a large table in the opposite, rear corner. Several retirement-age couples occupied center tables, but they were preoccupied with their meals.

Caroline shook her head. "I can still feel it."

"You haven't been getting out enough," Suzanne commented, then broke off at the arrival of their waitress. She ordered for them while Caroline continued looking around the room, beginning to doubt her own sanity when it became clear to her that no one was showing the least interest in her.

As they spooned down a first course of rich, New England-style clam chowder, thick with potatoes and cream and laced with sweet onions, Caroline still couldn't dismiss the feeling that she was being observed.

She ate slowly, concentrating on the warm spot in her stomach created by the deliciously satisfying chowder. But her mind kept wandering, analyzing the sense of . . . of what? It was more a feeling of not being alone, rather than being gawked at. It was a feeling she hadn't had since the early days of her marriage, when the golden glow of love filled every corner of her days and she'd believed, in her heart, that she and Rob would be together, forever. Back then, being alone had seemed an impossibility.

But now? Only at that moment did she realize how very desperate she had been for companionship during the past year.

Caroline finished and set her spoon down on the rim of the soup plate with a sigh, to wait for the next course.

"Hey, you ate that pretty fast," Suzanne commented, looking pleased.

"Guess I was hungrier than I'd thought."

"Well, I hope you saved room for your fish," the waitress said, removing the soup bowl and plate and placing a platter of crispy, broiled halibut in front of her.

Caroline blinked at the size of the serving. "I'll never make a dent in this mountain."

Suzanne laughed. "Give it a shot. You never know."

Zachariah hovered behind and slightly to one side of Caroline North's chair in the cramped little restaurant. The place was very different from the dinner spots he'd taken his dates. The restaurants in Hartford and the surrounding suburbs were calm, candlelit islands of colonial decor with miles of tables. The Fisherman's Den managed to squeeze eight tables into a closet-size storefront. The atmosphere was tacky, the air redolent with the odors of hot oil, fish in various stages of freshness or decay, discarded lobster shells, and beer.

Still, he had to admit, the establishment had its charm. And the young woman he'd been sent to watch over seemed more comfortable here than she'd been in her apartment.

The first thing he had done after Meher dismissed him was to alter his name, at least in his own mind, to something less dated, less Old Testament sounding. Zach, he'd decided, was more comfortable, more nineties, less immortal sounding. Making that one decision put him in a more positive frame of mind.

I can do this, he thought. *If they tell me this is my job, fine. I'll do it.*

Well, it wasn't as if he had any choice.

Then he'd wondered how he was supposed to get around. Meher had left before filling him in on the rules of the game. Was he to do all of his work from up in a cloud? Or was he supposed to return to the living world and guide Caroline North by physically manipulating her? If he did travel back to the realm of the living, would he be visible to all people, only to some of them, or to no one? If he spoke would they hear him? If he touched someone, would that person feel it?

So many questions remained.

He really wished that his induction had been more thorough. No welder, plumber or electrician worth his salt would have let loose an apprentice with as little training.

But he supposed there was a reason behind everything they did in Heaven. So he'd make the best of things and have faith that the system would work.

He thought to himself that if he was to help this woman at all, he'd have to get closer to her and observe her for a while. As soon as the intention entered his conscious mind, he found himself in the restaurant, standing beside her. He moved behind her chair and put his back to the wall, wanting to see the reaction of people in the room to his sudden appearance before he did anything else.

It didn't take him long to realize that, although others in the room didn't seem to be aware of his presence, Caroline North somehow knew he was there. She couldn't see him, any more than anyone else in the room could. But there was something about the level of her alertness. Her eyes seemed brighter, her attention shifted subtly away from preoccupation with her own pain. She ate with a healthy appetite.

Great, he thought, *I'm already doing her some good. This job will be a cinch.*

He looked around the room hopefully. Maybe Caroline's husband-to-be was in this room, this very minute.

The prospects didn't look good, though. Retirees, young couples with small, rowdy children, a group of six teenagers trying to look bored. That left only one other table of people, who seemed to know each other and were holding themselves aloof from the tourists.

He spotted one man at the long table who wore round, steel-rimmed eyeglasses and was speaking in a solemn voice to an older man at the table, something about widening one of the local roads to accommodate traffic between the Seaport and the glitzy gambling casino the Pequot Indians had recently built on land north of Mystic.

Zach moved across the room, noticing that he didn't have to avoid chairs or people. He passed straight through them. He stood facing the bespectacled man and thought very hard, *Look at the brunette across the room. She's gorgeous.*

He hadn't known if it would work. But, to his delight, the man's eyes lifted from his plate and drifted across the room toward Caroline. She met his glance, then looked away quickly. The man dropped his own eyes shyly and continued talking to his friend.

"What a wimp!" Zach fumed. "Hey, she's the hottest looking woman in this room. Don't you have a drop of testosterone in that body of yours?"

The man glanced again at Caroline and grimaced, looking uncertain and confused.

Then Zach noticed the slim gold band on the man's left hand.

"Sorry, fella," he grumbled. "Go back to your sandwich. She's not worth ruining your marriage."

Obviously he had to be more careful. He remembered the Archangel's words. This man Caroline was supposed to meet and marry, with whom she'd have a child, was very special. He wasn't just anyone he might match her up with. And he certainly wasn't the kind of man who would cheat on his wife to be with another woman. Zach decided he'd have to give this some more thought. He'd have to get to know Caroline better, and only set her up with a man he was very sure could fulfill Meher's requirements.

Zach watched as the two women finished eating and split the check. He followed them out of the restaurant and down a street lined with quaint shops. Staying close behind them, he tuned into their conversation. They were talking about the shop they owned, the Silver Whale, discussing inventory and the possibility of having a Labor Day sale.

He felt the need to practice communicating with mortals a little more before trusting his technique with a really important task. He decided to try another experiment.

When they came to an intersection and had to wait for the light to change, he noticed a young man who looked like every twenty-year-old lifeguard he'd ever encountered. He was with two other boys in T-shirts who looked much less muscular but every bit as on-the-prowl for the opposite sex as he had felt at their age.

Zach moved up closer to Caroline, who was holding a foam box containing her leftover fish. "That young hunk over there could be on 'Bay Watch,'" he whispered in her ear.

Caroline swatted at the air as if shooing away a pesky fly. Then the corners of her lips turned upward tentatively, and her soft brown eyes twinkled as they focused on the lifeguard. She touched her girlfriend on the arm. "Look at that guy over there," Caroline whispered.

Suzanne followed her gaze. "Which one?"

"The muscles." Caroline giggled self-consciously.

Suzanne's eyes widened, then turned to stare at her friend in disbelief.

"I mean, don't you think he looks like an actor from that TV show, 'Bay Watch'?"

Suzanne laughed out loud. "Caroline North—ogling men on the street! That's not like you at all." She stopped herself. "Actually it's an improvement. What kind of fish was that?"

Caroline's cheeks turned fiery red. "That's terrible—what I just said! I can't believe those words came out of my mouth."

"Don't get all bent out of shape." Suzanne grinned at her. "I think it's healthy that you're showing an interest in men. Even if this one happens to be ten years younger than you."

Caroline elbowed her in the ribs in retaliation.

Grimacing dramatically, Suzanne dodged away from her but returned to drop an arm around her shoulders as they crossed the street. "Now we just have to make sure you don't go overboard, girl."

Caroline shook her head, looking puzzled as they passed the lifeguard and his friends.

It was then that Zach decided working from the outside wasn't such a good idea. He'd learned he could manipulate thoughts, and instigate actions. But the result didn't seem very effective because he still had no concept of Caroline's personality. If he worked against her natural instincts, he'd make a mess of her life. He had to focus much more intimately on who she was and how she felt about her world, and the people and things in it. He had to find some way to become a part of her life...even if he, himself, were dead.

A few days later Caroline walked briskly along the second-floor hallway, hiking a heavy grocery sack onto one hip while she fumbled through her purse for her keys. Why did they always gravitate so maddeningly to the bottom, like burrowing animals intent on seeking the remotest hiding spot?

She felt the shape of her wallet, of her purse-size hairbrush with its sharp bristles, her checkbook and the small plastic zipper pouch in which she kept a lipstick, blusher and mascara. At last her fingertips flicked over the jagged, metal edges of her apartment keys, which she'd separated from her car key on her last trip to the auto repair shop.

Juggling purse and brown paper bag, she awkwardly shoved the appropriate key into her front door...right at the same moment the bottom fell out of her shopping bag, releasing a milk carton, box of cereal, tampons, a small bunch of bananas, a jar of instant coffee and an avalanche of apples across the corridor.

"Damn!" She tossed down her purse to scramble after a McIntosh that was rolling with obvious intent toward the top of the stairs.

A wide, tanned hand reached down and plucked the apple from the top step.

Caroline snatched in a quick breath, her eyes tracing the strong fingers upward to a muscular forearm that led, in turn, to rather impressive shoulders and a football player's neck. Dazzling blue eyes flashed. A magnificent smile beamed at her, and she realized she was down on her hands and knees, in a less than flattering position.

For some reason, her ungraceful pose seemed more important than spilled food.

"Oh," she gasped, grinning sheepishly as she struggled to her feet. "Thanks. It seems my groceries have sort of...escaped."

"Looks like," the man said, handing her the apple. "Your bag tore, did it?"

"Yes." She shrugged. "I knew I shouldn't have let them pack so much into one bag, but I figured it would be easier to carry in from the car."

The man bent and picked up what was left of the brown paper sack. It hung in pitiful, soggy shreds from his fingertips. "Looks like the condensation from your milk carton did you in."

"Well, now I know better." As great looking as the stranger was, she wasn't about to invite a male lecture on how to safely carry her food home. Then her glance landed on the box of tampons.

Hastily she scooped it up and clamped the distinctive blue carton between her ribs and elbow. She retrieved the plastic produce bag, still holding two apples and dashed around, picking up the rest of her fruit. When she straightened up and turned around, the man stood holding her milk carton. She sighed, thankful it hadn't split open in its fall, spilling milk all over her landlord's new carpeting.

"Maybe I should introduce myself," he said. "I'm Zach Dawson. I just moved in across the hall from you."

"Really?" She frowned at the brass 2B on her neighbor's door. "I didn't know the Schulzes had moved."

"Graham accepted a job transfer. I understand it happened unexpectedly. He and his wife wanted to sublet the apartment for a while, just in case they decide to move back within the year."

"They were fortunate to find a tenant so quickly," Caroline commented. She twisted the key she'd left dangling in the doorknob and used one toe to kick the door open.

Zach walked into her living room without waiting for an invitation.

She frowned, trying to figure out how to tactfully let him know she hadn't intended to ask him in. But he was holding half of her groceries, and was, after all, her neighbor. It didn't seem right to toss him out without at least welcoming him to the building.

"Come on in," she said, belatedly. "I'm Caroline North. If you need help finding your way around town—" she studied him as he crossed the room in three long strides and deposited his load on her kitchen counter "—that is, if you're new in town, just ask."

"Thanks." He hitched one slim hip up onto a bar stool and looked around with casual interest. "Your place is bigger than mine."

"I think the Schulzes have a one-bedroom. This apartment has two." She prayed he wouldn't ask any more questions. Her glance flitted automatically to her bedroom, hoping the unmade bed wasn't visible from his angle, then to Jimmy's room.

Her eyes immediately felt moist, and she turned toward the refrigerator. Opening the door, she stuffed the tampons inside, then marched in the direction of the bathroom, carrying the carton of milk. Halfway there, she realized what she'd done and stopped herself. For a moment, she pressed her fingertips against her eyelids, squeezing back the tears she refused to shed.

"Something wrong?" Zach asked.

"Nothing. I guess I'm feeling a little rushed today. I have to get back to my store to relieve my partner."

She felt him watching her as she retraced her steps to the kitchen. When she set the milk on the top shelf of the refrigerator, she didn't pull out the tampons. She couldn't imagine why she was being so bashful around the man. After all, he must be about her age. He must have sisters, girlfriends . . . hell, he might even be *married*. He'd certainly seen feminine products before.

Then she turned and found herself staring straight into his electric blue eyes, and she knew why she'd been so uneasy. He was looking at her so intensely, she felt sure he had a reason for following her into her apartment besides wanting to help her with her groceries.

Caroline shivered, suddenly aware that they were alone in her apartment, that she knew absolutely nothing about him. Who he was . . . what he did for a living . . . even if he was who he claimed to be: her neighbor. Didn't serial killers create credible scenarios and roles for themselves to put their victims at ease?

"I, um, I have to get back to work now," she said quickly. "Maybe another time we can chat a little longer."

"I'd like that." His voice was a rumbly baritone that made her toes curl, despite the warning she'd just given herself. "I am new in town, and I have a feeling living in Mystic will take some getting used to. I'm used to life in a large city."

She smiled hesitantly as he eased himself lazily off her bar stool. He had a way of moving that was at once gracefully catlike, and strong. In blue jeans and a plaid sport shirt with the cuffs rolled up, he reminded her of a Marlboro ad—slim hips and muscular shoulders, rugged. But his face, although suntanned, didn't have that craggy, weatherworn look of the cowboys in the advertisements. The line of his jaw was smooth, closely shaven, without scars to detract from his angular, masculine features. And when he smiled at her, as he was doing now, she felt a rush of pure energy pulse between them.

Caroline was shocked at the warmth of her reaction to Zach. It had been so long since any man had aroused any kind of strong feelings in her. The last had been Rob. *Look what happened with him!* she reminded herself. He'd abandoned her. She'd been serious when she'd told Caroline she wasn't going to set herself up for that kind of heartbreak again.

"So, where is this shop where you work?" he asked, turning toward her as she opened the door for him to leave.

"On Water Street, down by the river. It's called the Silver Whale. We sell gifts—high quality items, no lobster-shaped ashtrays. Stop in some time . . . it's easy to find, right off Main Street."

"I will," he promised. "You can count on it."

She closed the door behind him, then leaned against it, feeling slightly off balance, listening to the too-fast rhythm of her heart echoing in her ears. "No," she told herself, "you're not going to get involved with this man. Not him or any other."

Zach stepped inside the apartment he'd moved into the day before and let out a long breath. He shut his eyes for a second and tried to regain his composure. Although he'd gotten up close to her while he was invisible, the effect she had on him was different once he'd assumed a mortal form. He just hadn't counted on Caroline North being as attractive as she was. Or on seeing her smile at him that way—the way a woman does when she's attracted to a man.

He felt thoroughly rattled.

"Careful there, boy," he told himself. "Careful . . . careful . . ." If he did anything to encourage Caroline and she developed a crush on him, his job would become even more difficult. To move up from his lowly third tier and win his wings, merit badge or whatever Meher gave out for a job well done, he'd better not louse things up.

"Hey, did you see that?" Zach asked out loud. "Meher, old buddy, I did okay in the face of a challenge, don't you think?"

There was no answer.

"Guess you're not listening in right now," he mumbled. But he continued talking to himself as he constructed a ham-and-cheese sandwich on rye bread, adding a kosher dill, lettuce, tomato and onion slices. "One thing I discovered today, Mr. Archangel—living in a human body again sure restores the old mortal drives. Man, am I hungry."

But there had been parts of him unrelated to his appetite for food that had been kicking up pretty fierce back in Caroline's apartment. Hell, I can deal with that, he told himself. It's not like I'm some teenager fighting down runaway hormones.

He carried the sandwich with him into the bedroom. It looked a lot neater than the one in his old apartment, but then he hadn't moved in any clothing or furniture. He'd agreed to keep some of the Schultzes' furniture they hadn't wanted to sell or move. As to his old clothes, he assumed someone had disposed of them after the accident. He wondered who had been given that morbid job. Matt maybe? He hoped the chore hadn't weighed too heavily on the old man. He was a good guy.

Besides, he didn't need a closetful of duds. All he'd had to do was think about wearing comfortable jeans and his favorite shirt, and they'd appeared on his body. He'd envisioned a hearty sandwich, and the makings had appeared in the refrigerator.

The whole setup was pretty cool, when you came down to it. Just wish for something and there it was. Simple. But he assumed if things got out of hand—for instance, if he wished for a spanking new Porsche or a couple of hours with the covergirl from a *Playboy* magazine, the powers-that-be wouldn't approve. He instinctively understood that he would be granted whatever he needed to help Caroline, and nothing more.

As he ate, he looked out the window and down to the ground. From the front door stepped Caroline, her dark hair freshly brushed, blowing in soft waves around her pretty face. Her step seemed more self-assured than it had on the day he'd first observed her through the mists with Meher. Perhaps she was coming out of her depression on her own, without any help from him.

"No," he whispered, as the answer came to him out of nowhere, "she needs me. I've got to find the man Heaven has lined up for her."

He shoved the last bite of sandwich into his mouth, wiped the crumbs from his fingers on the sides of his jeans and walked with a surge of energy and purpose across the living room to the telephone. "The perfect man . . . the absolute right man for you, Ms. Caroline North . . ." he muttered to himself, picking up a pad of paper and pen from beside the phone.

It seemed unlikely that he'd been sent to pluck some guy's name out of a hat. If that had been the plan, Meher could have chosen anyone for the job. So there had to be a personal connection. From the little bit he'd already learned about her through a few days' observation, Caroline didn't seem to have an obvious circle of friends from whom he could select her mate. On the other hand, while he'd been alive, he had come into contact with a lot of interesting men because of his profession. Some he'd known, personally, for many years. Others he'd built houses or offices for, and he'd learned a lot about them in the process. Of the ones he most admired, several had strong traits that might appeal to Caroline and compliment hers.

When Zach finished adding to his list of names, he nodded at it with satisfaction. "One of you fellas is in for a treat," he mused, feeling pleased with himself.

Ten minutes later, he'd made up his mind. Reaching for the phone, he dialed Paul Cooper's number in New Haven.

Chapter 3

During the next week, Caroline caught only glimpses of her new neighbor. Zach seemed to keep himself very busy. Doing what, though, she hadn't figured out. One afternoon at the Silver Whale, she told Suzanne about him. "He's sort of a mystery," she added after filling her in on the basics. "He doesn't keep regular hours. Maybe he's self-employed, a writer or consultant of some kind."

"Maybe he's *un*-employed?" Suzanne suggested as she picked up a dust cloth and set to work on a row of porcelain figurines.

"How could he afford that apartment if he doesn't have a job?" Caroline asked. "The Schulzes must be charging him at least what they pay. The one bedrooms are six hundred a month."

"Is he cute?" Suzanne asked, looking at her slyly from the corners of her eyes as she flicked her rag at stray dust puffs.

Caroline grinned. "He's knock-me-down-and-drag-me-away handsome, and intelligent, and actually seems very nice."

"Then forget about how he makes his living. Go for it!"

Caroline frowned. "I'm not sure I want to go for *it*. I told you I really don't want to get involved with anyone, and starting a relationship with my neighbor might get awkward. Here, let me do that, you're just moving the dust around." She took the dust cloth from Suzanne and picked up a gnome playing a fiddle to give him a good cleaning. "Besides, I have a feeling Zach's avoiding me."

Suzanne propped her hands on her hips and looked at her doubtfully. "Why would you think that?"

"I offered to show him Mystic, and he admitted it was taking him some time to find his way around. But he hasn't called or stopped by." She sighed. "I'm probably just not his type."

"Don't count him out too soon," Suzanne advised. "He could be getting over a difficult relationship, or a divorce. Men take these things just as hard as women."

"Or maybe there's someone else in his life," Caroline murmured. She looked at Suzanne. "What are the odds a great looking guy like Zach isn't already attached?"

Suzanne shook her head. "You analyze everything. Don't think so much. It's just great to see you even a little bit interested in a man. It's a healthy sign."

"I suppose."

Caroline spent the next two hours helping customers choose gifts for family and friends at home, or collectibles for themselves. Even though it was only August, vacationers seemed to be on the lookout for gifts to put away for the holidays. Caroline couldn't help thinking about the previous Christmas. How horrible it had been.

Jimmy had died the week following Thanksgiving. For weeks afterward, she had been in shock and Rob seemed to be living with her in body only. They rarely spoke to each other. They never touched. The infrequent sex they'd shared for the past few years of their marriage stopped completely. In retrospect, she realized he must have made up his mind to leave her very soon after the funeral, maybe he'd been contemplating splitting up even before Jimmy died. But he'd stayed through Christmas.

Perhaps Rob had only hung around out of compassion, sensing how difficult it would be for her to face the holidays alone. Or maybe he was just afraid of what their families and friends would think of him if he ran out on her so soon. He'd always been concerned about what people thought of him. In a way, she decided now, it would have been better if he had just gone. The strain between them when they'd made their traditional family visits—to her mother's place in Philadelphia, to his folks in Bridgeport—had been unbearable. The way Rob had made a show of holding her hand in front of his mother, only to recoil from her when she'd tried to touch him on their way home in the car.

The awful silence that stretched between them for days on end. The accusing tone in his voice when he said his son's name in her presence. The way he soaked up his friends' sympathy—seeming to enjoy the attention he was getting at their son's expense. It was all too much for her.

The jingle of the bell over the shop's door pulled Caroline out of her downward spiral of grim memories. She looked up to see Zach stride through the door.

Quickly she glanced around for Suzanne, but her partner must have stepped into the back room. Caroline coughed lightly to try to clear the lump from her throat and moved around the counter, a polite smile pasted on her lips. "Welcome to the Silver Whale."

Zach's face broke into a wide smile. "Hey, there. Long time no see."

Another man followed him into the shop, and it took Caroline a moment to realize that they'd come in together.

Zach turned to his friend. "This is Paul Cooper. He's an architect from New Haven. An old friend of the family's, I guess you'd say."

Paul was at least six inches shorter than Zach. He had a friendly face and sensible tan eyes behind stainless-steel-rimmed eyeglasses. His eyes seemed to match his conservatively barbered tan hair. He looked like a figure taken from a sepia print and pasted into the colorful backdrop of her shop. "You must be the pretty neighbor Zach has been raving about," Paul said, holding out his hand to shake hers.

Caroline looked at Zach, surprised and unsure of what to say. If he'd thought of her so often, why hadn't he called or stepped across the hallway? "I'm at least his neighbor," she said, then changed the subject. "You and Zach have known each other a long time, then?"

"Well, not really, although what he said was true. The families have known one another for decades."

"Paul was good friends with my cousin," Zach put in quickly. He detached himself from them to wander around the shop, looking suddenly interested in a grouping of haloed cherubim on a shelf near the front window.

"See," continued Paul, "I went to high school with Zane Dawson. We were best buddies for years afterward, too. Kept in touch as we took off in our separate directions. I went straight into college and became an architect. Zane liked using his hands and took a construction job. Years later, he earned a degree in engineering." Paul stopped, and his hesitation told Caroline something was wrong, even before his eyes darkened.

"Did something happen to your friend?" she asked.

"Yeah," Paul said, nodding sadly. "A freak accident. He was killed on his own construction site."

Caroline drew in a shocked breath. "How terrible," she murmured. "I'm sorry."

"Yeah, well, I really miss the guy. He and I were pretty close for a long time, although I hadn't seen him in a couple of years. Funny thing is, when his cousin, Zach, called me last week, I was surprised because I didn't remember Zane mentioning he had a cousin. But they look so much alike, there's no doubting the family connection."

Caroline looked across the room at Zach, trying to imagine another man just like him, struck down in his prime years. A wave of melancholy swept over her, as if she herself had lost someone special. Determinedly she drove the disturbing emotions from her heart, afraid they would bring back other painful memories.

"Zach said you're from New Haven. What are you doing out this way?" she asked.

"Visiting my folks," Paul said, his voice brightening. "Zach caught me at my parents' house in Groton the other night and suggested I might like to walk around Mystic with him after we got in a game of tennis today. I figured I could stay a couple of extra days and just hang out in the area. I haven't taken a real vacation in a long time. And I feel a lot more relaxed here than when I'm in the city."

Caroline observed the tight web of lines around Paul's eyes and mouth. She guessed that relaxing wasn't something he took time to do very often.

They chatted for a few more minutes while she gave Paul a short tour of the shop. Then Zach rejoined them. "So have you two gotten acquainted?"

Caroline stared at him in surprise. He sounded as if he'd been trying to set them up. The possibility didn't really upset her; she was more curious why he'd go out of his way to matchmake.

"Paul told me about your cousin's unfortunate accident. I'm so sorry," she said.

"Yeah. It was tragic. Happened up in Hartford, earlier this month." He hesitated before looking at Paul and adding. "I wish I could have made it to the funeral, but there was a business trip I couldn't get out of."

Paul nodded, as if to say he understood.

"By the way," Caroline asked, "what kind of business are you in?"

Paul's glance fixed with interest on Zach, as if he knew no more about his friend's job than she did.

Zach's glance shifted away from them, across the shop. He grinned. "Hey, this must be your lovely partner!"

Suzanne put down the vase she had carried out of the storage room and walked over to them. Introductions were made all around.

"Say, I have an idea," Zach said after they'd talked for a while. "How about the four of us get together over dinner tonight. We can find a good restaurant or I'll whip up something at my place."

Suzanne grinned. "Hate to spoil the party, but my husband has a thing about my accepting dates with handsome strangers."

"Bring him along," Zach said magnanimously.

Suzanne shook her head. "Maybe another time. We're working on a special project at home." She spotted a customer across the shop and turned away to ask the woman if she needed any help.

Caroline stared after her, wondering vaguely what Suzanne had been talking about. Special project? When she looked back at the two men, Zach was studying her intently but glanced away as soon as she made eye contact with him.

Paul spoke up cheerfully. "I assume *you* don't have a husband to run home to?"

Caroline felt the bottom fall out of her stomach, but not before she caught a flash of horror in Zach's eyes. "No," she murmured thickly. "Not anymore."

A subtle male signal passed from Zach to Paul, who suddenly looked worried. "I'm sorry. I have a feeling I've said something in poor taste."

"It's all right," Caroline assured him, although the words raked like pitchfork tines across her throat. "I was married for a while, but my husband and I separated a year ago."

Paul looked a little pale. "I didn't know. Sorry."

But it was Zach's expression that drew her attention. He looked positively stricken. In his startlingly blue eyes she read sympathy and regret that went far deeper than embarrassment for his friend's minor faux pas. And she wondered if he knew not only about Rob, but about Jimmy, too. But then, how could he know unless someone had told him? She certainly hadn't brought up her son's death the one day they'd met.

The knot in her stomach tightened agonizingly, but slowly eased up as she realized what must have happened. Of course, someone in the apartment building must have dropped the information. Probably the Schultzes, before they left. It would only be natural for them to mention her if Zach questioned them about his new neighbors. And how else would they describe her? *The nice young woman across the hall—poor thing. She lost her baby about a year ago, then her husband walked out on her.* Those facts seemed to define her entire life, no matter how she tried to forget.

Caroline bit down on her lip, trying to settle herself. Even if, for a brief moment, she managed to escape the nightmare of losing her child, it seemed the rest of the world wouldn't let her forget. Suddenly she couldn't bear the thought of spending another evening alone with her memories.

"If you don't mind entertaining only one lady," she blurted out, "I'd love to come to dinner."

"Good," Zach said, looking relieved. He nodded with satisfaction at his friend. "Seven o'clock all right with you?"

Paul nodded enthusiastically, watching her from behind the lenses of his glasses as if he were afraid she might disappear in a puff of smoke if he let her out of his sight.

Zach turned back to Caroline, his blue eyes flashing, a recalcitrant lock of blond hair falling rakishly over one eyebrow. "Seven o'clock it is, then. At my place." He winked at her, and she gave him a wobbly smile, wondering if she'd bitten off far more than she could chew.

By 6:00 p.m. that night, Caroline was dressed and, at least technically, ready for dinner. She was also convinced she'd made a very foolish decision.

After being on her own for nearly a year and spending the previous four socializing as half of a couple, she had agreed to dine in a strange man's apartment, accompanied only by another man who was equally a stranger. She couldn't imagine why she'd agreed to the odd arrangement, except that, for reasons she couldn't fathom, Zach both fascinated her and had somehow made her feel she could trust him.

Still, the night's plans seemed the worst possible way to ease herself back into a social life.

Caroline picked up the telephone three times during the next hour, prepared to plead with Suzanne to drag Ralph along and join them—then chickened out before she finished dialing. Even though she felt perfectly justified for being jittery, she could imagine Suzanne teasing her mercilessly for weeks if she had to come to her rescue.

At ten minutes before the hour, she reached panic mode and snatched up the phone again, prepared to fib her way out of the dinner by claiming a ferocious headache. Maybe she could get away with telling Suzanne nothing. After all, she'd become preoccupied with customers before the date with Zach and Paul had been firmed up. And they had been too busy to talk about the two men later.

Her hands sweating, Caroline hastily punched in a 5...5...4...

There was a knock on her front door.

She frowned and slowly returned the receiver to its cradle. "Who's there?" she called out.

"The chef! Chow's on!"

Caroline sighed at the sound of his rich male voice. She'd waited too long. If she didn't eat the meal Zach had prepared, it would be rude.

"Dinner's getting cold," he called good-naturedly through the door. "Come on, you can't keep two hungry males waiting when something as serious as a steak is involved."

Caroline laughed, feeling suddenly less nervous about the evening. *He's a well-meaning guy who's just trying to be nice,* she decided.

Taking a deep breath, she walked to the door and opened it. Zach stood in the hallway, a chef's white paper toque perched cockeyed on his head, looking three sizes too small for him. Caroline raised her hand to her mouth to cover the laugh that bubbled out anyway. "You've really gone all out."

"Of course I have. You're a very special guest! Come on. Paul's pouring the wine." He grinned at her. "I think he really likes you. He's done nothing but talk about you for the past two hours."

Caroline rolled her eyes as she slipped her spare door key off of its hook and into her pocket. "Are you trying to set me up with him?"

"Don't you think he's a nice guy?" Zach asked, ignoring her question. He cupped her elbow in one hand, drawing her through her doorway, guiding her across the hallway.

"He seems nice, yes," she admitted reluctantly. "But I've only talked with him for a few minutes. It's sort of hard to judge a person after such a short time."

Zach pulled her to a stop before opening his apartment door. His eyes latched onto hers. "Do you believe in love at first sight?"

"Love?" Caroline stared at him, brought up short by the unexpected mention of the most private of all human emotions. Her body responded before her mouth could form a proper witty comeback. A subtle pulse throbbed in her throat and wrists as she stood looking up at Zach, wondering what had prompted him to ask her such a question. In his eyes she read an intensity that told her he thought her answer was important. The finely muscled contours of his face conveyed a secret urgency.

"Love at first sight," she repeated, trying out the words for herself. When she said them like that, flat out, they seemed fairly ordinary, harmless.

"Yes," he said, his eyes darkening to a midnight blue, not unlike the color of the ocean on a moonless night. "You know...two people meet, and right away they know they're perfect for each other. There's something magical there, some special chemistry."

Caroline swallowed, her mouth suddenly dry. Was he talking about himself, or her...or them? Or was this some kind of test?

A theoretical question that had just popped into his mind? "That's just animal attraction. It happens between men and women," she stated, trying for as casual a tone as she could muster.

Did she really believe what she was saying? Caroline wasn't sure. She wasn't sure of anything at the moment. And she realized the reason she couldn't think clearly was the incredible warmth she felt radiating from Zach's body. His crisp plaid cotton shirt and her fitted, knit jersey were just inches apart. His fingers had tightened around her elbow, and she had the sense that he didn't realize he was gripping her a little too tightly.

"Do you think so? It's just lust?" His gaze shifted away from her, and he looked thoughtful.

"Yes, that's what I think," she said.

"Maybe you're the sort of woman who has to get used to a man slowly," he murmured, as if he were talking more to himself than to her. He stepped back, studied her face, then, wearing a patient expression, announced, "Right. Fine, we can do that."

Laughing, Caroline pulled her arm out of his suddenly relaxed hand. She put out her hand to stop him from pushing open the door. "Do what, Zach? You're talking in riddles."

His bizarre mood vanished and he beamed at her enthusiastically. "Never mind. Everything is going to work out just great. I can tell. Come on, let's join Paul before the food really does get cold."

All through dinner, Caroline watched the two men suspiciously. At first, she wondered if there might be a boyish conspiracy of some sort between them. Perhaps they'd wagered on which one of them could win her over. But Paul seemed a shy man, and Zach made no effort to draw attention to himself and away from his friend.

With some encouragement from Zach, Paul talked about his work as an architect, but didn't monopolize the conversation or brag. He described a home he'd designed for a wealthy New York stockbroker, constructed on a tiny rock island at the mouth of the Thames River, near his parents' home in nearby Groton.

"It sounds very dramatic," Caroline remarked. "I'd love to see it sometime."

Paul glowed. "I can arrange a visit with the Kingsleys, if you like." He seemed almost too eager—a little boy wanting to be liked.

It might have been an endearing trait in a younger person, but she found it somewhat unnerving in a man in his thirties.

Zach broke in when the conversation seemed to lag as they finished their salads and started in on thick porterhouse steaks, baked potatoes and steamed green beans. "You know, it's plenty warm for swimming still, and there's a great beach over at Eastern Point, overlooking the Kingsley house. You still like to swim, don't you, Paul?"

Before his friend could answer, Zach turned to Caroline.

"Paul was on the varsity swim team his second year of college. At least, I seem to remember Zane saying something about the meets. Took a few medals for freestyle, didn't you, Paul?"

"Well, yeah, but it wasn't something I stayed with." He blinked apologetically at Caroline through his glasses. "I'm no jock. My studies were too important to me to throw away my time on swim practices."

"Very sensible," she agreed politely, taking another bite of her steak. Zach had prepared it on an indoor grill, and the lightly charred, delicately smoky flavor was wonderful. "By the way, this is very good. What did you season the meat with?" she asked, intentionally changing the subject. Paul seemed as uncomfortable with Zach's heavy-handed attempts to sell her on him as she was beginning to feel.

"Something that comes in a jar, labeled Steak Seasoning." He laughed. "Steak is the one recipe I don't botch."

Paul chuckled, shaking his head, eyeing Zach as if they shared a secret.

"What?" Caroline asked. She put down her fork and leaned forward against the table.

"Nothing," Zach said quickly. "It's a guy thing."

Paul's tan eyes glimmered mischievously. "Oh, you can tell her. She's a good sport." He took a sip of the Bordeaux wine he'd brought to accompany their meal and grinned at Caroline when Zach seemed reluctant to explain. "Zach here must share more than genes with his cousin. Old Zane, he used to grill steaks for his girlfriends, or at least for the ones who lasted more than two dates. First dates, he'd take out to a swanky restaurant. Seconds, he'd spring for a movie or concert, then drinks afterward at a club. If he hadn't gotten them into bed by then, the third—"

"Hey!" Zach laughed, nervously. "She doesn't want to hear about my deceased cousin's love life. Nothing like putting a damper on the perfect dinner party."

"I'd *love* to hear about your cousin," Caroline said, suspecting there was a reason Zach felt uncomfortable with the conversation. Maybe he feared some piece of personal information about himself would slip out. She felt wickedly justified in tormenting him. Fair payback for the way he'd made her feel in the hallway. "Go ahead, Paul. What about your friend's third dates?" she asked sweetly.

"On the third date, Zane always figured if the lady hadn't already slept with him, she was primed for the big move and, if she had slept with him, she was good for one last night—"

"Paul." Zach's voice had taken on a tight edge. He turned to Caroline. "I don't—"

"Family secrets make you nervous?" she asked playfully.

Zach rolled his eyes. "Fine. Go ahead and have your fun, you two."

Paul continued, chuckling to himself, obviously enjoying the story much more than Zach. "So, the third night, he fired up the grill on the patio. Steaks were the only entrée he knew how to cook, so if she was a vegetarian he was out of luck. As soon as she arrived, he'd kick me out with instructions to find an all-night cinema or bunk with one of our friends. And I'd better not show up too early the next morning—" Paul was laughing so hard, tears trickled from the corners of his eyes "—or I'd likely walk in on a scene of monumental debauchery."

Zach glared at Paul, then said solemnly to Caroline. "Zane was a really nice guy. He just liked to have a good time."

"Well, I think it's gallant of you to defend him," she said. "But my limited experience with dating before I married convinced me—men *that* obsessed with sex are usually pretty shallow characters and not worth bothering with."

Zach's mouth dropped open.

Paul got himself enough under control to come to his departed friend's rescue. "No, no really," he gasped, still sounding short of breath. "Zane was a good fella. The best. It was just that he liked women a lot, and they liked him. It wasn't like he tricked any of them into bed. I'm sure they had as good a time as he did."

Zach muttered something that sounded suspiciously like, "You can bet on it."

Caroline frowned at him. "What did you say?"

"Nothing," he snapped.

She studied him, amazed at how close the two cousins must have been for Zach to have taken Paul's comments so personally. His reaction aroused her curiosity in both of the Dawson men. "Tell me," she said, watching Zach's eyes with interest. "If you knew Zane that well, then you must know when or how often he broke his pattern and had a fourth or fifth date with a woman."

He shrugged. "Plenty of times."

Paul let out a crack of a laugh. "Yeah sure. Like, who was she?" He turned to Caroline. "Zane never got serious with a woman in his life. He liked things the way they were. No complications. Do everything his way. Marriage would have terrified him. And kids?" He waved his fork at her. "Forget it. He couldn't have handled a pack of *rug rats,* as he called them."

"Well," Caroline began, "that's a shame because children are wonderf—" She cut herself off and stared blindly across the room.

Paul put down his knife and fork, looking at her with concern. "Is something wrong?" he asked.

"No." She swallowed, then swallowed again, tears welling up hopelessly in her eyes. She played with her silverware, reached for her water glass and drained it.

"Caroline," Zach said, reaching across the table to lay his hand over hers.

"I'm all right. Really." She sniffled back the tears. "Kids are something I have a hard time talking about."

She felt Zach's eyes delving into hers, searching for a hold, a way to reach her. Then, strangely, the pain that had filled her heart to overflowing, faded. The feeling reminded her of a sunset so brilliant the colors hurt the eyes. A minute later, the hues pooled together, softening, then vanishing altogether in the dying light of day. She looked at him across the table, cluttered with plates, wineglasses and utensils, aware that her hand still rested warmly beneath his callused fingers. She liked the roughness of his skin, liked the contrast to the thin, soft flesh on the back of her hand.

For an instant, that was all she could think of…that skin-on-skin sensation. Then she pulled her eyes away from their hands, up to his face, and saw something she hadn't noticed before. It was an aura of sorts, a soft sheen on Zach's pale hair that seemed not so much a reflection of the dim lighting in the dining room, but a light from another source, almost as if it were emanating from within him.

Caroline drew in a sharp breath and blinked, trying to force her eyes to focus.

The soft glow disappeared.

Paul coughed politely, shattering the spell. "Look, I really didn't mean to tell family secrets that would embarrass or upset anyone. Sorry." No one answered, so he went on. "If everyone's done eating, I'll clear the dishes."

"No!" Zach shouted.

Paul stared at him, looking puzzled.

Slowly Zach withdrew his hand from Caroline's, taking away its pleasant warmth and comforting weight. He stood up, looking a little off balance, avoiding her eyes. "No," he repeated in a more controlled voice. "I'll take care of that. You two sit here and visit."

Once inside the kitchen, Zach wondered if he was being too obvious about setting up Paul and Caroline. Probably he was. But who could blame him? He'd always been too busy getting girls for himself to worry about how other guys made out—so to speak. And now he felt awkward, he felt like a damn klutz, actually. Like some kid on his first construction job who doesn't know a girder from an I-beam.

He set the stack of plates and salad bowls in the sink and ran hot water over them.

"Well, how am I supposed to know what I'm doing?" he whispered hoarsely, glaring up at the ceiling, wishing Meher would appear to help him out. He didn't. "You told me squat about this job," Zach complained bitterly. "Just do it, you said. This isn't some ad for athletic gear!"

Zach groaned in frustration. Closing his eyes, he thought about his orders again.

Maybe the situation wasn't as bad as he was making it out to be. So Caroline didn't believe in love at first sight. That might actually work in his favor. Paul was a down-to-earth, sensible kind of guy. He probably wouldn't fall for a woman overnight, either. Zach remembered how cautiously Paul had dated during their college years, going out with just one girl all their years in school. After that, he'd been exclusively with one other girl, but she'd eventually married someone else. To Zach's way of thinking it wasn't a big surprise. Waiting around for Paul for almost five years, she'd gotten impatient. Only after she'd left had Paul admitted he'd been thinking about asking her to marry him.

Thinking about it…for five years. He hoped to God it wouldn't take him that long this time!

Zach's ears perked up at the sound of conversation from the other room. He stepped close to the kitchen door and eased it open just wide enough to be able to make out their words and see Caroline and Paul at the table.

"—And we could swim, like Zach said, maybe grab lunch at my parents' house, then go tour the river house. I think you'd have a good time."

Caroline was smiling hesitantly. "I don't know. I shouldn't leave the shop for a whole day, and I feel sort of funny imposing on your parents. I don't know them at all … or you, very well."

Paul kneaded his hands in his lap, looking desperate.

"You're losing her," Zach whispered. "You've got to say something fast, or she'll back out and your window of opportunity will close. You're an architect, dammit. Make a blueprint. Figure it out!"

Paul glanced toward the kitchen, and only then did Zach realize his friend must have heard his warning—not in words, but in thoughts, just as Caroline had heard him on the street the other day.

"My parents are always entertaining—" Paul blurted out.

"Yeah, right," Zach muttered. "And hermits throw parties every night."

"R-r-really," Paul stammered. "They're always asking me to bring around my friends. Besides, Zach will be there, too. It's not like it's just you and me. Not like a real date or anything."

No! Zach thought, bursting through the kitchen door. "What's this all about?" he demanded.

Caroline jumped at his sudden appearance, nearly falling off her seat. "Do you always crash into rooms like a bull in season?"

Paul looked at him sheepishly. "I was just telling Caroline," he said slowly and with emphasis, as if trying to squeeze extra words between the ones he was actually speaking, "that *you* will be at my folks' house next weekend, too, so she shouldn't feel it's a big deal or anything. Just a bunch of friends over for a swim and lunch." Paul seemed to be holding his breath, waiting for Zach to get the message and come to his rescue.

Zach rolled his eyes. The guy was being so obvious, it was pitiful. Still, whatever got the job done.

"Oh, yeah," Zach agreed reluctantly. "Of course, I'll be there."

What else could he do? He didn't want to tag along to watch Paul put his moves—if he had any—on Caroline. But maybe it was for the best. If he were there, he'd have some control over the situation. At an awkward moment, he'd be able to lend a hand.

"I'll be there." He ground out the words between his teeth. "We'll have a good time."

Caroline looked at him thoughtfully. "Well, if Suzanne can cover for me at the shop for a half day, I guess we could arrange to get together one afternoon."

Zach let out a long breath of relief. Now things were starting to cook!

Chapter 4

"Well, this looks *very* promising," Suzanne remarked, cocking one brow meaningfully at the overnight bag Caroline carried.

"I don't want to hear it," she warned. It was ten minutes before opening time at the Silver Whale, and she had a lot of work to finish before noon if she was going to take the rest of the day off to go to the beach with Paul and Zach. "I couldn't find my old beach bag, so this will have to do for toting around my soggy bathing suit and towel."

"Well, if for any reason you're not able to make it back by tomorrow morning to open up, you just let me know." Laughing at the way Caroline's jaw dropped in shock, Suzanne dodged out of range before her friend could fling the Beluga whale-shaped pillow she'd grabbed.

Caroline glared at her. "All I'm doing is spending the afternoon at the beach. I told you that yesterday. With two friends," she added belatedly.

"Two?"

"Yes. You met them both last week—Zach and Paul."

Suzanne fanned herself with one hand. "Once you decide to have a social life, you sure make up for lost time."

This time Caroline didn't give her a chance to duck. With a flick of her wrist, she lobbed the pillow at Suzanne's head.

"Hey, watch the crystal!" she warned, giggling despite the possibilities for disaster. "So tell me, which one are you interested in?"

"Neither. I told you, I don't intend to get serious with anyone."

"So, who's talking about *serious?* Play the field for as long as you like. Have fun. Let a few nice guys spoil you a little...or a lot. Swimming and sunning at the beach. Dinner and dancing. Holding hands in the moonlight . . . you'll feel like a woman again."

Caroline bit down on her bottom lip. "That's the problem. I'm almost afraid to feel that way again."

Suzanne's grin stiffened and dropped away. "Oh, honey, why on earth shouldn't you?"

"Because I have a feeling that if I let myself go, if I ever let passion take over, I'll fall in love again. Fall really hard. What if he's another Rob? Or worse. What if he's really, really nice . . . the absolute right man this time? Then, if he wants to have a child with me, I won't have the strength to say no."

"And you really think the risk is that great of having another SIDS baby?"

Caroline nodded slowly, then stared down at the overnight bag at her feet. "Yes, I suppose I do. I don't know why, but I do. And—" she swallowed over the lump growing in her throat "—and I can't face that possibility."

Suzanne put an arm around her shoulders. "Look, about this afternoon. Why not just look at it as a chance to be with a couple of nice guys and have a little fun for a change. Nothing's going to happen with the two of them around. Enjoy yourself. Make friends. You deserve a chance to relax."

"I suppose." Caroline sighed and tried out a smile, knowing if she looked happier Suzanne would be pleased. "Maybe I'm making more of this than I should," she admitted.

"Exactly. Now, seriously, which one turns you on?"

Caroline choked on a laugh. "You never give up. Okay, if you want to know the truth—Zach. He wins, hands down."

"I thought you said he wasn't your type."

"I said, I didn't think *I* was *his* type. But that's not the point. You asked me a theoretical question, right? So I'm telling you.

Paul is too meek. He's intelligent and nice, but if I ever did get serious with any man—which I won't—he'd have to be someone with a very strong personality. Someone who knows what he wants, who can handle a crisis and not run away from life. I think Zach's that kind of man."

Suzanne studied her skeptically. "You want to know what I think?"

Caroline picked up her overnight bag to stow it in the back room. "I don't suppose it would do any good to tell you, I don't."

Suzanne breezed along as if Caroline hadn't spoken. "What I think is, you chose Zach because he's already let you know, in his own way, that he's off limits. Paul, on the other hand, is obviously interested in you. You made the safe choice—the guy you can't have. It's like nursing a crush on the village priest."

Caroline opened her mouth to object, but an insistent rapping on the shop's door interrupted her. Two women, standing outside, pointed at the sign in the front window, listing the shop's hours.

"We've got to open," Suzanne said. "You think about it, though. I'm right. You're playing it safe."

Caroline did think about Suzanne's theory. All morning she dwelled on her words with growing anxiety. Probably Suzanne was right: The only reason she allowed herself to admit the attraction she felt for Zach was that he was an impossible objective. For reasons of his own, he simply wasn't interested in her, at least not in a romantic way.

She decided to put him out of her mind. After all, a man and a woman could just be friends, couldn't they? No law stated they had to be lovers. That was a choice either of them should feel free to make, and he'd made life easier on her by making the decision for both of them.

Zach paced the boardwalk along the private beach at Eastern Point. Paul had said he would pick up Caroline at exactly noon, then they'd meet him at half past twelve on the short walkway that separated the ocean and sand from the beach road. But it was 12:50 p.m. now, and they were nowhere in sight.

"If he chickened out, I'll kill him," Zach muttered, spinning on the heels of his bare feet and picking up a splinter, which irritated him all the more. Taking a human form had its definite disadvantages—like pain.

He hopped to a nearby bench and propped his injured foot on his knee to study his wound. Luckily the sliver had only pierced the first layer of tough skin on the ball of his foot. But the end sticking out was short, and his wide fingers refused to grip it. He tried, cautiously, several times, aware that he'd probably bungle the job and break off the tip at skin level, then he'd have to suffer with the aggravation of a sensitive foot all afternoon, and eventually go back to the apartment and dig the thing out with a needle.

He hated needles.

"You're supposed to read the lines on your palm, not on the bottom of your foot," a sweet voice chimed out from above him.

Zach looked up to see Caroline grinning naughtily at him. Paul stood beside her, looking typically confused.

"This hurts like hell," he insisted, plucking ineffectively at the stubby splinter.

"Here, let me try," Caroline said. She folded her legs under her and sat on the rough planks in front of him, taking his foot gently in her hands.

While she figured out the best angle of attack, Zach looked down at her with new admiration. She was a natural beauty, her soft brown hair setting off fair skin and doelike eyes, but she was more than something pretty to look at. She was tender and caring, a born nurturer. He suddenly understood why Meher believed she'd be the perfect mother for a special child.

Then Zach's line of vision shifted past Caroline's face, dropping a few inches to the lovely swell of her breasts above the neckline of her jade green maillot. She wasn't a large woman, but her breasts possessed a pleasing fullness that was in perfect proportion to her narrow shoulders and slim hips. Her legs, he noticed, too, were long and sleekly shaped. Without intending to, he envisioned them circling his hips, pulling him closer as he lowered himself over her.

"No!" the word burst out of him, chasing away the erotic stirrings that had suddenly made him feel quite alive again.

"Did I hurt you?" she asked, frowning up at him.

"I—just a twinge," he lied. What could he say? You make me feel like throwing you down on the boardwalk and making love to you?

"I'll be careful," she promised.

Her innocent words only reminded him that he, too, must be careful, for her sake. Exquisitely careful. For he'd been given an important mission, and he dared not make a mistake because it could destroy her future as well as his shot at eternity. Any feelings he might have for her, carnal or otherwise, he must overlook. She would marry a man who was right for her, who would give her the baby she deserved—a baby Meher had promised was destined to make a difference in the world. All he, Zach Dawson, Angel of the Third Tier, could give her was a moment of pleasure and the deceptive and brief satisfaction that would come in its wake.

Sleeping with Caroline would be wrong, very wrong, given all he knew about her and her future. But as he watched, she used the soft pads of her thumbs to tenderly smooth the skin on the sole of his foot away from the splinter.

"Tweezers might help," Paul suggested helpfully, peering over her shoulder. "I could see if my parents have—"

"It's all right," she murmured, intent on her task.

Zach gritted his teeth, liking the feeling of her touch, but dreading the moment when she'd pull on the sliver and perhaps lose part of it under his skin. Childhood memories of his dad, roughly digging with a needle for a thorn buried in his leg, sent a shiver through him.

"There, it's out," she said simply, and stood up, flicking an infinitesimal speck from her fingertips.

"You got it?" he asked in disbelief. Grabbing his foot, he stared at its underside. He couldn't even find the place where the splinter had been.

"Gone," she repeated, turning toward the ocean. "Now that I've baked under this sun for a good ten minutes, I'm ready for a swim. That water looks delicious."

Zach looked at Paul. From the darkening in his friend's eyes, he could tell that what Paul thought looked delicious, was Caroline. Good, he thought. Where there's a spark, there's the beginnings of a flame.

"Great idea," Zach said quickly. Seizing Caroline's bag and the beach towel Paul carried over one arm, he suggested, "You guys hit the surf, I'll spread out the towels and be with you in a minute."

Caroline smiled and started down the slope of dazzling white sand, toward the gray-green water, her hips moving in seductive waves of their own.

Paul tossed him a grateful look and jogged eagerly after Caroline.

For a minute, Zach stood watching them. Caroline touched her toes to the ripples at the water's edge, then surprised him by racing headlong into the waves. In the blink of an eye, she dove and gracefully disappeared beneath the water.

Paul looked doubtfully at the chilly New England water, then back up the beach at Zach. Zach waved him forward. With a reluctant shrug, Paul marched bravely into the ocean. The water inched up his pale body until he was standing chest deep, his hair not yet wet, and he looked around for Caroline.

Zach chuckled to himself. "She's a handful, Paul, old boy. You'd better start showing some spunk if you want to hold your own with her."

He'd forgotten that when he addressed a person in his thoughts, his message was transmitted to them as clearly as if he'd picked up a telephone and dialed. When he'd spread out the towels and sat down on one, he looked up to find Paul gamely swimming after Caroline as she laughingly tried to escape him.

"Good for you," he whispered. "She needs to learn to play again, to heal and forget . . . and love again." The last words stuck in his throat.

To love again.

In a way, he supposed, he was jealous. She'd loved once before. Granted, it had been a misplaced love, but it was love nonetheless. He, on the other hand, couldn't really claim to have ever been in love with a woman. Oh sure, he'd *made love* to plenty of women, or at least he'd had sex with them. But the real thing, the kind of love you throw your whole heart and soul into...well, that hadn't entered into the bargain.

Caroline and Paul were now splashing each other and ducking under the water, trying to grab each other's feet. Then Paul sucked in a deep breath and dove, but he didn't immediately reappear. Caroline looked around with a puzzled expression. A second later, she squealed and flushed a pink so deep Zach could see the change in color on her cheeks from the beach.

He sat up straight and glared across the water, suddenly alert. What had Paul done? Had he dived down to the bottom and tickled her feet? Had he run his hand up her leg?

Zach knew what *he* would have done, had he been in Paul's place. He'd have patted that adorable bottom of hers. He'd have snaked his arm around her waist and gently pulled her under, then nuzzled his face between her luscious breasts . . .

Tearing off his T-shirt, Zach shot up off the sand and ran toward the water. A primitive beat throbbed through his veins. He had no idea what he intended to do. All he knew was he couldn't sit under the blazing summer sun and watch another man play petting games with Caroline.

He took three long strides into the water, tucked his head between his muscled shoulders, and dove into an oncoming wave. His sun-bronzed body sliced through the cool water, soothing his flesh but not his libido. In four strong strokes he reached them and burst through the frothy green water between clumps of brown kelp.

"Zach!" Caroline cried in surprise. "Where were you? We were looking all over for you." Without waiting for an answer, she flashed him an enticing grin and executed a neat surface dive.

Zach looked at Paul, who appeared to be out of breath, and lifted an eyebrow. "Hard work, killing time with a pretty woman, huh?"

Paul puffed out his chest as if pleased with himself, and more than a little aroused by their water games. "If you didn't feel like swimming, Zach, you could have stayed on the beach."

"Oh, I *definitely* feel like a good swim. I need the exercise. Important to keep in shape, you know. You ought to do laps up and down the beach. Builds great muscle tone, expands the lungs."

"Tell you what," Paul said slyly, "why don't *you* swim the laps, and I'll keep Caroline company."

Caroline had been trying to walk on her hands on the bottom. Only her feet and ankles stuck up out of the water, swaying with the motion of the low waves as they rolled toward shore. Zach watched her as she broke the surface, water sheeting off her dark hair, beads of the sea clinging to her eyelashes—and something inside of him ached.

"You look like a sea nymph," he said without thinking.

She smiled and dove again.

Paul scowled warily at Zach, as if he'd suddenly become aware of an unspoken competition between them. Then a triumphant glimmer lit his eyes and he ducked beneath the water.

What is he up to? Zach wondered, at first more amused than worried.

He tracked the other man's pale shape, gliding just beneath the surface of the shoulder-high water, heading directly for Caroline. In an intuitive flash, Zach realized what Paul intended to do. He was going to swim between Caroline's long legs and pick her up on his shoulders, as they'd done with UConn coeds at the campus pool. He remembered all too vividly how the girls' firm, young thighs had clamped around his neck. How, his passenger would sometimes lean forward while trying to balance on his shoulders, and innocently press the soft mound of her femininity into the back on his neck, sending erotic fingers of fire straight down to his—

It was all Zach could do to stop himself from diving in and intercepting Paul. *Anyway,* he argued with himself, *you wanted them to hit it off. Didn't you?* If Paul got a little playful, wasn't that a good sign?

Zach turned away and glared stonily at an oncoming wave, unable to stomach witnessing the moment when Paul caught up with Caroline. The wave moved slowly toward shore, not a big wave at all, just a shallow crest of spume like each of its brothers. Because of the sandbar farther out and the coving effect of the rocky shore, the waves at Eastern Point were never big enough to consider surfing.

As Zach stared at the low ridge of water, he thought, *I wish you were a monster wave. I wish you'd knock that jerk for a loop he wouldn't forget!*

He closed his eyes for half a second and let out a long, unhappy sigh, envisioning Paul threading his lanky body between Caroline's lovely legs. When he opened his eyes, the scene before him yanked the air out of his lungs.

An immense, churning tower of water, ten times the size of any wave that had hit the beach that day, boiled and curled dangerously toward the swimmers. *Dear Lord, what have I done?* he thought.

All around him, others began to notice the oncoming wall of water.

"Look out! It's a rilly, rilly big wave!" a teenage girl shrieked, sounding more excited than terrified.

Two younger boys took up her cry.

Dozens of swimmers scampered frantically for shore.

"Zach!" Caroline cried. He whipped around and spotted her fifty feet away from him, too far for him to reach her before the wave hit. "Dive under it! Dive!" she shouted, then curled her body tightly and sliced deep beneath the water.

Zach looked around frantically for Paul, but his friend still hadn't surfaced. He took Caroline's advice and ducked beneath the surface then jackknifed sharply and kicked hard, heading toward the sandy bottom. He felt the grit and pebbles surge between his fingers and under his belly, as the wave passed over, tugging fiercely at his body. Almost immediately, the water smoothed to a silky flow. Holding his breath, Zach shoved off the bottom and shot upward toward the eerie greenish light of the surface.

When he broke through with a silvery spray, he gasped for air and looked around to make sure everyone was all right. Several lifeguards had gathered in the shallows and were helping a dozen or so swimmers to their feet, but no one seemed hurt. Another pair of guards was taking out a rowboat to check on people who had been swimming in deeper water. Kids were laughing, finding the freakish incident cause for hysterical antics. He could already overhear a few rehearsing stories to be told to friends at home. Parents were counting heads, looking relieved.

Zach spotted Caroline twenty feet closer to shore than where she'd dived. She was smiling and gulping down air, looking around expectantly. "Zach! Oh, there you are! Wasn't that magnificent? I've never seen a wave like that here at the Point. Where did something like that come from?"

He thought fast. "Must have been the wake of an awfully big boat," he mumbled, staring solemnly toward the horizon. "Sometimes the ferries to Block Island, they kick up quite a—"

"No way!" She laughed at him. "The ferries pass by here half a dozen times a day, and I've never seen one do that." She looked around again. "Have you seen Paul?"

A nauseous feeling suddenly filled his gut, and Zach stared across the ocean's now-smooth surface, then down into the water around them. But he couldn't really tell exactly where they'd been standing when the wave hit, or where Paul might have ended up. Had he still been under the water when the breaker hit? Or had he surfaced at the wrong moment and taken its force, full in the face?

Zach stepped closer to Caroline. "He'll be okay." All he'd done was mumble something about wanting to knock him for a loop, right? Thank goodness he hadn't wished to knock him to Kingdom Come!

Tensely they scanned the wave tops, now meek and harmless, then the line of the beach, crammed with bathers, jabbing fingers seaward, still talking excitedly about the rogue wave.

"There he is!" Caroline shouted.

Zach followed her pointing finger to a shape squatting on the sand, coughing up ocean. He raced Caroline to the beach. They stopped in the water's edge in front of Paul, who tipped red-rimmed eyes sheepishly up at them.

"Boy, that one sure caught me by surprise." He choked out the words.

"Are you all right?" Caroline knelt beside him in the wet sand.

"I'll be okay, soon as I catch my breath." Paul shook his head, and Zach swore he could hear water sloshing in it. "I was swimming underneath you, Caroline, and you just disappeared. I came up to catch my breath and find you . . . and there was . . . there was this incredible mountain of water." He shuddered, still looking dazed.

Zach reached down a hand and helped Paul to his feet. "Sorry, old man. You took quite a tumble."

"Wasn't your fault." Paul brushed fingers through his wet, sandy hair. "Just nature at work." The attempt at smoothing his hair only made it bristle in a dozen different directions. "I don't know about you two, but I think I've swallowed enough ocean for one day. Let's go back to my folks' house and have that late lunch we'd planned on."

"Good idea," Zach said quickly. He glanced speculatively at Caroline, who was observing Paul. He tried to read her expression but couldn't. He hoped he hadn't shown his friend in such a poor light that she'd become disinterested in him. That hadn't been his intent, and it would certainly be counterproductive to his job. "Come on," he said, starting up the beach toward the towels. "Time's a wasting."

Caroline couldn't figure out what was going on. Zach had obviously set up the afternoon trip to the beach to bring her and Paul together. What his motive might be for playing matchmaker, she still couldn't figure out, but she was growing more and more determined to discover what made Zach tick.

One thing was certain—it wasn't going to be easy to get inside his head. He seemed to continually erect emotional blocks between them. She could feel them forming as solidly as the stone walls surrounding the beach. And his actions contradicted themselves. One minute he was practically pushing her and Paul together. But as soon as she was in the water with Paul, beginning to have a good time and flirt a little, Zach appeared out of the blue, inserting himself into their game as if he were trying to distract her from his friend.

That didn't make sense. Unless, she thought with a glimmer of comprehension, he was jealous. And that possibility intrigued her.

Agatha and Bernard Cooper must have been older parents by the time Paul came along. The couple appeared well past retirement age, and had a graying, settled look. They didn't seem interested in anything beyond the four walls of their white Cape Cod, two blocks from the ocean.

The house, Caroline thought, seemed mostly a storage area for Mrs. Cooper's collections. One glass étagère in the living room housed an impressive but jumbled assembly of Hummels. On shelves beside the fireplace were Precious Moments figurines. A homemade wooden case displayed crystal and porcelain carousel horses. David Winter's cottages ranged across shelves built into one entire wall of the dining room.

There hardly seemed room for two people to move between the glass-fronted cabinets and shelves overburdened with fragile figurines and miniatures. Caroline couldn't imagine the couple entertaining friends or family in the tight rooms. One careless move from an overexcited child or negligent adult could prove disastrous.

Caroline seriously doubted Paul's story about his parents craving company. But she thought it rather endearing that he'd wanted so badly to spend an afternoon with her, he'd been willing to fib.

The five of them—Caroline, Paul, Zach, and the Coopers—ended up on a flagstone patio in back of the house, around a redwood picnic table draped with a red-and-white checked plastic cloth. Mr. Cooper grilled hamburgers and hot dogs, and Caroline helped his wife bring out bowls of potato salad, pickles and relishes.

They ate in the shade of a huge maple. Paul sat on one side of her, Zach on the other. The conversation was light, peppered with comments about their adventure at the beach and the Humongous Wave Out of Nowhere, as Paul referred to the strange incident.

Caroline began to relax and enjoy herself. It had been so long since she'd socialized with anyone other than Suzanne and Ralph.

For years, all her dinners, treks to the movies or a concert, had been with Rob. She'd been perfectly content to let him arrange their nights out, which, in retrospect, were few—for her birthday, or as a substitute for the Christmas present he hadn't the ingenuity to choose. Even then, Rob paid for a meal in a restaurant begrudgingly. He hadn't liked to spend money on things that were *frivolous.*

"Why pay four times what you'd spend on groceries to put on a tie and sit in an uncomfortable chair and eat food that isn't as good as what you can cook at home?" he'd often say. Caroline could see his logic, but once in a while it would be nice to not have to labor for an hour or more in the kitchen after a long day's work, to have someone wait on *her.*

"I've visited your shop often," Mrs. Cooper was saying, and Caroline turned politely to listen as she took another bite of the juicy hamburger. "The Silver Whale is delightful. You've probably noticed that my collection includes several pieces from your store."

"Of course, I knew right away," Caroline lied harmlessly. Brand-name collectibles were so widespread, they could have been bought at any of six or seven local shops in Mystic, Groton, or nearby New London. "You have a real eye for quality, Agatha."

The woman blushed, her full cheeks plumping with pride. "I like to think so. If there's one thing I know, it's how to make a home special."

Her husband smiled companionably at her, but said nothing. Caroline wondered how he felt about living in a curio cabinet. But she sensed that the couple were happy, in their own way—comfortable with their clutter.

She felt Paul looking at her and smiled at him. He'd managed to comb down his hair and clean most of the sand out of his ears. He'd changed into Dockers and polo shirt. He had, more or less, restored his well-groomed, conservative appearance.

Paul winked at her in a way, she suspected, he thought of as roguish, although the gesture only emphasized his awkwardness. Smiling again, Caroline looked down at her plate and plucked a potato chip to pop into her mouth. As she crunched on it, she felt his hand settle on her bare knee.

It was a nice hand. Not at all groping, just warm and friendly. In a way, that disappointed her. Paul's touch didn't result in the heated streaks she imagined racing up her leg if Zach had been the one to get playfully fresh under the tablecloth. Paul's hand might as well have been her brother's.

Zach cleared his throat and announced loudly, "Hey, buddy, how about you and I clear the table for your folks and bring on the dessert."

As if fearful someone might notice, Paul quickly withdrew his palm from her knee. "I'm not sure everyone has finished eating," he said, hesitantly.

"Looks like your mom and dad are done, and your plate's pretty clean," Zach said with forced enthusiasm. He started retrieving the used paper plates nested in wicker holders.

Caroline shoveled the last two bites of potato salad into her mouth, just before Zach snatched her plate and plastic utensils. She looked up at him curiously. Had he done it again? She couldn't see how he'd have been able to see the subtle pat on her knee, but there was no other explanation for his sudden insistence on drawing Paul away from the table.

Amused by the boyish competitiveness between the two men, she hid a smile behind her napkin. Zach was even more complex than she'd at first suspected. She was intrigued, and decided right then and there, she wouldn't be satisfied until she found out *everything* there was to know about her new neighbor.

Chapter 5

Caroline slipped her key into the apartment door and stepped through. Tossing the canvas overnight bag in the direction of the louvered doors that hid her washing machine, she spun around to close the hallway door and came face-to-face with Zach.

"So, what do you think of him?" he asked, smiling expectantly, as if he were trying to coach the right answer out of her.

Caroline laughed, shaking her head. She hadn't realized he'd followed her into her apartment after she'd tossed him a "goodbye" over her shoulder in the hallway. "*What* are you talking about?"

"Paul. He's a nice guy, right?"

"He's very nice," she agreed. Unzipping her bag, she dropped her soggy bathing suit and seaweedy-smelling beach towel into the washer. A cloud of sand dusted her carpet between the bag and machine. Why was it that, as long and hard as you shook a towel at the beach, it always produced more sand once you got it home? "He's just not . . ." She absentmindedly fished for words.

"Your type?" He raised an eyebrow.

"I suppose that's what I was going to say. Besides, I told you, I'm not interested in getting serious with any man right now. And Paul seems a very serious sort of person, although he was trying to loosen up.'' Scooping detergent into the washer, she started it and turned to squarely face Zach, her arms crossed over her chest.

He squinted at her suspiciously. "What are you looking at me like that for?"

Caroline didn't answer immediately. She was too interested in what she saw. His blue eyes sparkled with an inner light that seemed almost unearthly. Almost *too* bright. She wondered if he wore colored contacts.

"It seems to me," she pronounced slowly, "that as eager as you seem to get me and Paul together, you keep doing things to obstruct us."

"Obstruct you?" He laughed tightly. "That's crazy. A wave washed him ashore, and the meal was finished."

"Aha!" she cried, lunging toward him, her finger raised like a prosecuting attorney who'd just made a crucial point before the jury. "So you *knew* he was playing with my knee under the picnic table."

Zach's face went blank. "Under the table?" he murmured innocently. "Really? What a sly devil."

She made a face at him. "Are you married, Zach?" she asked impulsively.

"Married?" He stared at her, looking suddenly wary. "No—why?"

"Engaged? In a relationship?"

"No. No, I'm not . . ." He began to look irritated. "What's this all about?"

Caroline shrugged but didn't answer him.

She wasn't sure why knowing anything more about Zach than she already knew was important to her. It just was.

Perhaps she wanted to define him and his effect on her, because she'd felt better during the weeks since he'd moved in across the hall from her than she had at any other time since her baby had died. She hadn't forgotten the pain of course, and not an hour passed that she didn't think of Jimmy—snuggled trustingly in her arms; smelling of baby powder, formula and that impossible-to-describe sweetness all babies seemed to exude; clutching wisps of her hair in his little fist, as if they were a lifeline. And she'd wept . . . she'd wept as recently as the day before. But since Zach had moved in across the hall there had been something to distract her, and she found the memories easier to visit without tumbling back into the inky void of her despair.

She couldn't explain the effect Zach had over her. Yes, there was a physical attraction—at least on her part—but it was more than that. The friendship that seemed to be developing between them was warm and easy . . . and comforting. She hoped he'd live across the hall from her for a long time. She hoped if there was a woman in his life, she'd either continue to stay away or be the very understanding type who wouldn't mind him having female friends. Even better, maybe his girlfriend—she was sure he must have at least one—would dump him. Then he'd be free to—

Her fists automatically clenched at her sides, and she stared at Zach, surprised by the sudden surge of longing and possessiveness she felt for him. Picturing another woman in his arms made her stomach churn.

You're insane, she reprimanded herself. It wasn't as if they'd ever been or ever would be lovers. They were friends . . . just friends! How could jealousy have anything to do with such a casual, neighborly relationship?

But Caroline couldn't ignore the questions that continued nagging her.

"So, *is* there someone you're serious about?" she asked. "You seem to be taking obvious interest in my love life. I guess I should be able to do the same for you."

She saw the unmistakable flicker of pain cross his features, just before he turned away from her. "This isn't something I can talk about now," he said stiffly.

Caroline bit down on her lower lip, surprised by his reaction. "I—I'm sorry. I didn't mean to pry, I was just curious, Zach. Honest. I'm sorry if I hurt you or brought back unpleasant memories." She could have kicked herself for being so insensitive. She, of all people, should know better.

"It's no big deal," he said, walking away from her toward the door.

"Listen, your personal life . . . that's yours," she called after him. "I had no right to ask you questions like that. We're neighbors. We're friends, and I know you meant well when you tried to start something between me and Paul." He stopped with his hand on the doorknob, listening to her but saying nothing. "Zach," she continued softly, "you've made me feel better, just by showing an interest in how I feel about my life and what happens to me."

"I have?" he asked, sounding a little more cheerful.

"Yes, you have. Really." She stepped closer to him and touched the back of his shoulder, lightly.

He turned toward her.

Caroline took in his sharp, tanned features; his eyes were so full of hope and meaning that she could only guess what they might be. He towered over her, casting a shadow across her features, for which she was grateful. She didn't want him to be able to read her feelings at that moment. He might mistake them for something more than friendship.

Abruptly Zach stepped forward and wrapped his arms around her. She was startled , but after a moment, pressed her cheek to his chest, heard the reassuring beat of his heart against her ear and felt instantly calmed.

"I'm glad I'm doing you some good, even if it's not exactly what they wanted."

"Hmm?" she murmured.

"Nothing. It's nothing important," Zach said thickly.

Then, just as quickly as he had embraced her, he let her go and stepped back. Before Caroline could recover from the shock of their unexpected contact, he'd let himself out the door and closed it behind him.

The next day, Caroline rose at 6:00 a.m. She had dozed only fitfully during the night, and it seemed unlikely she would sleep anymore. She showered and washed her hair, even though she'd already gone through the same routine after Zach had left the night before. She couldn't stop thinking about him.

He was physically appealing, to say the least. In stretchy swimming briefs, he'd take away any woman's breath. His shoulders, arms, torso were lean and ridged with muscle. He moved with athletic ease, like a man accustomed to physical activity. There was a kind of Spartan grace and agility about the way he negotiated any room—economical yet fluid, strong but controlled. She wondered if he was a good dancer, then remembered the way he'd held her and wished there had been music playing. With the excuse of dancing to a familiar tune, maybe he would have held her longer.

She spent the day at the shop, daydreaming about Zach. But when Suzanne asked her how the beach party had gone she chose her words carefully.

"Paul and his parents are very nice," she admitted. "We had a good time."

"Define 'a good time,'" Suzanne replied, her eyes twinkling wickedly.

"Nothing happened." Caroline laughed and shook a scolding finger at her. "Get that mind of yours out of the proverbial gutter, dear. We went swimming, then we cooked out in the Coopers' backyard, then Zach brought me home."

"*Zach* brought you home? Not Paul?"

"Yes. We do live in the same apartment building, remember? It was convenient."

Suzanne drew her lips into a pout. "Find out anything more about your mysterious neighbor?"

Caroline tilted her head back and peered down her nose at her friend with mock disdain. "I don't pry into other people's lives."

Suzanne held up both hands defensively. "Just curious. You said you liked him, and I thought maybe he'd come around and..." She must have caught the warning look in Caroline's eyes. "Well, never mind," she said quickly.

Over the next few days, Caroline saw nothing at all of Zach, and she began to think he might be avoiding her. Then, on the following Friday, when she returned home from the shop, she noticed the door to his apartment had been left open a few inches. Through the crack, she could see one end of a thinly furnished living room—a beige couch, a brass halogen floor lamp, an expanse of neutral wall-to-wall carpeting.

She was wondering if she should knock to make sure he realized his door was unlatched, when Zach pulled open his door and stepped into the hallway.

"Hey, neighbor, how's it going?" he asked cheerily.

"Just fine," she said, wondering if he'd been waiting for her, and why. "And you?"

"Great. Couldn't be better."

She narrowed her eyes at him. "So, what's up?" she asked.

"Up? Does something have to be up for me to say hello?"

Caroline sighed. "Zach."

"Well, in a way, I guess you're right. I did want to talk to you." He glanced down at her through thick eyelashes—a pale fringe over blue orbs that seemed to draw her toward him. "I've sort of obligated myself to participating in a fund-raiser for the new children's wing of the hospital in New London. It's the kind of thing people attend as couples, and I—well—"

"You need an escort?" she asked, smiling.

"It wouldn't be like a date or anything," he stated hastily. "I just thought, as friends, you know..."

"I'd love to go, if it would help out the hospital," she said quickly, meaning it. The emergency room staff had been so supportive the day she'd arrived with Jimmy in the ambulance— Caroline shook her head, storing the memory away for another time when she could deal with it, alone.

"Count me in," she said. "When is this thing happening?"

"Actually I'm giving you rather short notice," he apologized.

"How short?" Why was it men never planned ahead the way women did? Caroline tapped her toe and glared at him as if he were a naughty little boy.

"Like, tomorrow evening," he admitted meekly. "Cocktails and hors d'oeuvres, accompanied by a string quartet and a brief solicitation speech by Dr. Maxwell Pearson, Chief Surgeon and Chairman of the Building Committee.

She wrinkled her nose. "Sounds stuffy."

"I don't think it will be too bad. Besides, just think of all the wealthy prospective customers for the Silver Whale at a gathering like that. People will mix, strike up conversations. You can drop your shop's name into the conversation a few dozen times. Wouldn't do your business any harm."

"I suppose you're right," she admitted. "All right. What time will you pick me up?"

"Seven o'clock, if that's okay with you."

"Fine." She thought for a minute. "I guess I should wear something a little dressy?"

"I expect so. I'll leave the details to you." Looking as if his thoughts were miles away, he turned to leave, then suddenly swiveled around to face her again. "And thanks, Caroline. It will help a lot, your being there."

She shrugged. "I'm not sure why, but I'll be glad to lend a hand any way I can."

Zach closed the apartment door behind him and leaned against it with relief. He'd done it. He'd actually asked her to go with him to the reception, and she'd said *yes*.

For days he'd agonized over his list of prospective husbands for Caroline. Sure, Paul Cooper was eager enough to continue dating her. But, now that Zach had seen them together, he realized Paul, as well meaning and nice as he was, wasn't right for her. She needed someone stronger, a man who knew his own mind without coaching from the sidelines, a man with the means to support her and their child, to give them both the best life had to offer—from a beautiful and safe home for Caroline to the best education for their offspring.

At last Zach made his decision.

First step, he'd have to find a plausible excuse for telephoning Max Pearson. By asking around, he discovered Max was still involved with the new wing of the Southeastern Connecticut Pediatric Hospital that he—as Zane—had been asked to help build, before the accident in Hartford. He called Max and explained that, in memory of his cousin, he wanted to be counted on as a benefactor. That had gotten him on the right mailing lists and, as he'd hoped, an invitation to a reception that had already been scheduled soon followed, along with a pledge envelope.

He just hoped things would go more smoothly with Max than they had with Paul.

Zach had done a lot of thinking about that day at the beach. He recognized the mistakes he'd made. Paul had simply been too wishy-washy. He'd tried out halfhearted moves on Caroline that had been easy for Zach to thwart. Max was different.

For one thing, he had a lot more experience with women. He was older than Paul by fifteen years, although on meeting him few people would have believed he was closing in on fifty years. His silver-streaked hair was the only feature that hinted at his true age. He had sharp, inquisitive eyes, a competitive nature and a thirty-year-old's physique. He was a distinguished pediatric surgeon with a thriving career, who'd lost his wife three years earlier to cancer.

Eveline hadn't been able to have kids. Rumor had it, Max was ready to marry again, and he'd confided in his closest friends that he was interested in starting a family before he ran out of time. Max had been dating younger women, and Zach suspected it wasn't just because they appealed to him on a physical level. He was looking for the right woman, the woman worthy to be the mother of his children. Zach had the perfect solution to Max's predicament. Which would be, coincidentally, the perfect solution for his own dilemma of finding a husband for Caroline.

As promised, Zach picked up Caroline at 7:00 p.m. He hadn't mentioned anything to Caroline about Max Pearson. If he did, he feared she'd smell a rat and get defensive, maybe even change her mind about going with him. So he kept her occupied by chatting about the new wing that the donations would help fund.

"I think it's marvelous, what these people are doing for the children," she said, looking over the literature Zach had brought her, while they drove.

There would be an interactive play area, staffed with qualified teachers. Children able to leave their beds could play together under proper supervision. And one end of the space would be set up as a classroom for long-term patients who needed tutoring to keep up with their schoolwork while they recuperated from surgery, injuries, or illnesses.

"Just marvelous," she repeated in amazement. "But I'm not sure I understand your connection with the project." She looked across the seat of Zach's car at him, her cheeks rosy with excitement. She seemed to grow more and more alive with each passing day, and he enjoyed giving himself a little credit for that.

"I worked with Pearson on the original plans," Zach replied without thinking about what he was saying.

"*You* did?" She leaned toward him with interest.

"Yeah, I—" Only then did he realize how close he'd come to blowing his story. "I mean, well, to be honest I only had a little input. Zane—remember my cousin?—well, he was the construction engineer who was brought in to consult with the architects during the planning stages. He showed me blueprints and stuff, asked me what I thought."

"And what did you tell him?" she asked.

"Go for it!"

To his ears Caroline's laughter sounded as sweet and pure as harps singing. She ought to laugh more often, he thought wistfully. "Well, I'm sure your advice was *extremely* important to the project," she said in a solemn voice, patting him on the arm.

"I'd like to think so." He grinned at her and steered into the center lane to pass another car.

They drove across the Gold Star Memorial Bridge from the Groton side of the Thames River to the New London side. The water far below was a dark blue, almost black—the color of a natural sapphire. He thought immediately of blue eyes, but quickly decided he liked brown better. They seemed more real, more down to earth, reliable, richer with emotion. He glanced sideways at Caroline's eyes and smiled.

"What?" she asked.

"Nothing."

"I saw you looking at me. Am I dressed all right?"

"You're dressed just fine," he said as his glance dropped to her knees and the three inches of thigh between them and her skirt hem. "Well, maybe the skirt could be a little longer."

"You think?" She scrunched up her nose, considering the smooth expanse of her long legs.

"Well, they look just fine to me, personally," he said, feeling a heat wave start to build somewhere below his belt buckle. "I was just thinking of the rest of the guests. They'll be a pretty sophisticated crowd, I suppose."

She shrugged. "I'll bet I'm not the only one to show up in a short skirt."

But when they walked into the room where the reception was being held, most of the women were wearing elegant dresses that brushed their calves or ankles—not exactly formal in length or design, but far less casual than the red batik-print skirt and matching top Caroline had worn.

"Oh dear," she murmured under her breath.

"It's all right," he reassured her. "No one's going to throw you out. Besides, this way you'll stand out in the crowd."

"Maybe I don't want to stand out," she whispered in his ear, her grip tightening on his arm.

It's better if you do, believe me, he thought. He didn't want her to fade into the crowd, or Max would never notice her.

"Hmm?" She frowned at him. "Did you say something?"

"Never mind," he said quickly.

Taking her elbow, Zach steered her between groups of cocktail-wielding guests, toward the bar, then stepped to the end of the line of guests waiting to order drinks. He scanned the room for Pearson. For the first five minutes, as the line crept forward, he couldn't find the doctor anywhere. Then he caught sight of a tall, trim figure in a European-cut suit, topped by a head of distinguished silver-and-black hair.

Zach grabbed two glasses of wine from a waiter circulating with a tray. Handing one to Caroline, he took her arm and started moving her across the room.

"Could we stand still just long enough to have our drinks?" she asked. "I can't walk and swallow at the same time."

"In a minute," Zach said, urgently maneuvering between guests, toward Pearson, who had suddenly dropped one group and started off toward another. He was afraid he'd lose Max, and he was also worried that the shrewd doctor would somehow see through his charade of pretending to be his own cousin.

It had worked fine with Paul and a few other people who'd known him in his mortal days. He'd learned that friends and acquaintances who had heard of his accident, didn't look at him as if he were a ghost or the walking dead. People believed what they were told was true. To them, Zane Dawson was dead because they'd read it in the newspaper or someone who had been at the job site had related the horrifying details of Zane Dawson's demise to them. So, even though he looked just like himself, like Zane, they were willing to accept him as someone from his family who just happened to resemble his cousin.

Holding his breath, Zach moved Caroline around the last group of couples standing between her and Max Pearson. Almost in the same instant, Max looked away from the woman he was talking to, and straight at Caroline. The older man's pale gray eyes traveled admiringly up Caroline's long legs and focused on her face as she at last stopped to sip her wine, oblivious to the attention she was attracting.

Zach stepped away from her, to better observe the situation. *Thataboy,* he silently mouthed. *She's beautiful, isn't she? Has that artsy look you like, doesn't she? Come on over and introduce yourself.*

On cue, Dr. Maxwell Pearson excused himself from his friends and started toward Caroline. She turned just in time to see him stop in front of her and give her his most charming smile.

Then he turned to Zach. "I'd know you anywhere. You must be Zach, Zane Dawson's cousin. You're a dead ringer for him."

Gotcha, Zach thought with satisfaction. He shook hands with Max, remembering the firm grip that had impressed him when they'd met to discuss the plans for the children's wing. "It's good to finally meet you, Dr. Pearson."

"Max . . . always Max . . ." Pearson slapped him companionably on the back. "He was a brilliant engineer, your cousin. Very likable fellow, too. I was sorry to hear of his untimely end. So tragic—a man that young, with so much to offer the world."

"Indeed," Zach agreed, feeling a genuine twinge of sorrow for himself.

Pearson's glance smoothly swerved toward Caroline. "And is this your lovely wife, Zach?"

"I'm Caroline North." She stuck out her hand to shake his, but he cupped it in his own, placing his other hand over it, as if he were gently trapping a small bird. "Zach and I are neighbors," she explained, "and he needed an escort for tonight. I was game."

"Oh?" Pearson's salt-and-pepper brows rose a barely perceptible quarter of an inch. "And are *you* from this area, Ms. North?"

"Caroline," she insisted, her voice warm and encouraging.

Zach took another step backward, to better watch them. He knew Pearson was interested in her, but it seemed Caroline was also intrigued by him. *This is going great,* he thought gleefully. Meher was going to be thrilled.

"And what do you do when you aren't attending charity affairs?" Max asked.

"I own the Silver Whale, a little gift shop in Mystic."

"I've been in it!" Max cried, looking pleased with himself. "A cut above the usual souvenir vendor, if I recall correctly. A very pretty collection of Swarovski crystal. And, I think, an excellent but small grouping of authentic scrimshaw."

"Yes," Caroline said, smiling. "My partner and I pride ourselves on those pieces. Although, they're antique and not for sale. Real scrimshaw is carved from whale or elephant ivory. We don't condone the killing of animals to provide ornamental fixtures."

Max studied her for a moment. "That's a very responsible attitude. We humans should protect the other species."

Zach exulted silently. They were hitting it off super. He'd practically sewn up the whole job in one night's work! Meher might even bump him up two levels on the basis of his superlative performance!

Zach tossed off the rest of his drink. "I think I'll make a trip to the bar," he announced. "Anything for you, Maxwell? Caroline?"

Caroline raised her nearly full glass to signal she was fine with what she had. Max waved him off with a vague smile, the kind of hopeful grimace a man wears when he hasn't yet determined what his chances are with a woman he's just met.

"You've got more going for you than you know, Max," Zach murmured as he strode away across the room. "Not many men have Heaven in their corner."

Caroline took a long, slow sip of the white wine Zach had handed her a few minutes earlier, and listened with interest to Max Pearson. He described dramatically the progress they'd made toward financing the new wing, and confided his frustration with involving people in a local project, when it often seemed more exotic to support causes on foreign soils.

"But there is *nothing* more important than the health of our children," Caroline said, firmly.

"I couldn't agree more." Max took a swallow from his drink and observed her. His eyes assumed the hooded appearance of a male predator, and she realized that Dr. Maxwell Pearson might be a few years older than she, but he was a passionate and worldly man who probably got just about anything he wanted. She was fairly certain that, at least at that moment, what he wanted was her.

She twirled the stem of her glass between her fingertips, then sipped the tepid wine, hoping he wouldn't notice that her hands were trembling.

He must have sensed her nervousness because, when she looked up again, he smiled and said, "You're a very pretty woman, Caroline. You shouldn't feel ashamed when men admire you."

Caroline felt herself blush. "I don't feel ashamed, just a little awkward." She didn't want to explain her personal history, though, so she dove back into their discussion. "Tell me more about the program you've planned for the children's wing. I read about it in the solicitation brochure, but I'd like to know more."

Max nodded and took another swallow of wine. "We're addressing the health of all children, regardless of their family income," he stated. "The Urgent Care facility will not only deal with traumatic injuries, such as those suffered by victims of automobile accidents, but it will also be available to children whose parents don't have a regular physician or insurance to cover day-to-day problems. We'll offer first-aid and institute a well-child clinic with free inoculations for any child whose family can't afford to pay."

"That sounds wonderful," Caroline said.

She admired Max Pearson. Here was a man, she thought, who could have put all of his time into paying patients—which probably would have made his accountant much happier. But he'd chosen to set aside a large chunk of his life to look out for the less fortunate.

Max tilted his head to one side, a warm expression filling his clear, gray eyes. "I'll bet you have a couple of kids of your own—that's why you're so interested in the new wing."

Caroline pulled in a sharp breath, feeling as if he'd shot back his fist and punched her as hard as he could in the stomach. "N-no," she whispered, lowering her glance to the floor. "I have no children. But I do love them."

"Well, that's all that matters, right?" Max crowed cheerfully. "You're a young woman. You've got plenty of time to make a family."

He has no idea, she thought sadly. None at all.

Suddenly she knew she couldn't stand in the middle of that glittering room and explain the horror of the last year to him. She was about to excuse herself when a man stepped up to Max and told him it was time for him to give his speech.

"Fine, Keith. I'll be right with you," he said, then turned back to her after the other man had left. "Things are going to get pretty busy tonight, I'm afraid. But I'd enjoy talking with you again, Caroline. I'd like to hear your reaction to the plans we've just settled on." He lifted her fingertips toward him, and for a moment she thought he was going to kiss them. "May I call you sometime?"

Caroline smiled nervously at him and opened her mouth to make her usual excuses. But an odd sensation stole across her. A numbness seemed to paralyze her lips for an instant. Then the word "Yes" sprang out of her mouth.

"I—I'm at the shop most days," she babbled on. "Give me a ring there, Max."

"Will do," he said, beaming at her as he spun on his heel and walked away, humming happily.

Caroline frowned in exasperation, watching him climb the steps to a speaker's podium. What had gotten into her? She'd intended to discourage him. She didn't want to be around someone whose business was little children. She'd be constantly reminded of her own baby.

Swinging around, she spotted Zach watching her from across the room. For an instant, his figure seemed to waver in the light, as if he wasn't completely solid. Then he started toward her and the trick her eyes had been playing on her stopped.

Caroline stared into her wine flute. Half a glass certainly shouldn't blur her vision.

"Looks like you two hit it off great!" Zach chortled, raising his glass to her.

"I'm not sure our hitting it off is such a good idea," she sighed.

"Why the hell not?"

"Don't get me wrong, Max seems like a perfect gentleman, a talented doctor and a wonderful man who cares about his community. But I don't think I should get involved with him."

"Involved? Whoa, he works fast. What did he do? Invite you to view his scalpel collection?"

Caroline glowered at him. "Of course not. But he said he'd call me, and if he does, I don't want to let him think I'm interested in anything but a casual friendship."

Zach shrugged. "If I were you, I wouldn't burn any bridges. You never know how you'll feel after you get to know him."

"I suppose you're right," Caroline agreed reluctantly "Getting to know a person can make all the difference in the world. It's just that, with some people, it's hard to get close enough to learn much of anything about them.''

Zach looked puzzled. "I don't think Max is a great enigma. He's wealthy, successful, handsome, dedicated . . ."

"That's not what I meant," Caroline snapped, turning away from Zach to face the podium as a woman stepped up to the microphone to introduce Max.

She felt Zach step up behind her. His breath brushed her ear, sending chills down her spine as he asked, "What *did* you mean?"

She observed the striking doctor, standing beside his presenter on the stage. Why wasn't it Max Pearson who made her feel wobbly in the knees, who made her want to ignore her vow to play it safe and do without love in her life? Why was it Zach who made her feel as if her world was about to spin out of control?

"I don't know," she murmured. "I guess I don't know what I mean."

Chapter 6

Caroline felt as if she'd been riding an emotional roller coaster for weeks. On one hand, having a friendly, capable, trustworthy male within a few steps of her front door was comforting and convenient. When Zach was around, she felt safe, as if she were no longer alone or so terribly vulnerable to life's vagaries. More than once he'd given her a shoulder to cry on, when her thoughts turned to Jimmy during an unguarded moment and she hadn't been able to fight back the tears. And he seemed always available to lend a hand to bring in groceries or to mount a curtain rod in her bedroom or unplug the drain in her kitchen sink.

On the other hand, she became more and more frustrated physically whenever he was near her. Their bodies would brush in passing through a doorway, or he'd unthinkingly rest his wide hand on her arm. She'd want to sustain the lovely, tingling warmth she picked up from him, but he'd react as if she'd touched a lighted match to his flesh. It soon became obvious to Caroline that a natural intimacy was developing between them, but Zach was doing everything he could to ignore the mounting sensual tension.

As the days passed and Caroline followed her customary routine, working at the Silver Whale and passing her free time at home, alone, her curiosity about Zach grew into something of a wicked obsession.

When they bumped into each other on the street or in the hallway, she couldn't resist testing his limits. She'd mention her childhood and watch the interest grow in his eyes as she told him about the happy times she'd shared with her brother and sister. He didn't seem to mind speaking of his own boyhood, growing up north of Hartford. She'd bring up the hospital addition and, predictably, he'd latch onto the topic then steer it toward Max.

But when she asked him about his plans for the future: Would he marry? Did he someday want to have children? Would his job allow him to remain in Mystic? A heavy shadow stole over his handsome features, and a look of incredible sadness dulled the intense blue of his eyes.

She began to treat their meetings as a challenge. It gave her a wry sense of satisfaction to predict his reactions correctly. But she sometimes despised herself for bringing on one of his bleak moods.

A week passed after the fund-raiser for the children's wing, and Max Pearson didn't call. He was probably just being polite when he'd shown an interest in her shop, she reasoned. Perhaps he flirted with any moderately attractive woman. He'd undoubtedly dismissed her from his mind the moment he walked away from her that night. Caroline put the man out of her mind.

One evening after she'd locked up the shop, she stopped by the library to exchange one stack of novels for another. She read at least two books every week, preferring them to television for company. When Caroline reached her apartment, she glanced at Zach's door. It was closed, but a thin golden beam shone through the crack under the door.

She frowned at the light, wondering why she'd never noticed it before. It was almost as if it were more than a source of illumination, as if it were—how could she explain it?—a presence. She imagined Zach standing on the other side of the door, his warmth shining through toward her.

Caroline smiled and shook her head, amazed at the wild turns her imagination was capable of taking in the past few weeks. But she didn't have time to dwell any longer on strange perceptions. Her telephone was ringing inside her apartment.

Caroline gave her front door a shove then swung it shut behind her as she ran for the phone. "Hello?" she gasped.

"Is this Caroline? Caroline North?" a deep voice asked.

"Yes," she answered guardedly. If this was another credit card telemarketing pitch or someone trying to sell her yet another cemetery plot . . .

"I hope you'll remember me," the man said. "This is Max Pearson. We met at the hospital reception about a week ago."

Caroline felt herself relax. "Of course, Max. How nice to hear from you." Her eye caught a movement from across the room and she stared at her front door. It was slightly ajar. Hadn't she closed it all the way? Perhaps not. A draft up the stairwell must have blown it open when it hadn't clicked shut completely.

"There is a function coming up, on September 10," Max continued. "A dinner for which the Funding Committee is charging an atrocious $1,000 a plate. More money for the building project. I was wondering if I could interest you in attending with me?"

The first thought that occurred to Caroline was that she couldn't possibly afford $1,000 for anything, let alone an overpriced, catered meal.

"As my guest, of course," Max added, after her silence. Belatedly it dawned on her that Max was asking her out on a date.

"I'd love to." She blurted out the words before they'd fully formed in her mind. She clamped her teeth together. What was she saying? She'd told Zach she didn't want to get too close to Max, and she'd meant every word. Besides, they were from vastly different social circles. He was accustomed to tossing off a couple thousand dollars for a good cause. She was lucky if she broke even at the end of a month and had an extra ten bucks to treat herself to a couple of videos and a small cheese pizza.

When she and Rob had first rented the apartment, they'd pooled two incomes to afford the new, relatively spacious rooms with a view of the river. The place was, admittedly, much larger and nicer than she needed for herself now, but the idea of giving it up felt wrong, as if she'd be leaving behind the last traces of Jimmy. As long as she lived there, she could catch the faint scent of baby powder and stand in the doorway to his room, imagining he was still lying, sweetly, in his crib...waiting for her to come in and pick him up.

But making each month's rent, on her own, was a financial stretch.

"Good," Max was saying in his take-charge way, snapping her out of her private thoughts, "we'll call it a date. I'll need to pick you up by six o'clock to give us time to get to the dinner. It's being hosted by a couple from Stonington at the Hilton."

Still feeling a little dazed that everything seemed to be happening so fast, Caroline gave him directions to her apartment. As she hung up, she stared at the phone and mumbled under her breath. "I don't even know what to wear to something like that."

"A conservative silk suit might be nice."

Caroline jumped and spun around to glare at Zach, who was standing halfway inside her door. "How long have you been lurking around?"

"I don't lurk," he informed her, sounding offended. "I was just passing by and noticed your door was open. You know, you should always make sure it's locked, even if you're sure you're going right out again."

"I thought I had closed it." She stared at the door as if to make it behave next time. Then a thought struck her. "How did you know that was Max, asking me out?"

"Max? That was Max you were talking to? Great! What are you two love bugs up to now?" Zach crossed the room in two long strides and flopped down on her couch, a gleeful expression on his face.

Caroline gave him a daunting look and shoved his feet off her cushions as she swept past him on her way to her bedroom. "You're telling me you didn't know I was talking to Max?" she called out as she slipped off her shoes then shrugged out of her cotton blazer and hung it up.

"Of course I didn't know. How could I?"

"Your comment about wearing a silk suit to the dinner, that's why. Did you and he conspire over this date?"

Zach laughed. "You don't know Max Pearson very well if you think he needs moral support before asking out a woman. He's a man who knows what he wants and he's used to getting it."

Caroline nodded to herself. That was exactly the picture of the gifted surgeon she'd gotten. But that still didn't tell her how Zach had so quickly come up with a solution to a situation he hadn't known about.

She walked back into the room and looked at Zach as she might have her younger brother when she'd discovered him snooping around her bedroom. "So how did you come up with the silk suit comment?"

"You practically shouted something about having nothing to wear," he stated calmly.

"So you just threw that idea out without knowing what I was talking about."

"Right," he said, complacently propping his tennis shoes on her couch again.

"Right," she muttered. Had there ever been a more irritating man than Zach Dawson? She wished she could make some sense of him.

"So, tell me about this date you've agreed to," he said.

She looked at him thoughtfully. "It seems to me, I'm always telling you about *my* social life. How about you tell me something about yours, *then* I'll tell you something more about mine."

Zach set his feet solidly on the floor and stood up straight. His smile was gone. "I don't have a social life worth talking about."

"And I do?" she asked.

"You have a *life*—" He cut himself off abruptly and jerked around to stare out her living-room window.

Caroline frowned at the sudden bitterness in Zach's voice. "Go on," she whispered. "I have a life that . . . what?"

"Nothing," he growled. "You just don't know how lucky you are. The future is yours. All you have to do is recognize it, and take it."

She stepped up behind him. Beyond his shoulder she could see a lone sailboat drifting in lazy loops at the whim of the wind. Its sail was as white as a gull's wing, its hull a cornflower blue. It looked as if it were a plastic toy, floating on a cloud. Caroline took a deep breath and pressed her palm lightly against Zach's back. "I could say the same to you, Zach. We all have futures."

"Not all of us," he whispered hoarsely. "Not *all* . . . "

She focused on the back of his head. Each blond hair seemed charged with energy, gleaming with a light of its own. Must be a trick of the sunlight, she thought absently, but she was still mesmerized by the effect. Then her eyes descended slowly to the fabric of his striped polo shirt, stretched tautly over wide shoulders. She could trace the pleasing contours of his muscles through the cotton knit. She remembered the checked strength with which he'd held her while she'd mourned Jimmy.

Caroline found herself wondering what Zach looked like without his shirt, but she hastily shook away the tempting image.

"I'm sorry," she said. "I just thought it fair that we share information, instead of it all going one way."

Zach's shoulders heaved as he drew in a deep breath, held it for an impossibly long time, then slowly let it out. "You're right. It would be fair." He turned to face her, and his eyes were dark and troubled. "But there are things from my life . . . things I can't possibly share with anyone, Caroline. I wish it were otherwise, but it's not. It's just best if we leave them alone and talk about what's going on now . . . with you."

A sour taste clung to her tongue. He was shutting her out again, and she had no idea why. She took a step away from him, avoiding his eyes.

"Listen," he said, "I'm sorry. I must sound like a total idiot. But I really can't talk about myself now . . . maybe someday that will change. When . . . if I can . . . I promise, you're the one I'll come to."

Caroline's eyes snapped up to meet his. She was touched. Here was a man who had obviously been deeply hurt, so deeply he couldn't even express his feelings. Yet he trusted her enough to promise he'd confide in her before anyone else. The thought warmed her from the inside out.

What sort of pain he'd suffered she could only guess from her own experience. Maybe a woman he'd loved had abandoned him. Perhaps he, too, had lost a child, or a cherished parent. She already knew about his cousin's tragic accident, but there seemed to be more to the penetrating sadness that sometimes overtook him than just that. She wished she could help him . . . somehow.

After a moment, she thought, Maybe just being his friend is a beginning . . .

"I have an idea," she said hesitantly. "Max has invited me to a dinner. It sounds very formal, a thousand dollars a plate. I was just thinking when you showed up that I have no idea what to wear. We could go shopping together, and you could give me a man's perspective on a new outfit."

A smile slowly lifted the corners of Zach's lips. He nodded. "Sure. I could do that. When do we start?"

Zach drove his car, a late-model, green-blue Accord, while Caroline sat in the passenger seat beside him, flipping through the most recent department-store advertisements from the New London Day, humming to herself. He felt an aching in his heart, a longing to reach out and touch her...hold her...kiss the furrows from her brow, to protect her and all she held dear to her. It was the same all-consuming emotion that had assaulted him back in her apartment just an hour ago, when she'd asked him about his past.

More than anything, he'd wanted to confide in her. He'd ached to tell her about his own death, and how he wished he didn't have to help her get ready to go out with another man...because what he really wanted was to keep her for himself.

She can't be yours, he told himself. *She can never be yours.*

That was the bitterest of all truths to swallow. It wasn't so much dying that he hated. It was finding someone like Caroline who seemed so full of life and love, who had a future to share with some lucky man. Maybe it was only because he couldn't have her that she seemed so appealing to him, he reasoned. If he had lived and met her, they might have hated each other... Or maybe they'd have had something very special together.

All of those possibilities tormented him now, as he drove north on Route 32, toward the nearest mall.

They parked and entered through Jordan Marsh, the large department store anchoring one end of the mall's hundred-plus shops. "Where do you want to try first?" Zach asked, halfheartedly.

"Right here," she said. "Jordan's has a designer department with a private dressing area. I used to come here and spend hours trying on luscious outfits." She smiled, her cheeks glowing like a young girl's. "Then I pretended to the saleswoman that nothing they had was good enough for me. Of course the only reason I didn't buy an armload of dresses was because I couldn't afford anything."

Zach felt awful for her. "Can you afford a dress from here now?"

"Considering I haven't bought myself any new clothes in over a year, I guess I can splurge."

Zach flipped over a price tag as they passed into an alcove of smaller, fancier displays of dresses. The lighting in the salon was softer than throughout the rest of the store. Two women, who appeared to be sales associates were dressed in tasteful dresses that had the look of money about them. The price on the tag nearly made Zach choke.

"Must be a misprint," he muttered.

"If it seems impossibly high, it's probably right," Caroline said over her shoulder. She stopped at one rack to slide dresses on hangers around the chrome circle.

It didn't take long for one of the saleswomen to approach them. "May I help you find something in particular?" she asked.

"I need a dress for a formal dinner," Caroline said. "And I have no idea what I'm looking for."

The woman's eyes lit up. A definite date, Zach thought, meant an almost-sure sale. Desperate women facing deadlines were apt to settle for whatever was available, at whatever price. "For a very formal affair, we have some lovely chiffon and sequined gowns."

And some lovely prices to match, Zach thought, remembering the tag he'd seen that had been attached to a rather plain cotton dress. "What about a nice suit," he suggested. "Something simple, classy. Max is a sophisticated man with conservative tastes."

Caroline squinted at him, as if she wasn't sure. "He seemed to like the dress I wore the last time."

"The skirt was too short, remember?" Zach said quickly. "Something more sedate would be appropriate for a dinner like this."

"You're sure?" Caroline asked.

"Positive."

She looked skeptical but shrugged. "You probably know better than I."

She and the saleswoman moved on to another rack. To Zach's satisfaction it was ringed with tailored suits, some in soft wools, meant for the fall, some in muted fawn and olive colors of a softer fabric that looked like silk. Caroline held one up against her cheek.

"What do you think?"

"The color is great on you," he assured her. And the skirt, he noticed with relief, was long enough to brush her calf. The perfect outfit for the wife of a distinguished medical man. From what he knew of the AMA, they were as clannish and straitlaced as politicians. And Max was an officer in the organization.

Zach noticed the saleswoman offered no comment on his selection. He suspected that as long as the suit cost enough she wouldn't try to steer Caroline elsewhere.

"Well," Caroline said with an air of resolution, "I guess I'll try on this one."

On her way to the dressing room, though, she paused at two other racks and plucked garments from them. He caught a mischievous twinkle in her eye and guessed she was up to her old tricks. Trying on shimmering, high-priced gowns for the sport of it.

Let her enjoy herself, he thought, chuckling as he settled into one of the overstuffed armchairs strategically placed around the salon for gentlemen to await their ladies.

He slid down into the chair, crossed his ankles, stretching out his long legs in front of him, and wedged his hands behind his head. Closing his eyes, he prepared himself for a lengthy wait. A feeling of satisfaction swept over him, and he thought to himself, "You're definitely on the right track this time."

Max Pearson was the man Caroline needed. He had the wealth, the stability, the dedication to family to provide for her and her child. Max would love her and protect her.

But even as he thought the words, his mind revolted against the idea. *She'll be in another man's arms,* he told himself bitterly. *She'll whisper to him, "Darling, I love you ... only you."*

Zach sat bolt upright in the chair, his entire body rigid, fighting the picture of marital bliss he'd painted for Caroline.

He hated imagining her like that. But what exactly about his mental image ate at his soul so violently? That Caroline should find happiness, while he could find only success in a heavenly mission well done? Certainly he didn't begrudge this woman peace of mind after all she'd suffered. That would be unthinkably selfish.

Zach stood up abruptly and paced the plush tangerine carpeting between two racks of delicately sewn gowns.

No. It was more than selfishness, more than jealousy because she was alive and had a future, while he had neither. What his whole being yearned for was the opportunity to be the man who would take her into his arms and, ultimately, into his bed. He desperately longed to touch her, hold her, comfort her, to summon cries of passion from her soft lips.

"You jerk!" he muttered under his breath. Talk about wanting the impossible.

"What did you say?" a voice asked from the direction of the dressing rooms.

Zach spun on his heel. Then his mouth dropped open.

There in the doorway stood Caroline, draped—or nearly draped—in a filmy gown. Its hem swept the carpeting at her heels, before curving upward to brush her thigh at one side and reveal an exquisitely tapered leg. The fabric seemed almost an extension of her skin, barely concealing, teasing the eye and shimmering over her graceful arms and shapely body.

"Good grief!" he gasped.

"You like?" she asked, pirouetting once for him, her eyes dancing.

The gown undulated and slithered around her. Was that her breast he glimpsed through the sheer stuff? Or a layer of flesh-colored fabric? He squinted, unable to tell.

"Like it?" he stammered, feeling a tropical high settle in his groin. Were angels supposed to react this way to half-naked women? He'd always thought angels were supposed to be sexless, or at least free of mortal needs! No, he reminded himself, he'd already discovered he had entirely human responses to certain situations. "Maybe you should take that off," he suggested.

"Really?" she asked, looking suddenly serious. She reached up for a glistening thread that seemed to be serving as a shoulder strap.

"In there, in *there!*" he cried, frantically waving her toward the back rooms.

"Oh." She turned to leave and he felt a wave of relief wash over him, but then she swiveled back to face him. "Maybe you should come back here and help me choose *before* I try on. That will save time."

He felt as if every ounce of blood drained from his body at the thought of entering the dressing room with her. All too vividly, he could envision Caroline disrobing, revealing even more of her than he'd seen at the beach or through the tantalizing gown.

"N-no, I really don't think I should."

The saleswoman appeared, smiling. "The dressing parlors are quite private, sir," she murmured. "There's a lounge and modeling area outside of each changing room."

"Oh," he said, "of course there is. Well, that's fine." He turned sheepishly to Caroline, sure she must think him a complete fool. "If it will help I'll—" But she had already taken his hand and was drawing him through a curtained passageway.

Zach wished he could see the expression on her face. Was she teasing him? Or was her request for assistance genuine?

If it were the latter, he'd offend her if he let on he'd been aroused when she'd modeled the first dress for him. He must keep his cool, behave appropriately, simply give her his honest, impartial opinion as to the appropriateness of the dress for the occasion.

"I can do that," he grumbled under his breath.

"What?" she asked over her shoulder, which was now totally bare, since a shimmer of fabric that had drifted over it a moment ago had slipped off entirely.

"Nothing," he said shortly.

They stepped from the passageway into an intimate lounge furnished with a small table and two comfortable-looking chairs upholstered in ivory brocade.

Zach pulled his hand out of Caroline's and gratefully dropped into one of the chairs, feeling out of breath and cornered.

"I'll be right back," she murmured, disappearing behind a lacy Victorian curtain along one side of the area.

He waited, humming a song he couldn't place, then wasn't even sure it *was* a song. Drumming his fingers impatiently on the arm of the chair, he waggled one loafered foot in counterpoint to the off-key notes.

At last, Caroline reappeared, still in the sheer gown. She carried with her two dresses and held one up in front of her. "Now this one is a very nice color, don't you think?"

"But you can see right through the blasted thing!" he roared. "Look, it's worse than the one you have on." What was the woman thinking? A heavy sweat broke out along his hairline. He could feel droplets trickling down the back of his neck.

"Oh." She sighed. "You're right, of course. No telling what the good doctor would think of me if I wore something *that* sultry."

"Exactly," Zach snapped, leaning forward in his chair, his fingers curling tightly around the armrests. "You want to show him you have character and good taste. The goal isn't seducing the man."

"You're quite right." She nodded solemnly, but there was a touch of wickedness in the curve of her lips.

Zach squinted, trying to see behind the mask of concern she'd drawn across her face.

"Then, *this* one would be the better of the two?" she asked.

"What happened to the suit?"

"Oh, it's back there," she said lightly. "I'll try it on in a minute. I just thought a dress might be more feminine, more me."

"Well," he laughed, "there certainly is a hell of a lot more *you* than dress in that outfit."

She giggled. "It is rather more flirty than I'd thought," she said, turning a few degrees to the north.

Now he was sure it was the side of her breast he was seeing through the fabric. "Go try that...that other one on in your right hand, if you must. *Then* the suit."

"Okay," she said, a little too brightly for him to relax.

Zach didn't sit down this time. He paced.

Dammit, he had to make sure she didn't walk out of the store with anything like that first gown. Pearson would be shocked...his friends and colleagues would be appalled. Meher would rightly hold him responsible for a second failed attempt at finding Caroline a mate.

Zach agonized for what seemed an hour. He glared at his watch. Only five minutes had passed. Still, he didn't understand why tearing off one nothing-of-a-dress and zipping up another took so damn long.

"How about this one?"

Zach froze in his tracks almost afraid to turn around. At last, he slowly revolved on the spot where he stood.

He had thought that this next dress, which had actually looked quite substantial on its hanger, could only be an improvement over the first. But that had obviously been an illusion.

"Th-that neckline—"

"I know," she said, tilting her head to one side in an attempt to view her own bosom. "It is a bit daring, isn't it?"

"A bit?" He made an effort to clear his throat. "The damn thing drops clear to your navel! And—turn around, let me see the back!"

She obeyed. Just as he thought, the rich wine-colored velvet flowed over the crests of her shoulders and drifted down, down, down in a backless design that finally ended somewhere below her natural waist, well into the swell of her hips. Barely an inch, he'd guess, above the crease of her bottom.

A stream of sweat dribbled down Zach's back, and his pulse rose dangerously.

A giggle escaped from Caroline's lips.

Zach's eyes narrowed and fixed on her face. "You've been doing this on purpose!" he accused her. "You little tease!"

"Can't take the heat, Mr. Dawson?" She moved toward him, her hips swaying enticingly, and he automatically fell back a step.

"That's not funny," he said. "I'm just glad you weren't serious about wearing one of those getups to Max's dinner."

"Who says I'm not serious. A dress like this might provide some interesting dinner conversation."

"Sure, it would," he agreed, glaring at her, "as well as some rather dramatic action. That's a drag-me-into-the-nearest-bedroom-and-take-me dress! And you can bet after a man like Max sees you in that, he'll never call you again."

"You think I'd be *that* bad in bed?" she asked sweetly.

"No, I don't think you'd be bad in bed at all," he growled. Why on earth did his jeans choose this moment to start pinching *right there?* He shifted his weight from one foot to the other, but it didn't help. "I think you'd make any man go out of his mind with lust. But if you wear something that revealing, you'll send Max the wrong message. He won't take you seriously."

"I told you, I don't want to get serious. I'm not looking for a husband."

That's what you think, he fumed silently. "The point is..." What the hell was the point? He was having trouble concentrating with her standing there, half-clothed, looking incredibly delicious. "The point is, you want to be respected as a woman, not treated like a sex object and mauled on your first date. Right? I mean, that's what you women are always griping about."

"I haven't griped once today," she objected.

He hated her playful tone. He hated the way she made his insides feel. He hated that he was helpless to do any of the dozens of things he wanted to do to her.

Zach's eyes fixed on the portion of the V-neckline that hugged the swell of her breasts. As an engineer, he contemplated the lack of visible support, and wondered why she didn't simply fall out from beneath the fabric. He itched to slip his hand inside and investigate.

"How about trying on that suit for me," he suggested, feeling suddenly exhausted.

Caroline eyed him slyly, then gave a little shrug. "Fine."

As she turned to leave, he couldn't tear his eyes away from the sweet scoop of velvet that dipped to the matching dimples on her backside. Zach gritted his teeth, planted his feet and held onto his composure as best he could until she'd disappeared behind the lace curtain.

He counted to ten.

He muttered to himself, then cursed. Then growled low down in his throat, "There's too much depending on your not screwing up."

But even as he alternately warned and chastised himself, Zach could feel the beat of his own heart escalating, the heated surge of blood through his veins. He could sense his willpower leaking away, like air from a punctured tire. She'd been tormenting him, playing with him . . . and he liked it, he admitted to himself, even as he despised his own helplessness.

Zach looked around, then peeked into the outer salon. He couldn't see either of the saleswomen, but could hear one of them talking to another customer. It probably wouldn't have mattered if the clerk had been standing right beside him. Nothing could have stopped him.

In an impulsive rush, Zach lunged through the lace curtain.

Caroline was standing on the other side, waiting for him, a huge grin on her face. She hadn't started to unfasten the wine-colored dress.

"You think you're so very clever," he raged, wavering between equally strong desires to strangle her and pull her into his arms. "Think you can seduce a man, just by showing a little skin?"

She coyly ran the tip of her tongue across her upper lip. "I think so."

"Well, you're wrong!" he snapped. "It takes more than a few flashes of skin and a trashy dress to drive a man to lose control. It takes some subtlety. It takes some class, for a man of substance to respond to a woman."

"Trashy?" She pointed at the price tag dangling from the sleeve. "I'd hardly call fifteen hundred dollars trashy."

"That's not the point!" he roared, bearing down on her. "The point is... The point is..." Why did he keep losing track of his line of thought? His eyes dropped to the lovely, long slope of white skin sandwiched between curves of wine-colored velvet, and was mesmerized by the rhythmic rise and fall of her breasts. He could smell her, standing this close. He breathed in the lingering trail of her perfume, light and flowery, and an underlying fragrance of soap and something essentially feminine, and intimately animal.

With a shudder, Zach staggered forward and clasped his arms around her, crushing Caroline to his chest. Before he could consider the consequences or stop himself, he lowered his head and pressed his lips over hers.

He felt Caroline brace herself, then relax and accept his kiss. *Stop it, Dawson. Stop it now!* he commanded himself.

But he couldn't. Something basic and needful inside him, something male and imperative took over, and he was powerless to resist it, even as he knew that what he was doing was wrong.

Caroline's arms came up around his neck and she caressed his sensitive nape with cool, soft fingers. He felt her breasts, warm, small but perfect against his stomach, fitting neatly into the hollow below his chest. Her hips pressed forward, almost shyly, against his thighs. And he felt himself grow and harden, and rivers of scalding blood raged inside him. He'd never wanted a woman more.

"No," he moaned, so low he, himself could barely hear the words.

"Zach—" She kissed him again, opening her mouth to his, running her tongue experimentally along his teeth—then looked up into his eyes. "This is nice."

"Mm-hmm."

"I'd thought I could do without sex, indefinitely." She sighed, resting her cheek against his chest, and he had to stop himself from pressing her to him even more firmly. "But . . . maybe it would be all right. Maybe . . . I don't know. I haven't been with a man since before . . . you know . . ."

"I know." He swallowed. What he wouldn't give to be the one to satisfy the longings he sensed must have built inside her.

But that would mean ignoring his mission. That would mean taking advantage of Meher's trust, and the chance the Archangel had given him to move up through the ranks of angeldom while helping Caroline find the man who was really meant to make her happy.

With an effort, Zach pushed himself away from her, his hands bracing her shoulders and holding her at a distance, to make sure she wouldn't try to cling to him. "Why don't you just take the suit with us and try it on at home," he said tightly. "I have a feeling it will fit great."

She frowned up at him, her eyes questioning, disappointed. Her lower lip trembled for a moment before straightening itself out. "All right," she agreed, her voice controlled even though the pain of rejection showed in her soft brown eyes. "Just give me a minute to change back into my street clothes."

Chapter 7

Caroline sat stiffly in the passenger seat of Zach's car. She couldn't remember ever having been angrier with a man.

The entire time they'd been in Jordan's dress department, she'd read all the right signs in Zach. The hunger in his eyes as they roamed her figure. The grating tone of his voice—his words coming with effort. And every time they'd passed within three feet of each other—that supercharged atmosphere between them. There was no doubt in her mind that he was attracted to her, despite his repeated efforts to put her off and convince her otherwise.

Of course, breaking away from their embrace in the dressing room was undoubtedly the sensible thing to do. They weren't guaranteed any privacy, and Caroline would have been mortified if one of the saleswomen had walked in on them. But why, she wondered, hadn't Zach suggested they go back to his apartment, or hers, and pick up where they'd left off? Instead he'd behaved like a schoolboy pilfering from the teacher's desk! It was almost as if he were convinced someone was watching them, waiting to snitch on him to the principal.

Caroline was furious.

And her anger fed her confusion and made his rejection sting all the more. She glared out the side window as Zach drove.

After a while, her head cleared enough so that she could start sorting through the events of the day and her feelings. More than ever, she needed to understand why Zach was behaving so maddeningly.

She'd seen no evidence that he was involved with another woman. And she wouldn't have believed him for a moment if he'd announced he was gay. So why had he drawn an invisible line between them that he himself constantly fought crossing?

Then there were the barricades she had drawn. What was she going to do about them? Caroline asked herself. How would she have handled Zach if he'd actually succumbed to her flirting? Modeling the gowns for him had started out as a game, a joke. But somewhere along the line, she'd gotten carried away. Had she even considered what she'd do if Zach threw her into his car and announced they were heading straight to his place to make love?

By the time they reached the apartment parking lot, Caroline felt she'd definitely made a mistake by toying with Zach's masculine pride. He hadn't spoken a word to her or so much as glanced at her all the way home. But she refused to apologize for what she'd done. A little teasing seemed fair punishment for his stubborn silences and refusal to explain himself to her.

Caroline climbed the stairs from the lobby to the second floor, three steps ahead of Zach. She turned toward her door, and heard him viciously jam his key into his own lock. Impulsively she spun around.

"Come in for just a minute," she heard herself say.

"Huh?"

Intuitively she knew that if she let him go his own way after what had happened in the store, she'd never see him again. Suddenly her anger sluiced away like rainwater after a summer storm. "I—uh, want you to see how this suit looks on. I'm really nervous about it fitting me."

Zach observed her solemnly. "It will fit perfectly. Take my word for it."

For some reason, she believed he was right. But it didn't matter. She just didn't want him to go away, still angry with her. Maybe there was some way she could smooth things over.

"Come in just for five minutes while I try this on," she repeated. "I need your opinion."

The lines around his mouth and eyes looked stressed to the point of snapping. He swore under his breath. "All right. Five minutes, then I have to get going."

Caroline let him in through her front door. Zach made a bee-line for the living room, plucked a magazine from her coffee table and sat down to wait for her to change. She carried the plastic-covered suit on its hanger into the bedroom.

Swinging the door closed just enough to shield herself from his view, she tossed the suit on the bed along with her purse, then kicked off her shoes.

"Men," Caroline stewed. Impossible creatures.

As she removed the protective covering from the silk jacket and skirt, she peeked into the living room. Zach was looking through a magazine—his motions abrupt, too packed with power for the little task of flipping pages. His eyes vacantly skimmed the glossy pages.

"What's going through that thick skull of yours, Mr. Dawson?" she whispered to herself, stepping back from the door. "Why do you keep coming back to me, if being near me upsets you like this?"

She stepped out of her skirt, balled it up and tossed it furiously on the bedspread. Unbuttoning her blouse, she yanked it off and flung it in the general direction of the bed, too. From the other room, she heard pages rustling, the sound of heavy, uneven footsteps muffled by her carpet.

She unhooked her bra, dropped it to the floor as she muttered a few choice expletives against the male gender, and was about to reach into her top drawer for the lacy, beige bra she'd wear with the suit—when she became aware that Zach was speaking to her.

"—And, hey, I'm sorry about that scene in the store—"

Caroline whipped around in time to see Zach push open her door and step into her bedroom.

For an eternity, she stood absolutely still, wearing only her bikini panties and an astonished smile. It seemed to take Zach just as long to react to her near nakedness, but his mouth kept moving as if he were powerless to control it.

"I—I really...shouldn't have kissed you...like that...and..." His eyes drifted from her face down her throat to her breasts, her stomach, and lower still, driving primal chills through her body.

"Oh Lord—" He let out one long breath and stared pleadingly up at the ceiling. "Don't do this to me."

"Do what, Zach?" she asked softly.

"This is too much."

"Too much what?"

"Temptation," he growled.

His reluctance perversely fed her rising desire. She took a step toward him. "I don't understand, Zach. You want to make love to me, don't you?"

"Ye-s-s-s." He hissed out the word.

"Are you holding back because of me? Because I told you how I feel about starting a relationship?"

He shook his head, as if it wasn't he who was controlling it, then reversed the gesture by nodding. "Something like that." He took a step back. She stepped forward. "I need to leave," he said, as if he were informing himself, more than her.

"Please," she whispered. "Just hold me." Tears, hot and steamy, welled up in her eyes. She felt utterly ashamed of herself for being so weak. What was wrong with her? Had she no pride at all? "It's been such a long time, Zach," she stammered. "I didn't think I'd ever again need a man's arms around me. But now ... there's you ... and I ..." She couldn't finish.

Zach glanced desperately over his shoulder at the bedroom door, as though the apartment were under siege and this was his last avenue of escape. Then a look of resignation passed over his eyes, as if he'd made the most important decision in his life, and he rushed to her, pulling her into his embrace.

"Help me ... stop me," he gasped into the soft hollow of her throat as he bent over her.

"I don't *want* to stop you," she whispered throatily. "Make love to me, Zach. It will be all right. If you have nothing with you...for safe sex, I mean ... I think there are condoms in the night table." How had she remembered that Rob had kept them there?

Zach scooped her into his arms, carried her to the bed and deposited her gently on it. She gazed up into his eyes, feeling suddenly vulnerable, naked but for her panties, lying before him.

His eyes had turned a hard, crystalline blue. He had only one thing on his mind now, she could tell.

As she watched him fumble with the buckle on his belt and unzip his jeans, revealing a flat, muscled stomach, she told herself that what was about to happen was for one reason alone. She needed a man to whom she could entrust her body, who would take her thoroughly and drive away the bitter memories of a bad marriage and the worst year of her life. If they made love, hard enough and long enough, there wouldn't be any room in her mind or her heart for anything but their passion.

Zach tore his T-shirt off over his head in one swift yank, wedged off his athletic shoes with his toes then practically jumped out of his jeans. White cotton briefs hugged his hips. He disposed of them so swiftly she caught only a flash of fair curls nesting around his arousal before he covered her with his body, crushing her mouth beneath his moist lips. Raising her hips, he removed her panties with a single tug that took her breath away.

It was as if they shared the same urgency, understood the same set of unspoken rules. No words passed between them to break the intense charm woven around their lovemaking. Touches, gestures were the only language they needed. They moved quickly, as if each feared the other would suddenly change his mind and put an end to the dance of passion they'd begun. And, at that moment, to stop kissing, touching, feeling each other's body seemed as impossible as choosing not to breathe.

Caroline gazed up at Zach as he rolled her onto her side with him, to better support his own weight. His eyes hungrily traced the line of her throat, to her breasts, and he reverently laid a hand over one nipple then slid down on the bed to lower his mouth over the tight, pink bud and draw it between his lips and teeth. Caroline cried out with pleasure, arching her back as she reached blindly for him. Her trembling fingertips raked the length of Zach's hard chest, down his stomach, and lower still, at last reaching her destination. She timidly touched his rigid response, then wrapped her fingers around him possessively. With her thumb, she circled the engorged tip, and knew that Zach was more than ready for her.

The mere thought of his entering her sent a short, sharp spasm of fire through her center, even before his palm smoothed over the velvety triangle between her thighs.

As she whimpered, recovering from the unexpected, initial wave of ecstasy, Zach moved his fingers over her, probing gently, stroking the intimate folds of her womanhood, driving her upward again through a tempest of glorious sensations. Suddenly he withdrew his hand, leaving her hot and wet and aching for more.

"Zach!" His name exploded from her lips. "Please don't stop!" She caught a momentary flash of doubt in his eyes, but knew at once that he'd only moved his hand away to reposition himself.

He covered her mouth with his own, smothering the impatient little cries of anticipation that bubbled up through her throat as he reached into the bed-table drawer. It took him only two seconds to rip open the foil packet and unroll the condom over himself, staying as close to her as possible all the time. As Zach shifted his body back over hers, he slipped his hand between her thighs to position himself. She felt the hot, stiff column of his male flesh touch the moist lips of her femininity, and she wrapped her long legs around his strong hips, making it easy for him to find her.

With a force that made her gasp with pleasure and shock, he thrust himself inside her. It had been such a long time, the tight, unused muscles resisted for a second before giving way to him. Then he pressed himself deep, as deeply as she could contain him, retreated, and thrust again, and yet again . . . again . . .

Caroline soared on a cloud of pink gossamer, clutching Zach to her, no longer able to separate one dizzying wave of her orgasm from the next. When she at last peaked in a fiery, liquid rush she heard herself call out Zach's name and soared . . . soared into realms she'd never known existed.

Tendrils of molten lava retreated slowly through Zach's limbs, gradually pooling in his center, slowly losing their heat and leaving him spent . . . and strangely different from his former self. He felt as if he'd been reshaped in some indefinable way by Caroline's body.

Her fingernails softly traced circles on his shoulder blades, although he was certain she wasn't even aware of their subtle motion. He was still inside her. He buried his face in the soft flesh of her breast and moaned his pleasure. -

Stroking his nape she whispered, "Thank you." And suddenly, he felt like kicking himself.

She was thanking him for giving her a few moments of carnal pleasure, when she should be cursing him for destroying her life. Because that was exactly what he'd done.

Caroline had been destined to meet and mate with a man who would bring her happiness and a child to mend her broken heart. And what had he done? Instead of delivering her to the man of her dreams, he'd jumped into bed with her! He'd literally screwed up Heaven's plans!

What kind of an incompetent angel was he?

Caroline was murmuring sweet things in his ear. He tried to shut them out. He had to concentrate on salvaging what he could of the situation.

Slowly Zach eased himself out of her silky warmth. Leaving her softness, her tender arms, was almost like leaving life itself. But he had to do it for her sake, and the sake of her future.

He felt her tense as she realized he was leaving her bed.

"Is something wrong?" she whispered.

"No. Nothing," he returned gruffly.

He retrieved his jeans, shirt, underwear from the floor and retreated to the far side of the bedroom to dress. He forced himself to not look at her, knowing if he, even for an instant, glimpsed her lovely body, bare against the sheets, flushed pink with their lovemaking, he wouldn't find the strength to step through the door.

"You're going so soon?" she asked hesitantly.

"Yes. I have to."

He felt rather than heard her sigh of disappointment. "You don't have to run away," she said. "I don't expect you to marry me just because we had sex. I don't expect any kind of commitment."

Her words brought him up short, and a fierce anger and resentment bubbled inside of him. He spun on her, his entire body tense with emotion. "You should *expect* a commitment!" he shouted at her. "A woman like you, Caroline... you should demand nothing less from a man after what he did—what I just did—to you."

She stared at him, blinking. He knew he wasn't making a lot of sense, but he couldn't help plunging on.

"You *deserve* a man who can stand by you, through the worst life has to dish out, as well as for great sex! You deserve—" Dear Lord, she deserved the best of everything, and he had nothing to offer her, not even a future. He lifted his hands in a pleading motion, then let them fall limply at his sides in defeat. There were no words that could explain what he had to do, or how deeply he felt his loss.

Caroline sat up in bed, letting the sheet fall from her breasts. He felt something jerk inside him—a combination of lust and a longing to simply hold her and comfort her.

"What you're trying to say," she whispered, "is that you're not that man and never can be that man?"

"Right."

She studied him, looking unconvinced. "If you say so," she said at last.

Something about her lack of acceptance of the situation annoyed him. He felt compelled to shock her into recognizing what had to be. "Wake up, Caroline! What happened between us was a physical reaction to my seeing a beautiful woman, naked. What man wouldn't have wanted to make love to you?"

She shook her head and smiled wryly, at last tugging the linens up over her chest as she rested back against the pillows. "It seems I've been missing a lot in the past year or more."

"That's what I've been trying to tell you." He pulled up his jeans and snapped them. "You should be dating, having fun, making yourself available for the right man whenever he comes along. You have a future to prepare for. There will be a man who will love you in every way you need to be loved. Who knows, he may be looking for you this very minute."

"And here I lie in this bed with you," she murmured, studying him almost coolly.

"Exactly. That's why our having sex is wrong."

"Wrong." She repeated the word as if trying to define it, as if it were from a foreign language she hadn't yet mastered.

"Yes," he said firmly, tucking in his shirt and buckling his belt. "Don't misunderstand. What we did felt great. But it wasn't love, it couldn't have been love."

She nodded, keeping her thoughts to herself now, cloaking them as if to protect her feelings from his destructive mood.

"I'll let myself out," Zach said stiffly, lunging for the bedroom door.

Back in his own apartment, Zach stood in the middle of the living room with its neutral decor and pile of *Architectural Digest* magazines on the coffee table. He squeezed his eyes shut and raised his fists in the air.

"I'm sorry!" he shouted at the ceiling. "I didn't mean for that to happen. Help me make things right. Please!"

For a moment he pictured Meher's ethereal glow, blending into the general whiteness of heaven. Then he was suddenly there, back in the cool mists of Eternity.

"You saw what I did, didn't you?" Zach groaned. "Of course you did. I've made a bloody mess of her life! Take me off this job, give me another one."

The answer came to him on a sweet zephyr. "No."

"Why not?" he demanded. "If you want her to find her perfect man, you should use someone with more experience than I have. Someone who won't leap into bed with her at every opportunity."

"Return to her and try again," instructed Meher.

Zach felt a gnawing fear in his gut. "Please, don't make me do this," he rasped. "When I'm with her, I can't help feeling things that I know I'm not supposed to feel. She deserves an angel who's got his act together."

"Go," Meher rumbled.

Immediately Zach felt the air around him turn heavy. Then he was back in his living room.

His head ached horribly. He dropped onto the couch and buried his face in his hands. "Why are you making me do this?"

He waited, hoping for an answer. There was none.

Perhaps, he thought, he'd been chosen for the job *because* it would be difficult for him. Maybe there was no other way to earn your stripes in Heaven, except by doing what seemed impossible.

With an aching heart, he gazed across the room at the wall closest to Caroline's apartment. He thought about her...and Max. As desperately as he wanted to ignore Meher's directive, he knew his duty.

Chapter 8

The Silver Whale stayed busy all week, and that made it much easier for Caroline to stick to the decision she'd made the night Zach left after making love to her. She would dismiss him wholly from her thoughts and her life. If the man was so confused about his own feelings, he couldn't recognize a woman who honestly cared for him and had to hide behind a subterfuge of concern for her future... then he deserved a lifetime of meaningless one-night stands.

Caroline threw herself into her work. She reordered the crystal dolphins that had been selling so well since a new exhibit had opened at the Mystic Marinelife Aquarium, as well as more of the hand-dipped bayberry candles, porcelain angels and framed prints of scenes of the seaport. She and Suzanne unpacked case after case of Christmas ornaments, collectibles, Victorian greeting cards and wrapping paper. For the next two months they would be launched into nonstop activity. Not until after New Year's would things slow down—and that was just fine with Caroline. The longer hours she worked, the less time for dwelling on Zach.

One morning, as Suzanne tied the strings of her candy-cane striped apron, she asked briskly, "So, what's up?"

Caroline grimaced. "What makes you think anything's *up?*"

"You're so easy to read. All week you've been glowering at every customer who walks through the door, and giving one-syllable answers. Every emotion shows on your face and in your voice. You're mad as hell about something."

Caroline rolled her eyes. "My mother used to say exactly the same thing when I was in junior high school. The typical adolescent pout, I suppose. I gave my parents a hard time when I was a teenager, I'm afraid."

"Didn't we all." Suzanne prodded her toward the rear door leading to the storage room. "Come on. While we have a break between customers, let's take time out for a cup of tea. Regular or herb?"

"Herb," Caroline said absently. "Something soothing." She wondered if there were a blend capable of wiping one's memory blissfully clean.

While Suzanne prepared their tea, Caroline opened a plastic bag of cookies she'd baked the previous night. They were her favorites, Snickerdoodles—all sugary and cinnamon, with a mild vanilla bite to them. She picked one up and munched on it, wondering where to begin—because Suzanne wouldn't let her interrogation drop until she picked every last detail from her brain.

By the time a steaming mug sat in front of her, Caroline still had no idea where to start. All she could do was plunge right in.

"Zach and I had sex," she stated as blandly as if she were quoting the stock market.

Suzanne didn't even blink. "I wondered if that was it. Was it good?"

Caroline chomped down hard on her cookie. "That's just it, it was fantastic. It was more than fantastic. It was as if we'd been made for each other," she growled.

"Well, that *is* awful news." Suzanne snorted and shook her head. "How can you sound so dismal about something like great sex? Zach is a drop-dead gorgeous guy. He obviously likes you a lot. And he's great in bed! What more could you ask for?"

"I don't know," Caroline admitted.

"Are you looking for marriage?"

"No!" She laughed a little too loudly. "No," she repeated, controlling her volume a little better the second time. "I told you I can't risk getting pregnant again, or trusting a man enough to fall in love with him. But it's . . . I don't know . . ." She drifted in her thoughts. " . . . it's a feeling that Zach is a man I *should* trust and *shouldn't* be afraid to be with."

"I say, go with gut instincts," Suzanne stated.

"I did that with Rob, and look where it got me," she said pointedly.

"I've told you—all men aren't like Rob. Most men aren't like Rob, thank goodness. If you like Zach and he likes you, why not give it a shot and see what happens?"

Caroline gazed into the dark amber tea in her cup. It smelled like chamomile, but she wasn't sure. She could almost see her reflection in it. She wished with all her heart that she could see into the future.

"It's not that easy," she murmured.

"Why?"

"After we made love, Zach bolted for the door like a wild animal sprung from a cage. He couldn't get out of my apartment fast enough."

"Typical male panic syndrome."

"What?"

Suzanne laughed. "That's what happens to men when they're faced with commitment."

"I didn't ask for a commitment."

Suzanne leaned back in her chair, observing Caroline over the rim of her tea mug. "No, I expect you didn't. But if he's a decent man, he probably got hit smack in the face with a truckload of guilt as soon as he finished with his orgasm. You told him about Rob and the baby. And he's been playing Cupid, trying to set you up with someone dependable, right?"

"Right."

"Then he acts on impulse and you two end up in bed. He's being a gentleman, obviously. He knows he's not the permanent type, and he's trying to stay out of your way, not cramp your style."

Caroline stared at Suzanne, wondering if she could possibly be right. She remembered what Zach had blurted out about her right to expect a commitment from a man who had made love to her. "But I felt as if we were so right together. When he touched me, it was as if the whole world went away with everything bad in it, gone forever. There were the two of us—nothing more, nothing *hurt* anymore."

Suzanne laid a hand on her arm. "Chalk that up to good sex, sweetie. So Zach is an experienced lover. I have a feeling Rob was never very good for you. It would have suited his personality. Selfish men make lousy lovers."

Caroline opened her mouth to protest, but Suzanne waved her to silence.

"Listen, if he never comes around again, at least now you've had the experience and you know what a good man can feel like. Count yourself lucky. Some women never get that opportunity." She sipped her tea for the first time since they'd sat down. "Now, tell me about this date you have with the Doc."

Caroline couldn't help smiling. Suzanne always made her feel better, in her cavalier, come-what-may sort of attitude toward life. She rarely let anything anger her. When something did strike her wrong, her temper was frightening. Luckily that didn't happen often.

"Dr. Maxwell Pearson is a pediatric surgeon, and I think he's rich."

Suzanne leaned across the table, grinning like a cat that's just discovered a new mouse hole. "Tell me more."

At last Saturday arrived. Caroline watched the clock, feeling more excited about the evening than she dared to admit. Max had called and confirmed their arrangements. He'd pick her up at her place, and they'd drive directly to the dinner. She felt like a teenage girl looking forward to her first real date.

An hour before closing, the bell over the door of the Silver Whale tinkled, and Caroline looked up as she handed a woman her purchase.

It was Zach.

Although she'd steeled herself against the inevitable moment when she'd run into him again, her heart plummeted to her feet. She swore she could hear its leaden thump.

He wore cutoff jeans that displayed his great legs. A short-sleeved shirt bared his biceps appealingly. The faint smell of suntan lotion—coconut oil and bananas—wafted across the room. Caroline glowered at him and spun away.

"Hi!" he said cheerfully, coming up behind her.

"Hello," she muttered, stooping down. She started stacking gift boxes beneath the counter, using more energy than was necessary as she slapped them, one on top of another.

"All ready for tonight?" he asked.

She nodded. "I'm surprised you remembered about the big dinner."

"I was planning on going myself, so it was on my mind."

Caroline frowned up at him. "Why are *you* going?" Her voice sounded overly sharp to her own ears, but she didn't like the idea of Zach haunting her night out with Max.

"It's a good cause," he said casually, gazing around the shop as if he wasn't really paying attention to their conversation.

Caroline stood up and stepped around the counter to face him, her hands on her hips. "Zach, why did you come here?" she demanded angrily.

His head snapped around and his eyes widened, as if her question frightened him. "What?"

"Why did you come to the shop today?"

Relief showed on his face. "Oh, you mean, just now—here. I came to see if you were nervous about your date with Max. I had a feeling I'd given you mixed messages about him and . . . well, about me, too."

She squinted at him. "You could say that. Encouraging me to date him then screw—"

"I'm sorry." He interrupted her as a look of panic crossed his eyes. "I told you that before. It was a terrible mistake."

"Terrible?" She couldn't help letting a wicked smile lift the corners of her lips. But inside her, the anger kept building. "Terrible?"

"Not terrible in any way except that I—" He raked a hand through his short, blond hair and blinked at her helplessly. "Let's just say I had no right to do what I did. And I apologize. I guess I felt I should stop by today to make sure you were all right."

"I'm fine. What's in the bag?" she asked, pointing to a small paper sack he'd been clutching since he entered the shop.

He looked down, as if he'd forgotten about it. "Oh, well, I know how busy you get in here on Saturdays. I brought you a little lunch." He stuck out his hand, looking once more like a little boy, this time offering to share his lunch with his best pal.

Caroline thought it an endearing gesture, but she refused to succumb to his charm. "Thanks," she said stiffly, snatching the bag away from him.

"Maybe I'll see you tonight," he added quickly, backing toward the door. "Hope you have a good time with Max."

She nodded and was still staring at the door he'd disappeared through when Suzanne stepped out from behind the curtain separating the public area from the back room.

"Was that Zach I heard out here?" she asked.

"Yes," Caroline snapped.

"What did he want?"

Caroline peered into the sack. A New England-style grinder made just the way she liked it—generous layers of salami, provolone cheese, lettuce and sliced tomatoes, onions, smelling of olive oil and oregano—looked back at her. "He brought me my lunch."

Suzanne stared at her. "At four in the afternoon?"

Caroline shrugged. "That's what he said."

"The man is crazy about you."

"You think?"

"I know."

At the last minute, Caroline debated rushing back to the mall to purchase a dress she felt more comfortable in than the staid silk suit Zach had picked out for her. But she supposed he knew what he was talking about when he said Max had conservative tastes and would appreciate her toned-down dressing.

Then she saw the look on Max's face when she opened her apartment door to him.

"Oh," he said, his pale eyes traveling over the finely tailored jacket and skirt of dimpled plum silk. "That's a very... nice outfit."

"Thank you," she murmured, suddenly wishing the skirt were three inches shorter, or there was a strategic slit in the front to at least show a little of her slim legs and add a stylish flare.

She glanced at Max for a reassuring sign. But the sparkle in his eyes had dimmed.

It wasn't as if she needed a man's approval to feel good about herself. It was more a matter of her intuitively knowing she was improperly dressed for the night. As they drove to the Hilton, Caroline began to feel truly frumpy.

However, if Zach had been right about the type of guests at the banquet, she expected she'd blend in. Perhaps Max just didn't like plum.

Minutes later, though, as she stood beside him under soaring chandeliers in the hotel's foyer, scanning the crowd of doctors, politicians and local professionals, her stomach tightened into a hard ball. The room positively glittered. Many of the women wore formal gowns, resplendent in sequins and beads. Others had chosen simple black sheaths that reached to the floor, that seemed intended as backdrops for their dazzling jewelry, which she suspected was real. The men all wore tuxedoes.

"Oh dear," she breathed.

"Something wrong?" Max asked.

"I'm sorry. I'm very much underdressed, again."

He patted her fingers, curling around his arm. "Nonsense. You look just fine."

Just fine, she thought miserably. That's probably what you say to terminally ill patients. *You'll be just fine.*

She'd strangle Zach the next time she saw him.

Hungering for revenge, she searched the foyer for Zach. But there had to be over five hundred guests in the room, two hundred fifty of them in tuxedoes. There was no way she could single him out.

"Here are some people I'd like you to meet," Max said, guiding her across the room toward a white-haired couple who looked stunning in black.

It turned out Walter Fanning was the CEO for Roberts & Co., the huge pharmaceutical company located in Groton at the mouth of the Thames River. His wife, Margarite, was running for mayor. Caroline had heard she had a good chance of winning.

"I've often wondered why Groton hasn't been able to rejuvenate its waterfront shops on Thames Street, like Mystic has been able to do with its tourist district," Margarite commented, sipping slowly from the crystal stem she held lightly between two fingers. "A few good restaurants, an antique shop or two, perhaps some tasteful gift shops... like yours..." She studied Caroline shrewdly over the rim of her wineglass. "You wouldn't by any chance be interested in relocating the Silver Whale?"

Caroline could feel Max watching her, even as he pretended to give the CEO his full attention. "We have excellent customer traffic on Water Street," she said carefully.

"In other words, it would be too much of a risk to start from scratch in an unproven location," Margarite said thoughtfully.

"Yes. I'm sorry."

"Oh, don't be." She smiled and sipped her drink, her black eyes never leaving Caroline's face. "Shows you have good business sense, my dear. What about acting as an unofficial advisor to an economic development plan for Groton? I'm gathering information on what it would take to resurrect a shopping and restaurant district on Thames Street."

Caroline felt a twinge of excitement at the challenge. For decades, the historical dock area of Groton had languished, a strip of closed bars and forgotten, struggling merchants. "I'd be very interested in helping in whatever way I can," she agreed.

Ten minutes later, when Max steered her away from the Fannings, a smile graced his narrow lips. "Well, you certainly charmed the pants off of Margarite. Did you mean what you said about helping her bring back the waterfront?"

"Of course I did," Caroline said. "I wouldn't have said it if I didn't."

Max nodded. "You realize, you sly woman, you've also won yourself a flock of new and devoted customers. Knowing Margarite, I expect she'll show up at the Silver Whale to pick out gifts for her campaign staff within the week. And she'll talk the place up to everyone she knows."

"That's not why I offered to help," Caroline assured him.

He shrugged. "I guess it doesn't really matter. It will probably mean good things for both of you. You're both shrewd women, although neither of you will admit it."

Caroline felt vaguely uneasy after Max's comments. She wondered if he viewed her shrewdness as a plus... because he prided similar qualities in himself. But she forgot her concerns as the evening progressed from welcome speeches to seating the guests for dinner.

As the main course was being served, Caroline finally spotted Zach across the room. He was seated at a corner table, and his eyes locked with hers across the banquet hall, as if he'd been seeking her out, too. For a string of heartbeats, they absorbed each other from opposite sides of the room. All sounds faded from Caroline's ears, every other person in the hall seemed to disappear. There was only Zach, looking devastatingly handsome in a flawlessly pressed, black tuxedo, his blue eyes latching onto hers with a possessiveness that contradicted everything he'd said to her. Then he shifted his chair around and turned to the matronly woman beside him.

Caroline watched him for a few minutes, while he chatted in a friendly way with the woman, then with several others at his table.

Why weren't they right for each other? she wondered. What was it about her that sent him running for shelter? What was it about him that, despite his rejection, drew her inevitably toward him. Even now, she could feel an undeniable pull from across the room. It grappled with her unwilling heart, with her tormented soul, beckoning to her, holding her against her will.

"I'm losing my mind," she muttered into her napkin as she raised it to blot her lips.

"Excuse me?" Max turned toward her.

"Nothing," she said. "It's nothing. Delicious squab, Max. The orange-honey sauce is marvelous."

After the food had been cleared away and a parade of speakers had alternately thanked the guests for their support of the new wing and begged for more money to continue the work, an orchestra began to play. They seemed to favor romantic old ballads and dance favorites of the thirties and forties, but mixed in some newer "oldies" along with one or two Top 40's, toned down to a sedate style.

It had been ages since Caroline had last danced to live music, and she loved feeling the vibrations work their way up through the soles of her shoes and inside her stomach. The blare of the brass and sexy rhythm of the drums moved through her, making her feel restless and playful.

She looked up at the side of Max's face as she danced with him. He seemed much less interested in her that night than he had been at the reception just a few weeks earlier. Her choice of attire had obviously dampened his spirits. If all that mattered to him were clothes, she reasoned, then she could do without his company.

Still, it was nice to have someone take her out for an evening and buy her a fancy meal. And she enjoyed being around interesting people.

A moment later, she felt Max's arms stiffen then drop away from her, even though the music was still playing.

Puzzled, she looked up at him, then saw Zach standing behind his right shoulder.

"Mind if I cut in?" Zach asked smoothly.

Max waved him forward. "If the lady doesn't object, it's fine with me."

Caroline hesitated, not trusting her emotions enough to step into Zach's arms, but unwilling to make a scene over something so innocent. Zach didn't wait for her to make up her mind. He took her in his arms and guided her smoothly across the dance floor.

"What are you doing?" she asked.

"Dancing. What does it look like?"

She moaned in exasperation. "I mean, why are we dancing when you made such a point of fixing me up with Max and letting me know you weren't interested in me."

"I never said I wasn't *interested* in you." Zach corrected her stiffly. "I said we weren't compatible, or I just wasn't right for you or—" He broke off, looking flustered. "Listen, I can't remember what I said . . . it doesn't matter. Can't two people dance without becoming romantically entangled."

"We seemed pretty entangled in my bedroom the other day," she stated, not bothering to lower her voice.

The couple nearest them turned and stared. Caroline felt her cheeks grow hot, and she buried her face in Zach's shoulder. She could hear his heart pounding and feel the muscles in his arms knotting as he tightened his grip on her.

"That can't happen again," he whispered. "No matter how much I might want you, Caroline. It can't happen again."

"Why?" She couldn't bear to look up into his face, afraid of seeing her own longing mirrored there . . . but more afraid of not seeing it there.

"It just can't."

"Another woman?"

He hesitated. "Let's just call it another obligation. Believe me, I have only your happiness in mind."

She gritted her teeth, tears of frustration springing to her eyes, and tried to push him away. But he held on, continuing to sway gently with her in his arms as the music swelled, the male singer belting out Sinatra's "Fly Me to the Moon."

"Let . . . me . . . go!" She ground out the words.

"No. You're angry, you'll make a scene."

"I won't make a goddamn scene!"

"Watch your language, you never know who might be listening," he whispered in her ear.

"My language is just fine, given the circumstance." She pushed with all of her strength at his tuxedoed chest, and was amazed with what ease he kept her trapped in the warm circle of his embrace. To anyone nearby, they probably didn't appear to be struggling. "Zach, if you don't let me go by the count of three, I'm going to knee you in the groin. One . . . two . . ."

He lifted his arms away and stepped back, just as the music stopped. "Satisfied?"

"Perfectly." But when she spun around to walk away, he unexpectedly gripped her wrist and turned her back to face him.

"It's *not* that I don't care about you, Caroline. Don't ever think that. It's because you are so important that I can't let anything go wrong for you. You're special, in more ways than you know. Just believe that. Believe that and open yourself up to love."

Before she could analyze the rough catch in his voice, or begin to figure out what he was talking about, Zach had slipped away into the crowd.

Zach felt as if he were treading on red-hot coals, forcing himself to take each step across the dance floor, away from Caroline. More than anything, he wanted to stay with her, but he knew what he had to do. He must somehow salvage the fragile bond he'd started to build between Max and Caroline, even if their being together seemed to him the most unnatural thing in the world. Even if watching her fall in love with another man destroyed him.

Turning at the far end of the glittering banquet hall, he stood and watched Caroline, who looked so quietly lovely in the soft plum suit he'd picked out for her. He knew now why he'd chosen it.

Aside from complementing her coloring perfectly, it held her back in the shadows and kept her covered...sheltered was maybe a better word. What had he been thinking? Had he subconsciously tried to hide her away for himself? To make her less attractive to Max and other men?

Clearly he was still struggling with his runaway desire for her. Even now, as she stood listening to the conversation in Max's group, her head tilted in concentration, her face aglow, he ached to gather her into his arms and kiss her... right there, in the middle of the crowd.

This taking on a human form definitely had its drawbacks. How the hell was he going to keep his hands off her now? Now that he knew what she looked like, naked...how her flesh felt beneath his hands... how wonderful making love to her was?

Zach squeezed his eyes shut and prayed.

He couldn't remember the last time he'd even thought about saying a prayer. Probably it had been when he was still a little kid, reciting a bedtime litany of blessings for his mother, father, himself... his dog. And how had that little rhyme gone?

Four angels to my bed,
Four angels round my head,
One to watch, and one to pray,
And two to bear my soul away.

He hadn't realized he still knew those words from his childhood. Now, with all his heart, he begged for the strength to do the job he'd been sent to do.

When he opened his eyes, a blond woman in a gold-beaded dress stood in front of him. "Are you tired already?" she asked. "It's early yet. We'll have more dancing, soon as the band returns from its break."

He blinked at her. "Huh?"

"Just letting you know I'm available... to dance, I mean," she cooed coyly. The woman tipped one hip provocatively and gazed up at him through thickly mascaraed, amber eyes.

"Oh." He looked distractedly over her head, trying to keep track of Caroline in the crush of guests, as Max started to move them back toward their table.

It occurred to him that, during his preangel years, the woman who was so eagerly flirting with him would have aroused a lot more interest in him. She was flashy and reeked of sensuality. She was practically offering herself up on a plate. If he asked, she'd probably leave with him right then. But Zach felt only irritation that she was getting in the way of his concentrating on Caroline.

"Excuse me," he murmured, stepping briskly around her.

He eased his way between guests, picking up a glass of something that turned out to be champagne as he crossed the room, closing in on Max and Caroline. When he was no more than fifteen feet away, he stopped beside a table displaying a scale model of the projected Children's Wing and looked down, as if to study it. But from the corner of his eye, he could easily view Caroline's table.

Max was talking animatedly to two other men and seemed totally oblivious to Caroline, who was making small talk with one of the wives. Whereas Max had held Caroline's hand and gazed at her with clear interest at the reception, tonight he was behaving politely but coolly. *Not good,* he thought. *It's that damn suit. I blew it big time.*

But there was nothing he could do about her outfit now. Zach thought for a moment, then concentrated on Max and passed a thought to him: *Caroline North is the most beautiful woman in the room. She doesn't need sequins to shine.*

Max's shoulders shifted, then straightened, and he looked around at Caroline, seated beside him. Slowly his expression altered to a smile of comprehension. He reached out one hand to touch the small of her back and slid his chair closer to hers.

Good, Zach congratulated himself. *Now for her.*

He focused on Caroline. *Tennis. Tell him that you used to play tennis.*

Caroline gave Max a puzzled look as the others in the group kept up the conversation.

He met her softly questioning brown eyes. "What is it?" he asked.

"I don't know," she answered hesitantly. "For some reason, I had this odd impression someone had mentioned tennis." She shook her head, smiling.

"Do you play?" Max asked eagerly.

Good boy, Zach thought. *Now we're back on track.*

"I used to," Caroline admitted. "I never got particularly good at it, but it was fun when my friend Suzanne and I used to hit a ball around on Sunday afternoons."

Max grinned and turned to the man beside him. "Listen here, Barry. Caroline has brought up another good idea for a fund-raiser. A tennis tournament. We could talk to Jeff Malcolm at the club about it." He looked at Caroline. "Jeff is our resident pro. How about your being the first player to sign up?"

Caroline laughed. "Me? I don't think so, I'm so rusty."

"A little practice will put you back in form," Max suggested heartily. "Come on, you can come to the club with me and I'll whip you into shape."

Caroline looked doubtful but nodded in agreement. Then she turned, as if aware she was being watched and looked straight at Zach.

He raised his champagne glass to her and smiled. Archangel Meher would be so pleased.

Chapter 9

Caroline woke slowly through a thick champagne haze to a persistent pounding sound. She rolled over in bed and cracked open one eye, aiming it at her alarm clock. It was only 7:00 a.m., and the light through her window seemed painfully bright, and the sea gulls over the Sound were screeching several decibels higher than they normally did, she was sure.

She wished the noise would stop, but it kept up, growing louder. And she finally realized it was coming from her front door.

"Go away!" she shouted, then imagined a list of emergencies that might bring an early visitor. The shop had burned down overnight. Suzanne and Ralph had been in a car accident. Her mother had had a heart attack, and her sister hadn't been able to reach her by phone because the line was dead.

With a groan, she tossed aside the bedsheet and plucked her robe from the hook on the back of the door. "Oh, all right, keep your shirt on. I'm coming," she called out grumpily. Her first waking moments were never her shining best.

As she passed the mirror in her living room, she caught a glimpse of a barefoot, mussed brunette wearing a rumpled pink robe and a face decorated with pillow creases. Caroline rose on her tiptoes and pressed one eye to the peephole. Standing on the other side of the door, looking collegiate and perky in tennis whites with a racquet propped on one shoulder, was Zach.

She unbolted the door and opened it for him. "What are you doing here at this hour?" she grumbled. Swiveling around, she stomped off to the kitchen without waiting for his explanation. Coffee suddenly seemed a necessity.

She heard Zach step inside and close the door behind him.

"I thought you might like to warm up a little for Max. You said you were rusty."

She stopped cold, her hand on the kitchen faucet. "How do you know I said that? How do you even know about the tennis tournament?"

He shrugged, making a show of counting the strings of his racquet by walking his fingertips across them.

"You were *spying* on me at the banquet," she accused him.

"I wouldn't call it spying," he said. "I happened to be standing nearby, enjoying my champagne."

"I see," she said dryly. She measured water into her coffeemaker and grounds into the filter, then flicked the switch to start the coffee brewing. Facing Zach, she leaned against her kitchen counter. "I don't know why you're doing this!"

"Doing what? Inviting you to hit a few tennis balls?"

"No, you jerk. Why you're acting so damn irrationally. One minute you're beating a hasty retreat after making love to me, the next, you're looking for excuses to hang out together. What's going on, Zach? Does being around me scare you or threaten you in some way?" She stepped toward him.

He backed away a step. "No, of course not."

"But you're attracted to me... *a lot.*"

"Yeah, I guess I am," he admitted.

"Enough to make love to me."

He flushed and held the racquet in front of him, as if for protection. "Having sex isn't the same thing as making love," he said tightly.

"Oh, is *that* what that was... well, pardon me!" she shouted. "I'd forgotten the convenient male ability to separate the two."

"Now, Caroline," he said, in a placating tone she'd heard herself use with a difficult customer, the same one nurses employed on patients under strong medication. "I apologized for the other day.

I shouldn't have walked into your bedroom like that. I shouldn't have let your state of dishabille get to me, but I ... I—''

"You what, Zach?" She was having trouble standing in one place she was so furious with him. She wanted to run around the room and throw things to work off her frustration. "Was it really just hormones running rampant? Was that all it was for you?"

A muscle jerked and tightened along his jaw, and he closed his eyes and drew a shuddering breath. When he opened his eyes again, their blue was intense and cold—all emotion shut out of them. "Yes," he snapped. "That's it, just hormones. It would have been the same with any other woman who was moderately good looking."

She glared at him. "You're lying! You *felt* something. I could see it in your eyes, Zach. You weren't just going through the motions."

His eyes started to soften, but he turned away and started for the door. "If you want to hit some balls, I'll be down at the apartment courts."

She stared down at her hands, studying the uneven chips in the edges of her polished nails, listening to the door shut behind him, his footsteps fading down the corridor. At last, she could stand still no longer. Caroline ran to the window and watched Zach stride along the paved path that led to the apartment complex's tennis courts, swinging his racquet fiercely, as if miming an explosive slam through a concrete wall.

They played tennis for almost two hours. As the autumn sun warmed the courts, Caroline shed her jacket and remembered the satisfying feeling of forcing her body to push itself to its limit. Her muscles and tendons lengthened, and knots that had lived in them for months seemed to ease away. Her own body heat created a natural sedative effect, calming taut nerves. She pulled off another layer of clothing, and played for the last half hour in T-shirt and shorts.

Her frustration with Zach worked to her advantage, bringing out an aggressiveness in her playing that surprised her. When the sweet spot on her racquet strings connected with the ball, her shots zinged across the net, dropping sharply within the lines and giving Zach a run for his money. She was secretly pleased with how exhausted he looked at the end of their session.

Fair payback, she thought.

"Let's do this again tomorrow," she called to him coyly across the net.

Zach grimaced and rubbed the calf of one leg, which appeared to be swelling up rather nicely, she thought.

Two days later, Max called and asked if she'd like to play him in a friendly match at the public courts. She agreed to meet him for a few hours around lunchtime, if he picked her up at the Silver Whale and delivered her back there by 1:30 p.m.

Later that day, Zach stopped by the shop, ostensibly to sample the line of colonial-recipe jams and jellies they'd just added to their stock. "So how did tennis with Max go?" he asked.

Caroline squinted at him. She was almost certain he hadn't been watching her this time. "Not very well," she admitted.

Suzanne breezed through, carrying a tray with pretzel sticks and tiny fish-shaped crackers to accompany the sample jellies and cheeses she was putting out for customers. "Try the jalapeño havarti, Zach. It's great," she said, setting the whole tray in front of him.

"Thanks." Zach popped a fish cracker into his mouth and looked at Caroline. "So what happened? You lose your serve again?"

"Just the opposite," she answered with a wry smile.

"She beat the pants off the good doctor." Suzanne winked at him.

"Oh?"

"Yeah," Caroline admitted. "Max talks a good line, but he's not much of a tennis player. I just hit down the line to him the way you and I had, and the more points I won off him, the more furious he got." She shrugged. "By the time he dropped me off here, he was hardly speaking to me."

Zach looked worried. "You bruised his pride."

"Well, what did you expect me to do? Throw the match to feed his male ego?"

Suzanne used a pretzel to scoop up a dollop of creamy horseradish spread. "I told her, Zach, she could have pulled just a few shots to keep the man happy."

"Why should I do that?" Caroline cried. "If Max can't stand a little healthy competition—"

"You're right." Zach broke in, rubbing his chin thoughtfully. "If Pearson doesn't have the strength of character to hold up under a friendly game of tennis, he's not the right man."

"The right man?" Suzanne asked. She looked from Caroline to Zach and back to Caroline again. "The right man for you?"

"He's matchmaking again." Caroline sighed. "You'd think he were my mother or something."

Suzanne quirked an eyebrow and tilted her head to better ogle Zach's broad chest and long, lean legs. "Doesn't look like any mother I know."

Zach rolled his eyes. "You're as bad as any guy on a construction site."

Caroline laughed at the offended look on his face. "Listen, all of this dating nonsense is just too much work. I mean, why should I have to please some man by second-guessing his taste in clothes or trying to find just the right level of performance on a tennis court. I have to dress sexy, but discreetly. I have to be good enough to impress him, but not good enough to beat him."

Suzanne munched on another pretzel. "It's all part of the game," she commented philosophically.

"Well, I *hate* it," Caroline said, throwing up her hands. "Why can't I be myself, and still be attractive to a man."

"You *are!*" Zach burst out.

Both women stared at him.

He looked as if he wished he'd kept his opinion to himself. "I mean, you're a reasonably attractive young woman, Caroline, with a business of your own and a good head on your shoulders. Why shouldn't some man be interested in you?"

"Boy, he sure knows how to pile on the flattery," Suzanne muttered, popping three more pretzel sticks into her mouth.

"Stop it! You're going to eat all of our samples." Caroline snatched the tray away from her and moved it to a low oak table closer to the door.

Suzanne shrugged. "I've got to bring another tray out anyway." She disappeared into the back room.

Caroline slanted a questioning look at Zach. His eyes briefly met hers but quickly drifted away to fix on a small, stuffed bear with a lace collar.

As if needing an excuse to change the subject, he picked up the stuffed animal and held it out toward Caroline. "This is what dating is all about."

"Teddy bears?"

"Kids," Zach said.

Caroline felt the warmth drain from her cheeks. "That's one place this conversation isn't going," she stated firmly. Turning toward an already tidy stack of Victorian lace doilies, she started refolding them.

"It's true," Zach persisted. "I know you had a terrible experience. Losing a child isn't easy."

Caroline refused to look at him, but she was no longer able to check her emotions.

"How would *you* know?" she raged at him. She shook out a doily and slapped it down on the table, folded it once, twice, three times, pressing in each crease with the hot, moist palm of her hand. "What right do you have, Zach, to pry into my life and make judgments about what I should or shouldn't do with it?"

"I've never lost a child, it's true," he admitted gently. "But everyone has lost . . . has lost *someone* dear to them. And—" he stepped up closer behind her "—it's not as bad as those who stay behind think. It really isn't. Your little boy is happy. He's at peace and being taken care of. He has no pain . . . no worries."

"*I* took care of him. *I* protected him!" Caroline punctuated each sentence with a fist pounding the tabletop. She spun around to face Zach. "Jimmy wasn't in pain while he was alive. He was healthy and happy with me." She sobbed, tears flowing down her cheeks, puddling on the doilies. "There was *no* reason he had to die. *None!* It was unfair, unnecessary! I'll never understand why it had to happen!"

Zach stepped forward and, before she could dodge away from his outstretched arms, he'd enclosed her in a warm embrace. She wept openly into his shirtfront, vaguely aware of the scent of him, letting waves of grief wash out of her heart. Zach let her cry, holding her, rocking their bodies gently, resting his chin on top of her head.

He offered no explanation, no excuses for life, but she felt as if he were lending her his strength in his own silent way.

After several minutes, her tears slowed, then dried to a trickle.

"Children," Zach whispered, "are a gift from heaven. Sometimes, for reasons we can never hope to understand, heaven needs to take them back."

"My baby..." Caroline whispered shakily against his chest through trembling lips, and it felt as if her soul were escaping with the words.

"You will have another baby. A beautiful baby," Zach assured her, "who will grow up to bring you and others joy and pride."

Caroline swallowed; her mouth tasted salty, hot. "How can you say such things? You have no idea what the future will bring." She looked up into his face, and was astounded by the compassion and intense concern she saw in his eyes.

"I believe it to be true," he said simply. "And if someone like me can have faith in the future, then someone like you, who is a much better person, should understand how it has to be. Everything happens for a reason, Caroline. You are loved, and you're being watched over."

She couldn't believe she was hearing him right. The words seemed totally out of character with the rakishly handsome bachelor who lived across the hall from her. But something in his tone of voice, in the way his eyes locked on hers, never wavering, instilled complete confidence in her. As long as Zach stood there, holding her, she felt certain that everything he said must be true.

"Hey, you two, knock it off!" Suzanne called from the doorway, balancing another tray on one hand, while she carried a bowl of spiced punch in the other. "You'll scare away the customers. Come on, I could use some help running this shop."

Zach's arms dropped away from Caroline, letting in a thin sliver of cool air. He was still watching her as she stepped away from him, as if to make sure she was steady on her feet.

"I'm all right now," she whispered, giving him a weak smile. "I'm going to be all right."

Later that day, as the sun set over the river and long after Zach had left, Caroline and Suzanne closed up for the day. Only under the influence of a warm buzz encouraged by the leftovers of a second bowl of punch they'd mixed, then spiked with white wine, did Caroline allow herself to recall Zach's mysterious words.

She wondered, did it really matter whether or not he actually could predict her future? Wasn't it enough that he believed good things were going to happen for her? Shouldn't that alone comfort her? If he could believe that strongly, why shouldn't she?

Another baby.

She scooped up the lace-collared teddy bear. It had rich brown fur as cuddly as lamb's wool, eyes stitched in soft black yarn and a nose that begged to be teethed on.

Why did the possibility of carrying and giving birth to another child seem less terrifying now? She felt as if she really *had* drawn invisible strength from Zach's words... or, maybe it was from his touch... or the way he'd seemed to be able to communicate hope to her in ways beyond words.

Taking the bear along with her, she went to her purse, counted out the cost of the stuffed toy and put the money into the cash drawer. "You're going home with me," she told the bear, feeling pleasantly Chablis-dizzy. "You're going home to wait for... for whoever comes into my life who most needs you."

And all the way home, as she walked the darkening streets of Mystic, breathing in the misty sea air, humming softly, she thought about Zach and wondered how she might return his favor by doing something nice for him.

Zach sat, watching out his living-room window, a plate of microwave macaroni and cheese propped on the wide windowsill in front of him. He felt not at all hungry, but supposed he'd better eat something. Without food he wouldn't be able to think clearly, and it was imperative that he keep alert for Caroline's sake.

She'd scared him in the shop earlier that day. When she'd broken down and dipped into the dark corners of her life, remembering her little boy, Zach feared he'd lost her. He thought he'd never be able to pull her out of her despair.

But from somewhere inside him, or perhaps beyond him, the soothing words had come. He'd merely held her and let his own soul flow out over hers, absorbing her grief. In that instant, he'd suffered her pain as if it had been his own. Her grief had overwhelmed him, making his own death seem, at first, inconsequential. He'd told her that her baby, Jimmy, was happy in Heaven, for he somehow knew that was absolutely true. Then, with her in his arms, he relived his own death and understood the magnitude of the loss he'd suffered, for by leaving the world of the living, he'd relinquished every chance of sharing a life with Caroline.

When he walked out of her shop that afternoon, he'd carried with him not only the weight of her sorrow but his own. Being an angel, he thought, was not as easy as it might seem.

He'd busied himself around his own apartment, while biding time for her to come home. And while he waited, he tried to think of ways to continue her healing process. He had to prevent her from sliding back into her pit of despair ever again. He had to find some way to help her move from the bleakness of the past into the light of the future.

It was 6:30 p.m. when she appeared on the walkway between the nearly leafless maple trees bordering the parking lot, her hair blowing in the autumn breeze off the ocean, shining with reddish highlights from the setting sun. Her step appeared bouncy and upbeat. A little smile played with the corners of her lips, and he was thankful that the effect of his comforting words and touch had lasted.

Then he saw the teddy bear clamped under her left arm, and he smiled. "Good girl. Think to the future."

Zach wolfed down the rest of the cold macaroni and cheese, and tossed the plastic plate into the trash can. He grabbed his keys from the kitchen countertop and bolted toward the door. Just as she unlatched and pushed open her door, he skidded into the hallway.

"Hi!" he said brightly.

Caroline turned with a smile. "Hi, yourself. I see you're hard at work as usual."

He laughed at her wry humor. "I've never told you about my work, have I?"

"No, you haven't."

"I'm an independent consultant."

"A consultant," she repeated, eyeing him skeptically.

"Yeah." What else would you call an angel who roamed around, straightening out people's lives?

She nodded but looked unconvinced. "I guess all consultants grow muscles like those." She poked a finger into one of his biceps.

"I work out," he said quickly.

Up close he could see pale gray fatigue shadows beneath her eyes but he didn't dare leave her alone that night, not while her emotional state was still so fragile. He caught a faint, sweet whiff of fermented grape on her breath, and guessed she and Suzanne had been sampling punch. In her condition, a little alcohol might push her over the edge into melancholy.

"You look pretty tired," he said. "How about letting me take you out to dinner. Say, the Fisherman's Inne?"

"Zach—" she said, "we have to talk."

"We will, over dinner. I'll tell you more about my job."

"I mean about us. Really talk. Things are happening between us, and I don't understand them."

He frowned. "Are these things making you feel bad?"

"Not at all. That's just it." She fiddled with the teddy bear's lace collar, smiling faintly. "When I'm with you, I feel wonderful, as if nothing on earth can harm me. All the pain goes away—even the worst kind, like today. It just evaporates. And I'm filled with this feeling that's so hard to explain. It's as if I know that everything will be fine. Life will work itself out. I'm at peace with myself."

"That's good, right?"

She gently lofted the little bear through the door, toward her couch, then turned back to face him. "We might as well leave right away if you're ready," she said. "I'm pretty hungry."

Zach kept in step with her, down the stairs and through the lobby. "You didn't answer my question. Isn't it good—the way you're feeling?"

She bit down on the pink inner flesh of her bottom lip. "Yes, while you're with me. But what happens when you go away? I mean, *forever* go away. What then?" A spark of determination lit her eyes. "I refuse to be dependent upon a man in that way."

He hadn't let himself think about the time when his assignment would be complete. Of course, he'd have to leave her and go where Meher next sent him. But by then she'd be with her new husband, and *he* would take care of her.

"I wouldn't worry about it," he said tightly.

"But it will happen," she insisted softly, as if she sensed the inevitable as surely as he knew it. Caroline's walk slowed as they crossed the parking lot. "It sounds as if a job like yours might require some traveling, might even take you away from Mystic, and even if it didn't you obviously aren't the kind of man to stay with one woman for long."

"People follow their own destinies," he muttered, not knowing what else he could say.

"And yours and mine aren't the same?"

"No." He sighed. "I'm pretty sure they aren't."

She said nothing while he opened the passenger side door for her and waited for her to climb in. Running around the outside of the car, he dropped down into the driver's seat, buckled his seat belt and slipped the key into the ignition.

Caroline's hand closed softly over his. "Tell me why, Zach."

He closed his eyes. The cool touch of her fingers on his hand sent pleasant chills up his arm, down through his chest and into the depths of his masculine being.

"Zach, tell me what it is that stands between us. You must feel what I'm feeling—the way we react to each other when we're together. It isn't something you could miss or ignore easily. Like right now. You want me, and I want you."

"It can't happen again," he said shortly.

"Why not?"

"It just can't."

"Tell me why." She wasn't nagging or prodding. She was asking for a simple, logical explanation, which she needed to rebuild her life. Even so, he was sure that if the punch's effects had totally worn off, she wouldn't have worked up the courage to confront him.

But her reasons for needing an explanation from him were strong. One man had turned the tragedy of losing their child into an even worse nightmare. She was asking Zach to unravel the mystery of the male gender for her, so that she could learn to trust herself to love again. It wasn't so much to ask. But revealing why he'd come to her and why he must leave was not something Meher would allow.

"Are you terminally ill? Or—" she whispered hoarsely. "Do you have a disease you're afraid of passing on to me?"

"No. Nothing like that." He was struck by the irony of her concern and nearly laughed out loud. She worried about his health, when he was already dead.

"But the truth is too painful to talk about?"

"Something like that," he murmured, unable to look at her. Death is a pretty sensitive topic, he thought, especially when it's your own.

Around them, the parking lot crept from dusk to dark. The lights from the apartments and a few weakly glowing parking lamps cast a dim silvery luminescence across the expanse of pavement and unmoving vehicles. Through the windshield, Zach could hear the sound of water sloshing in the cove nearby. Caroline leaned closer to him, across the padded console that separated their seats. He could feel her wine-sweet breath on his face.

"I want you to know that you've helped me a lot . . . at the store today...other times, too," she murmured, looking up into his face with a soft smile.

It was all he could do to not enfold her in his arms. He kept his voice level, unemotional. "You were sad, I happened to be there. I'm glad I was."

"No," she said, "it was more than that. It was as if you were *meant* to be there for me. I haven't felt that awful about my baby since before you moved in across the hall. Our friendship has taken my mind off the past. You've been good for me, Zach."

The light in her eyes was beautiful, enticing, and suddenly provocative. He could read what she was thinking, and her needs mirrored his own desires perfectly.

Quickly he reached in front of her and turned the key in the ignition, starting the engine. He couldn't allow himself to dwell on those eyes, reminding him so vividly of how it felt to make love to her.

Just as quickly, Caroline reached out and twisted the key in the opposite direction, shutting off the engine. The car rumbled to silence. "Zach, I want to please you. Call it my way of thanking you."

He didn't have to ask what she meant—he knew. And the idea appalled him, sending a bolt of panic shooting through him.

But . . . damn, she looked delectable in the dim glow of evening, sitting so close to him. Her cheeks were flushed, her eyes wide with anticipation, her breathing shallow and irregular. Great heavens, how could he be expected to refuse such an offer?

"Caroline," he croaked, "we can't."

"We can."

"It's not just a matter of sex," he said. "I lied about that, in your bedroom. This whole thing is much more complex than—"

"I realize that." She interrupted him. "If all I felt for you was lust, I couldn't have let you touch me the way you did. And I couldn't do this." She brushed her lips lightly over his. Her mouth felt incredibly warm, full and moist. "And this." She drew her lips down the side of his neck into his shirt collar, raising goose bumps all over his body. "Or this." Easing open the top buttons of his shirt, she planted feather-light kisses across his chest, nipping at the tufts of pale hair as she worked her way downward, toward his belly. "Or this," she murmured throatily as her fingers came to rest on the zipper of his jeans and her lips started to follow.

"Caroline, no!" he growled, clamping his hands on either side of her head to stop her descent.

"You don't want me to make love to you like that?" she asked innocently. A slightly drunken smile curved her lips. "I've read that most men enjoy it." There was playfulness in her voice, but it didn't lessen his own tension.

Zach shuddered with the effort to restrain himself. The image of her warm, wet mouth closing over him, drawing him between her lips was almost too much for him. He ached to let her do what she had in mind. But he'd already slipped up once. How many mistakes would Meher allow before he reacted with a vengeance that would make a ton of steel on his head feel like a feather pillow?

Zach kept her head immobile between his palms. "Of course I'd like you to... oh, Caroline," he moaned. "It's just that it's... it isn't fair to you if we—"

"Who's to say what is fair for *me*, but *me*?" she argued lightly, her fingers moving busily as she spoke. He looked down. His belt buckle was undone, the button of his jeans open. She eased down his zipper and began sketching silky circles with one polished fingernail, beneath the elastic of his briefs.

"You don't understand!" he sputtered. Afraid he'd hurt her if he gripped her any harder, Zach moved his hands to the steering wheel and held on for dear life.

"If there's another woman you're being faithful to, tell me and I'll stop," she whispered, bending low to plant a kiss in the wiry curls at her fingertips.

"No...no other woman," Zach gasped. His head suddenly felt too heavy to hold up. He let it fall back against the car seat. Shutting his eyes, he concentrated on the ripples of fire radiating from her touch, through his flesh.

"And you like this very much," she murmured hypnotically.

"Yes, very much." How could this woman have been left by any man in his right mind? he thought desperately. She was driving him mad . . . the best kind of mad.

Zach's fingers clenched and unclenched and clenched again around the steering wheel. He'd been trying to stop himself from touching her, but he could hold himself back no longer.

With one arm he cradled her between his body and the steering column, as she closed her mouth over him. His free hand instinctively negotiated skirt, panty hose, panties, seeking out her liquid center. Then the tips of his fingers were moist with her, and she was moving so deliciously over him, he hadn't a chance in the world of resisting the power she held over him.

All he could do was sink with her into the leather cushion and watch helplessly as she worked her magic on him . . . and it wasn't long before the world exploded within him and ecstasy hummed through his veins.

Caroline felt Zach's body grow rigid and quake beneath her as he moaned deep down in his throat. She gloried in the pleasure she was bringing him but, in the next minute, found herself distracted by the sensations of his hand stroking her, lifting her onto her own wave of rapture. She had expected nothing from him in return for her gift, but somehow, through the urgency of his own rapture, he'd thought to repay her in kind. As his strong fingers discovered the moist, throbbing pulse of her womanhood, she buried her face in his pungently damp lap to stifle her cries of delight.

For what seemed to her an eternity, neither of them spoke. Then Zach gently lifted her into a semireclining position, supporting her gently in his arms, burying his face in the velvety curve between her cheek and shoulder.

"You didn't have to do that," he whispered hoarsely.

"I know. I wanted to." She nuzzled against his bare chest where his shirt lay open, inhaling the smell of man underlying with his spicy after-shave.

"That felt wonderful," he said, after a while.

She couldn't stop herself from giggling. "I sort of guessed it had." She hesitated. "Zach?"

"Yeah."

"I just want you to know, it was never like this for me . . . with Rob."

"No?"

He seemed incapable of speaking more than one syllable at a time.

"Not at all. Rob was very . . . I don't know . . . controlled . . . difficult to please. It's hard to explain."

"But he satisfied you?"

"You mean, did I climax every time?"

"Yeah."

"No. I did once in a while. I didn't expect anything more from sex. I didn't know making love could feel so . . . so important."

He laughed a loud, rich laugh. "*Important?* I've never heard it called that."

She felt only a little offended. "Well, yes. It wasn't any big deal . . . wasn't *important* whether I had an earth-moving climax or not. Sex seemed to me mostly a marital gesture. I'm not sure what it was for Rob."

"Such a waste," Zach murmured into her hair, inhaling deeply. "If I'd been married to you, it would have been different."

She held her breath, waiting for him to go on.

But he didn't, and little pieces of her heart chipped away in the silence strung between them.

At last she found the words to say what she'd tried to ask before. "Zach. There is a reason, isn't there?"

"Yes," he admitted, his voice strained. "There's a very special reason."

She looked up into his face and found emotions that terrified her, even though she couldn't define them. "Go on," she whispered.

"I can't explain now, Caroline," he said. "But I promise that as soon as I can, I'll make everything clear to you."

"I can wait," she said softly.

Chapter 10

The Fisherman's Inne wasn't as crowded as it often became on summer weekends. After Labor Day, the restaurant was frequented mostly by locals—a cozier, tamer crowd.

Caroline had always loved the colonial-style ambience. The historical building was part of the Mystic Seaport, a replica of the real eighteenth-century whaling port that had once thrived on the same site. A candle shop, general store, barrel maker, blacksmith and cottages—crusty wheat loaves baking in blazing stone hearths—lined the cobbled streets. The *Morgan,* an ancient whaling vessel, was permanently docked on the river. The town square, with its pretty white, balustraded cupola, hosted concerts and reenactments of ship-to-shore rescues and town meetings. All of the seaport, with its buildings and authentically costumed staff, formed another world into which twentieth-century visitors could dip their senses.

Every year Caroline had purchased a season pass, and she'd wander up and down the quaint paths, soaking up another era. She loved feeling the continuity of life, the flow of time through her veins. Living, back then, had been exciting, challenging, full of love and yes, tragedy, too. Women often produced ten or more children, only to lose more than half of their beloved brood before they reached adulthood. Disease, the trauma of childbirth, the perils of travel and daily living claimed souls early in life. It was soothing to her, even while she and Rob were having their difficulties and she wondered if their marriage would be a lasting one, to stroll among the cottages and wave a friendly hello to a young woman much like herself, garbed in the clothing of two hundred years earlier...and wonder what it would have been like to live back then.

After Jimmy had been born, she'd bought a family pass and pushed his stroller from one exhibit to the next, excitedly pointing out the toy shop, a tiny lending library, the one-room schoolhouse—although she knew he couldn't possibly understand any of it. But after he'd been taken from her, she'd lost all interest in visiting the village. It seemed too cruel a reminder of his absence. The setting that had once been comforting to her then seemed to shout harsh lessons: *Time goes on. People are born; people die. Life never changes.*

Was there no reason or logic to life? Was all left to chance? Were the innocent punished as harshly as the wicked?

She'd exhausted herself, asking those questions.

Now, as Zach pulled his car into the parking lot across the street from the Seaport entrance, she could see a few early-evening visitors strolling between the Museum Shoppe and the sail-maker's shed. A twinge of doubt assaulted her, and she subconsciously tensed.

"Something wrong?" Zach asked, his voice still a little husky, reminding her of the intimacy they'd shared only moments earlier.

"No, I . . . I just used to bring Jimmy here for walks."

He nodded. "I know."

She turned in the seat to face him. "You know?"

He seemed to consider his next words carefully, then said. "I suppose it's a popular spot for a lot of families."

"Yes," she said, following his gaze to a young couple who were pushing a stroller. A second child, about three years old, was leashed to the stroller frame with a braided harness.

Caroline couldn't help smiling at the little girl's impatience to dash off in every possible direction except the one her parents intended.

"That one looks like a handful," Zach commented, letting himself out of the car.

He walked around to the passenger side and opened Caroline's door for her while she was still watching the couple and their children. "My niece in Pennsylvania is about that age," she said wistfully. "She's such a doll baby."

"When did you last see her?" Zach asked.

Caroline had to think for a minute. "It's been nine months...no, almost a year. My sister sent me photos of Kerry's birthday party in July. I couldn't believe how she'd grown." She smiled at the thought of the little golden-curled girl who had brought so much joy into her sister's life.

"You should drive down and visit them," Zach suggested as he tucked his wide hand into the small of her back and guided her across the street. "Wouldn't Suzanne be able to cover for you at the shop for a week?"

Caroline looked at him and smiled. "Why are you pushing kids at me all the time?"

Zach shrugged. "Like I said before, you're a nice woman who deserves to be happy. Children are an important part of a full life."

"And nothing more?"

"To have a family you need ..."

"That's not what I meant, Zach, and you know it," she said firmly when they'd reached the other side of the street. "*You* have something at stake here. I can feel it. I'm important to you, but I don't understand why." She stopped in the middle of the sidewalk and drew a finger down the beard-stubbled line of his jaw, studying the shadows deep within his blue, blue eyes. "What do you feel when you're with me? Why are you trying to straighten out my life when no one, including me, has asked for help?"

His eyes clouded over, veering away from hers. "You're imagining things." Grasping her hand, he moved it away from his face, dragging her along with him as he strode toward the restaurant, two blocks down the street.

Caroline gazed up into his troubled face, sure she was right. But he had erected his protective shield and stepped behind it. She wished she knew his secrets.

Suddenly Zach began talking again in a calm, even voice, as if what he was saying was part of an ongoing conversation they'd started days earlier. "There are some Native American tribes who used to believe, perhaps still do, that when a brave travels alone through the wilderness, a spirit guide walks with him."

"Really?" she whispered.

He nodded solemnly. "The brave's companion stays with him through lonely days, weeks, months of hardship. It advises him when he loses his direction or can't find game. It comforts and heals and, they say, it even follows him into death."

"That's a reassuring fantasy," she murmured, watching Zach's face, wondering what he was really trying to say to her.

"I've read interviews with men who claimed to have spirit guides. The braves who spoke of them could describe in detail what they looked like, but each one was different."

Caroline immediately thought of the experiences people had written and spoken of in recent years, involving angels. Each one special, mysterious, taking a different form. Some angels were reputed to be mere flashes of pure white light, others took the shape of a protective animal or a person of authority, or were only a voice that directed their charge to safety or gave strength.

"Suzanne once told me a story," she said softly as they climbed the stairs toward the inn's massive oak door. Zach held her hand, guiding her upward, his wide fingers warm and reassuring around her smaller ones.

She looked at him again when he didn't respond, but he seemed to be hearing only half of what she was saying, as if another voice had caught his attention and he was trying to listen to both of them at the same time.

"Maybe it's just one of those urban myths that seems to be circulating these days," she mused. "The story goes that a young girl was taking a bus home across the city. It was night time, and very dark, and she became aware of a man on the bus who changed seats to sit closer to her. He stared at her, muttering things under his breath that she couldn't make out but somehow knew were evil.

"When her stop came, she stood up to get off, praying he'd remain behind on the bus. But he rose and followed her down the aisle. The bus pulled away, leaving her alone with him on the dark street corner. No one was in sight. And she had nearly a half mile to walk to her house.

"She waited to see which way he would turn, so that she could take a different direction. He stood silently, glaring at her, a crooked smile on his lips, then took a step toward her. She started to walk away. He followed."

Zach watched her lips move, as if he were trying to catch her words from the shapes her mouth formed before sound escaped it. "And then?" he asked.

Caroline felt her own pulse quicken in response to the urgency of the little girl's plight. "Just when the man's long strides caught him up to her, out from between two buildings ambled a huge, white sheepdog. It was so white, it seemed to glow with its own light—an unusual dog for the city, because it would be impossible to keep clean or exercise.

"The girl had always been afraid of dogs, especially large ones. Strays prowled her neighborhood in packs, searching for scraps, and they were not friendly creatures. But she was more afraid of the man than of the dog, and she didn't try to run when it approached her."

Zach brought them to a halt on the top step, as if wanting to hear the ending of her story before they were interrupted by the hostess on the other side of the door. "Go on," he prompted, watching her expression intently.

"The dog walked alongside the terrified girl, his big head beneath her hand. He accompanied her all the way to her house, and the threatening stranger, perhaps thinking the dog was hers and would be too dangerous an obstacle, disappeared into the shadows." Caroline looked up at Zach, trying to read his reaction to the tale, but his features were blank.

"What happened to the dog?" he asked.

"The girl went inside to bring it some food and water. When she returned, the dog had gone away, and she never saw it again. Neither did anyone else in the neighborhood, although she asked around frequently."

Zach touched Caroline's cheek with his palm. His hand felt warm against her cool skin. "What does that story mean to you, Caroline?"

She frowned up at him. "I don't know. I'm not sure." She drew a thin ribbon of chill night air between her teeth, and tasted the sea's salt lingering in it. "I've never believed in ghosts, things that go bump in the night, angels or phantoms or devils. I guess I'm too logical a person."

"Maybe you don't have to *believe* to have a guardian angel," he said. "Maybe, like the little girl in your story, all you have to do is be a good person and need help."

She heard in his words a strange ring of truth, but her sense of reality struggled with them. If everyone had a guardian angel, where had hers been the night Jimmy died? Why hadn't it stopped that ultimate evil from casting a black pall over her entire life?

To some questions, there are no answers, a voice whispered through her thoughts.

Caroline looked up sharply at Zach, but his mouth was closed. She peered into the dark around them. They were alone on the steps. Nevertheless, she felt oddly comforted by the words.

Smiling up at Zach, she asked, "Are you hungry?"

"Very," he said, reaching down for her hand and enclosing it warmly within his. "Come on, let's eat."

The meal was marvelous. They chose two traditional dishes from a simple but hearty menu. Zach had Yankee pot roast, swimming in thick brown gravy, his plate piled high with the potatoes, carrots and whole pearl onions that had been roasted in the pan with the meat. Caroline ordered Boston scrod, broiled and drizzled with herb butter, served with a side order of baked beans, seasoned with sweet molasses and bacon.

They ate in comfortable silence, with the hum and clatter of diners around them—mostly families with children. A little girl with red curls looped with a bright blue ribbon, sat at the next table. She turned around every few minutes to bat her eyelashes at Zach, although her parents repeatedly instructed her to, "Pay attention to your meal, Becky. Leave the nice man alone."

But Zach seemed as taken with the little girl's flirtations as she was with him. And he encouraged her by making atrocious faces at her.

"I think she likes you, Zach," Caroline teased. "Is she your type?"

"Maybe in twenty years." He laughed, shaking his head in mild embarrassment as the toddler again squirmed around in her high chair to grin at him.

"Let's see, by then you'll be what? Fifty? I'd call that a May-December relationship."

He blushed, and she decided she liked teasing him. But another part of her felt a twinge of jealousy. What the hell *was* his type, if she wasn't it?

She'd seen not one woman enter or leave his apartment. Yet she never once doubted Zach's strongly masculine nature. And on the occasions they'd made love—like that very night—it was clear he'd had plenty of experience and enjoyed being with a woman.

Caroline considered asking Zach, straight out, about his sexual history. After all, this was the nineties. Prospective lovers were supposed to talk about such things, if only to protect themselves from disease. Still, she felt reluctant to demand such intimate information from him. If the most she could ever hope to share with him was the friendship and stolen moments of passion they'd already shared, maybe she'd have to be satisfied with that.

They ate, talking about everything and anything that came to mind, except their future. "Aren't kids great?" he asked when the family with the little girl got up to leave. "You can't bottle that joy and enthusiasm for life."

"I know," she agreed, and for the first time in what felt like forever, she was able to understand that simple truth. Love automatically came in the bargain with children, and that love didn't cease to exist when a life ended.

She thought about Jimmy, remembering the dizzy, drooly smiles he'd give her when she swung him up over her head. Remembering how he'd entwine his chubby fingers around a lock of her hair and hold on fiercely.

By the time Zach led her outside, tears clung to her eyelashes, but they were tears of joy, not of mourning. She brushed them away with the back of her hand before he could see them.

"I have an idea," Zach said. "How about we see if there are any interesting movies showing."

"It's been a long time since I've actually gone to a theater," she admitted. "It might be fun."

"We can drive over and take pot luck," he suggested.

They followed Route 1, a two-lane road that laced through the wooded lowlands hugging the Connecticut shoreline. In Groton there was a modest four-screen cinema that shared a parking lot with the Stop & Shop grocery store.

Zach glanced at the digital clock on his dash board. "Eight-thirty. Good timing. Most places have shows starting around nine."

Caroline leaned forward, reading the marquee. *"Ultimate Force?"*

Zach rested his wide chin on the steering wheel. "The new Arnold Schwarzenegger movie. High action, lots of buildings blowing up."

She frowned. "Somehow two hours of destruction doesn't suit my mood."

"What about *Super Dad?*"

"What's that one about?"

"I think it's sort of a cross between Superman and Bill Cosby-style humor." He paused for her to answer, and when she didn't he suggested. "Let's try that one, it's a good family flick. I saw the previews on TV."

As if on cue, a family with three lively youngsters stepped out from the glass doors. The older girl and boy were running circles around Mom and Dad, playing a wild game of tag amidst squeals of excitement. The youngest, a little boy who was walking unsteadily but refusing assistance from either parent, seemed intent on leading the way. The determined expression on his face warmed Caroline's heart.

"What a wonderful crew that is," she murmured, only realizing she was speaking out loud when Zach responded.

"They are beautiful," he said. Something different in his voice caught her attention.

"You've never been much into kids, have you?" she asked.

He looked momentarily embarrassed, then he laughed. "No. I guess not. I spent my adult life avoiding them."

"Why?"

"Like any male in his twenties, I suppose I saw them as part of an elaborate trap called marriage. I didn't want to give up my freedom."

"Your freedom to never get tied down to one woman?" she asked.

"Something like that, although I suppose it's more complex than simply an issue of being free to sleep with whomever I wanted. I felt as if I had a lot to prove to myself, and a lot to accomplish in my career."

"Consulting," she supplied.

He shifted uncomfortably in his seat. "Yeah. I'd better get tickets. You want to come or wait here?"

"I'll wait," she said, settling down deeper into the smooth leather cushion.

Caroline watched Zach ease himself up out of the car. He pushed down the latch, locking her in for safety. It was a small gesture, but she liked his natural protectiveness.

Beneath the lights of the marquee, Zach strode to the ticket booth, took out his wallet and purchased their tickets. He looked lean and muscular in the shadows that played across the parking lot. In jeans and a leather aviator jacket with the collar turned up against his jaw, he appeared to have a bit of the rogue in him.

She liked thinking of him in that way—the bad boy a mother wouldn't want her daughter to date, but she would anyway.

The air was growing more densely chill. It was the first week of November, and the weather was primed for winter. Caroline thought of how warm she felt when Zach held her in his arms.

And how hot she'd become, touching and kissing him in his car outside her apartment building.

What had possessed her to do that to the man? The lack of inhibition she felt when they were together shocked her. When Rob had suggested satisfying him in that way, she'd been reluctant. In fact, it had never worked out well, had seemed awkward and embarrassing for both of them, and they'd given up trying. Once she'd voiced a bashful desire for him to kiss her "down there." He'd refused, saying he didn't like that sort of thing.

But Rob was behind her now. And perhaps she shouldn't really dwell on the future any more than on the past. If she and Zach weren't meant to be, she thought again, why push for anything more than what they had at the moment?

A blur of black leather caught her eye. She turned to see Zach moving toward the car, his blue eyes sparkling as he waved a pair of tickets at her. Caroline smiled. Whatever he was to her or could never be to her, he was still the man who had dredged her up from the depths of her own despair. She would always remember that and thank her lucky stars that he'd come into her life when he had.

She swung open the car door and, checking to be sure he'd taken the keys with him, locked up then dashed across the pavement to meet him halfway.

As it turned out, they didn't have any trouble finding decent seats because the crowd was so light. The film was a comedy, but the underlying message was obvious. Fatherhood was every bit as challenging, and warmly rewarding, as motherhood.

Caroline thought about the tender scenes between the young father in the film and his daughter and son. One early episode, in which he dragged himself out of bed at the crack of dawn to lift his infant daughter from her crib, got inside her and worked magic with her heart. The image of a man in pajama bottoms, cradling his infant daughter to his bare chest, was so endearing she'd sighed out loud in the theater.

As they walked to the car, she slipped her fingers into Zach's and felt his hand close around hers. She could imagine Zach, his wondrously sculpted chest and shoulders flexing as he gently scooped up a baby... tickled a toddler... wrestled on the ground with an energetic second-grader. He'd make a wonderful father—as protective of their children as he was of her...

The stars' light from above seemed to dim momentarily, then brighten again, just as electrical lights do when there's a power surge. She looked up for a moment, wondering why her eyes were playing tricks on her.

"Penny for your thoughts, miss," Zach asked, taking her hand to lead her across the parking lot.

Caroline felt her cheeks grow hot. "I was just thinking how nice the movie was," she lied.

"Nice? In what way?"

"It captured what families are all about—caring for each other, helping each other grow, getting through the rough times as well as having fun together."

He nodded. "I thought the mother and father had a super relationship. They were doing everything they could for their kids, but they still had that young-and-in-love attitude about themselves when they were alone together. Even after years of marriage."

"Yes," Caroline said, watching him as he unlocked the car door for her. "I think that's the ideal relationship. But how often does that happen in real life?"

"I don't know." He looked puzzled. "I used to think never. But maybe..." He looked down at her, his eyes full of questions. "...maybe..."

For a long moment, she thought Zach was going to say something more. But a sad shadow passed in front of his eyes, and he just stood back and waited for her to get into the car. They drove back to Mystic in silence, each buried in dreams and doubts and thoughts too private to share.

The weeks that followed were hectic, and Caroline saw very little of Zach. The Silver Whale had to be readied for the holidays. She and Suzanne spent every minute they could spare away from waiting on customers to restock shelves with Thanksgiving, Christmas and Hanukkah treasures. Each work day seemed to grow longer than the one before it.

There were fanciful turkey candles and silver dinner bells that tinkled cheerfully when lifted from their pedestals. Cranberry chutney and herbed cheese spreads were set out for sampling. Jugs of cider arrived from an orchard in Stonington. The shop smelled of cinnamon, bay leaf and pine through the weeks before Thanksgiving. Caroline sometimes left for only six hours, to go home, eat and fall into bed, then return to work in the quiet morning hours before opening the doors to another rush of holiday shoppers.

"You can't keep this up. You're exhausted," Suzanne told her one evening as she was preparing to leave. It was after 10:00 p.m., and Caroline had announced she'd be staying another hour or more to catch up on paperwork. "Let the bills wait, take some time for yourself. It's only going to get worse after Thanksgiving."

"I'd rather keep busy," Caroline told her. A crystal poinsettia lay on its side on the shelf in front of her. She reached out to set it up straight. But the fragile glass stem slipped from her fingertips. Red and green shards exploded across the floor. "Oh, no!" she cried, stooping to try to pick up the pieces.

Suzanne gently took hold of her arm and pulled her to her feet to study her face. "You have that hollow look you get when you're sliding downhill again."

Caroline didn't have to guess what she meant. As Christmas approached, she often thought how wonderful that time of year was for families, and how lonely it could be for people on their own. It would have been Jimmy's second Christmas...and the realization tugged at her heart.

"I'll be fine," Caroline assured her. "I just need a little more sleep. I'll catch up soon."

Suzanne shook her head doubtfully. "I don't want to lose a business partner, any more than I want to lose a friend. Take care of yourself."

"I will, just stop worrying." Caroline reached behind the counter for the dust pan and whisk broom.

Suzanne stopped her. "Leave it. I'll sweep up and bring another flower from the back room. What's happened to Zach? Isn't he around to coax you out of your moods and help you to unwind?"

"He stops by almost every night," Caroline admitted.

"And?"

"We talk for a few minutes, then I usually ask him to leave because I have to get some sleep."

She had to admit that Zach had been particularly careful about checking on her, making sure she ate, trying to lighten her moods. But the holidays pressed heavily on her spirit. She sometimes found herself in the baby's room, and couldn't remember how long she'd been standing there.

Caroline felt Suzanne studying her again. "I know you're bursting to say something. You might as well just come out with it."

Her friend nudged a chunk of glass out from under a table with the toe of her shoe. "That man really cares for you. Can't you see that? Why are you keeping him at arm's length?"

"Because that's the way he wants it," Caroline told her with a wry twist to her lips. "There are some things in the world, no one can change. And Zach Dawson is one of them."

Chapter 11

Zach kicked up billows of clouds, wondering what was keeping Meher. It seemed as if he'd been waiting forever for the Archangel, but maybe it had been only minutes, or seconds. He had no concept of time when he checked in upstairs, but that didn't help his impatience.

"I know you have a lot of folks to keep track of," Zach muttered. "But you said Caroline North was *important*. It's going all wrong. I need *help!*"

No sooner had he thought the words, than he felt Meher's presence hovering close to him. He swung around to face the white, formless light.

"We know." The familiar voice resonated with displeasure.

"It—it isn't my fault," Zach stammered. "When I'm around her, my emotions get all tangled up. I can't think straight. I can't make the kinds of decisions that have to be made to help her."

"You are in *love* with her," Meher stated.

"No!" Zach protested. "It's nothing like that. I've just taken the human form, and with it comes some...distractions." It occurred to him that if the Archangel knew how deeply he cared for Caroline, he'd take him off of her case. Then he'd never see her again. Unless they met in eternity—and that wouldn't be the same as sharing little pieces of her life with her, as he'd been able to do for the past weeks.

Meher was ominously silent, his light dimming for a moment, then growing in intensity.

"So, what should I do?" Zach asked. "I need some guidance here."

"You must remain true to your mission," the Archangel stated. "You must find the ideal mate for Caroline North."

"But can't you help me out a little here? Just tell me who he is . . . or at least what he looks like." Despite the soothing zephyrs that shifted among the heavenly mists, Zach felt himself begin to sweat. He raked the fingers of one hand through his hair and huffed in exasperation.

"Help will come when you need it. Have faith in yourself and trust your instincts."

"I trusted them twice, and came up with two losers named Paul and Max!" The light began to fade again, but this time continued to grow dimmer. "No, wait!" Zach pleaded. "I really need your advice!"

But it was too late.

Zach was alone, but for a group of six cherubs playing on a nearby puff of candy-cotton cloud. He wondered if one was Jimmy and suddenly felt sure he was among them. He wished with all his heart that Caroline could see them and know her son was happy.

It was even later than usual when Caroline arrived at her apartment that night. Zach heard her letting herself in and he rushed across his living room and out into the hallway, but she'd already closed the door behind her. He knocked.

"I'm too tired to talk tonight, Zach," her voice drifted out through the door. She sounded so tired and down, it nearly broke his heart.

"How about popcorn and a movie?" he suggested. "I rented a good video."

"No, thanks." Her voice sounded still more distant, as if she'd moved into her bedroom and shut yet another door between them.

Defeated, he turned back into his own apartment.

* * *

The next morning, Zach watched from his kitchen window as Caroline emerged from the building's front door and headed on foot for Water Street. The sun wasn't even all the way up.

He was at a loss for what to do for her. He sat down at his kitchen counter with a cup of coffee and considered making one final plea to Meher. He was still sitting there a half hour later, on his third cup, when someone knocked on his door.

Puzzled, he walked over and opened it. Suzanne stood, her hands clamped on her hips, looking past him as if to make sure he was alone.

"Come on in!" he said, smiling. Then a terrible thought occurred to him. "Nothing's wrong with Caroline, is it?"

"Nothing we can't fix," Suzanne retorted, her voice snapping with determination. She stormed past him, into his living room. He shut the door behind her, wary of the momentum she had obviously started building before she reached his apartment.

"What's that mean?" he asked.

"It means..." Suzanne spun around to face him. "It means, Caroline thinks she can never love again, but I know better... because *she's already in love.*"

Zach stared at her. "She is?"

"Absolutely. Care to guess who the object of her affections might be?"

"I'm not sure I dare."

"She's in love with *you,* Zach."

"With me?" he asked weakly.

"Yes, and if you can't see it, you're blind. Totally blind, like most men I've known." Suzanne crossed the room to his window and glared out into the rosy dawn. "The thing is, she doesn't know it, or won't admit it. And it's eating at her while she's already feeling miserable because the holidays are here again, and she's still mourning her baby."

"What do you expect me to do?" Zach asked, dropping onto the couch.

"How about telling her you love her?"

He looked away from her. "That would only make matters worse."

"I see," she said. "Well, if *you* can't fall in love with *her*, you can at least take her mind off her troubles."

"I've been trying to, but she won't let me."

"You haven't been trying *hard* enough," she said pointedly.

Zach stared in shock at Caroline's friend. Was she suggesting he start sleeping with Caroline on a regular basis? That he use their physical attraction as a kind of therapy?

He saw from the dark twinkle in her eyes that was exactly what she had in mind. "Oh," he said.

Zach thought about Meher's cryptic answer to his plea for help. He'd told him he'd find help when he needed it. Was Suzanne the help the Archangel had been referring to?

Maybe what Meher and Suzanne were both suggesting, was if he could first take Caroline's mind off her pain and loss, then perhaps he'd have a better chance of successfully introducing her to another man . . . the right man this time.

Zach coughed into his hand, finding himself more than a little bashful about discussing his and Caroline's love life with Suzanne. "I have a feeling you've got some definite ideas about how to best help your friend," he said.

"You're right. There's too much here, in Mystic, that she can't forget," Suzanne explained. "She's in the same job, living in the same house, walking the same streets. Everything is the same as when she had Jimmy, before her coward of a husband left her. How can she separate herself from her pain when everything reminds her of what she's lost?"

It suddenly hit Zach, what she was suggesting. "You want me to take her away from here."

"Exactly."

"Where?"

Suzanne rubbed the bridge of her nose. "I don't think that matters a whole lot. Just take her away for a week and keep her busy. A change of scenery and time spent doing anything other than work will do wonders for her—I guarantee it."

Zach considered this. "But now is one of the busiest times of the year for your shop. Caroline would never leave you with all the work."

"She'll have to if I tell her how crazy she's making me. And I can cover for her better now than right before Christmas, which is when she'll collapse from exhaustion if she doesn't take some time to pull herself together. There are plenty of students, housewives and retirees looking for part-time jobs to supplement their incomes around the holidays. I'll have no trouble finding a couple of eager helpers." She jabbed a finger at him. "You just look after Caroline."

Zach stood up and found himself nodding as if he were an obedient schoolboy. A thought came to him. "How does an early-season skiing vacation sound?"

"Great. I'll tell her she has to take off all next week, that way she won't be moping around her apartment on Thanksgiving Day. Can you arrange something that fast?"

"No problem," he assured her with a grin. "I have great connections in the travel industry."

"I can understand your wanting time off at Christmas," Caroline argued. "But why do *I* have to take off Thanksgiving week? I can wait until after the holidays, when things slow down."

Suzanne sighed as she stuck a bow on the box she'd just finished wrapping for a customer. She handed the brightly wrapped package to the woman with a smile. "See, it's more complicated than just wanting a vacation. Ralph is determined that we drive down to Florida and visit his parents for Christmas. I put him off last year and the one before. Now he's asking again, and I feel as if I can't tell him no."

"Then go, I'll be fine," Caroline insisted.

"But I'll feel guilty as hell," Suzanne insisted. "I can't leave you alone with the shop unless you get equal time. Besides, all the ordering is done and most of the stock has arrived. We're just ringing up purchases and throwing things in bags. Anyone can do that."

"I suppose," Caroline murmured. "But what will I *do* for a whole week?"

Suzanne rolled her eyes. "Come on. Your mom would love to have you for Thanksgiving. Or you could go visit your sister—you've wanted a chance to see your niece again. Heck, book a week in the Bahamas!"

Caroline shook her head. "Rob and I used to drive down to be with my mother. I'm not ready to make a solo holiday visit yet. You know my mother. She means well, but she can't help bringing up Jimmy whenever I see her. You know . . . Jimmy would have loved this, or Jimmy could have eaten with us at the table this year. And my sister will have her hands full with her in-laws this year."

"Well, in that case, maybe you should plan a trip to somewhere sunny, Cancún or someplace. A singles week. What about Club Med?"

"You know I'd hate that—pairing off with strange men for a one-week fling... People who take trips like that, go with one thing in mind."

"So, what's wrong with that? Sex can be fun. It can make you forget a lot." Suzanne giggled. "Like your name."

Caroline punched her playfully in the arm. "Knock it off. If I go anywhere for this enforced vacation, it will be by myself."

Suzanne shrugged. "Suit yourself."

Caroline ate a peanut-butter-and-banana sandwich, standing over the sink to catch the crumbs. She was sliding the last few drops of milk down her throat when the doorbell rang. Rinsing the glass, she put it into the dishwasher rack and walked to the door.

She checked through the peephole. Zach was standing in the hallway, bouncing impatiently on the balls of his athletic shoes, looking like a nervous teenager come to call on his girl. *What now?* she thought grimly.

"I'm tired," Caroline informed him through the door.

"Oh." He sounded so dejected, she took another peek at him. He'd shoved his hands into the pockets of his Dockers. As he turned away from her door, his muscular shoulders slumped, and he stared at the carpet. "I was hoping you could help me out," he muttered. "Never mind."

The disappointment in his voice awakened her maternal instincts. Help him out? How often had he comforted her during her dark moments? And he'd been there to help her with little things, like lugging groceries from the car or mounting a picture on her wall. It didn't seem right to turn him away when he needed help.

Caroline unlatched the dead bolt and opened the door for Zach. He turned back to face her, then hesitated. "You sure it's all right? I don't want to be a bother."

"You're not a bother, Zach. Just come in and tell me what's happened."

"This," he said, dropping an envelope on her coffee table as he swung past it on his way to the sofa. He sat down heavily.

Caroline picked up the envelope. In the upper left corner was an insignia that looked like a mountain with a pine tree sprouting from its side. Handwritten on the front was Zach's full name and a brief inscription: *Hope you enjoy your stay with us. Enclosed are your room reservations and lift tickets.*

"I don't understand," she said.

He rubbed his hands over his unshaven face. "I'd made plans to go away next week. My friend backed out at the last minute."

"Your friend?" So he did have a girlfriend after all. No, she changed her mind, it might just as easily have been another guy, like Paul. Someone he'd just looked forward to skiing with. She wished she could see his eyes, but he wouldn't look at her. She decided it would be tactless to pump him for information, especially while he was so dejected.

"It was going to be such a great time," he said mournfully. "A whole week at Killington in Vermont—skiing, kicking back in the pubs, relaxing in the Jacuzzi after a day on the slopes, eating great food every night . . . I was really looking forward to it."

"But your friend can't go?"

"Looks like if I want to ski, I'll have to do it alone. It just won't be the same without someone to share the fun."

Caroline pulled the reservations out of the envelope. They were for Thanksgiving week. She frowned, vaguely uneasy at the coincidence.

A long, mournful sigh from Zach brought her back to the problem at hand. "Zach, I'm sorry you're so disappointed. I really am."

"I know. You're very nice, but I shouldn't be bothering you with my problems. You have enough of your own." He started to stand.

She pushed him back down on the sofa and sat beside him, pulling his hands onto the shelf of her knees. "Listen. I may not be exactly what you'd been hoping for, but as it happens, I'm free all that week."

She thought she glimpsed a shadow of a smile on his lips, but it disappeared as quickly as it had come. "What are you saying, Caroline? *You* want to go skiing with me?"

"I've only skied a few times," she admitted. "But at least I'd be *some* company. We could have a good time, help keep each other's blues away."

"You think so?" He still sounded doubtful.

"Sure," she said with growing enthusiasm. "This way you'll get in some great skiing, have a dinner and pub companion . . . it'll be great!"

Zach grinned at her. "Somehow, I knew you'd come up with a solution."

They planned to start driving north the Friday before Thanksgiving. Although Caroline agreed to take off seven days, she couldn't in good conscience stay away the Friday after Thanksgiving—the biggest shopping day of the year.

"We can drive back from Vermont early that morning," she suggested, "and be back in Mystic by ten when the Silver Whale opens."

"Fine with me," Zach said. He called the reservation hot-line at Killington and adjusted the dates of their stay, and they were all set.

It made Caroline feel good to be doing something to help Zach, for once. She wished he trusted her enough to confide in her totally, but that was another issue. The few times she hinted that she was available to listen if he'd like to talk about anything, he either changed the subject, or looked so bleak she didn't press for details.

She couldn't help thinking that he'd feel better if he got off his chest whatever seemed so troubling to him.

Still, being a friend meant knowing when to back off and leave well enough alone. And they were friends, weren't they? Sometimes she felt so close to Zach, she wondered how they'd gotten so far, so fast. It was as if he'd always been a part of her life—there when she most needed him. Something like a big brother, but more . . . much more.

Now, as they drove, she thought about the two times they'd taken their relationship past friendship, to the ultimate levels of intimacy. She turned away from him, looking out the passenger window so he wouldn't see the flush she felt creeping across her cheeks. How she'd loved the feeling of him against her skin—stroking him, being caressed by him...

Caroline squeezed her eyes shut. The images floating through her head summoned up waves of remembered pleasure. A surge of heat flowed deep within her, and she gasped in surprise.

"Something wrong?" Zach asked casually, as they sped along Route 32, headed due north through the Connecticut countryside.

"No." She forced out the word, then bit down on her lip. *Yes*, a voice inside her corrected her. *Yes, something is very wrong*. She'd decided she was through with men, or at least she would never give her heart away or risk getting pregnant. Then along came Zach Dawson, and suddenly she was lost in an undertow of emotions. "Yes," she said softly, "something is very wrong."

"Tell me."

"I don't want to get your hopes up," she said quickly.

"My hopes?" he repeated.

"Yes. You see, that night in the parking lot—"

"That was very nice," he interjected, his voice gravelly again with remembered lust.

"Yes, it *was*... I'm not sure nice is the right word, but I have to admit I enjoyed it and—"

"Then there's nothing wrong with what we did, right?"

"No, Zach. There was something wrong. You see, I'm not the kind of woman who does that sort of thing. I didn't even do *that* when I was married. I've read magazines, seen...well...manuals, that sort of thing. So of course I knew about oral sex, but I didn't really *know* what I was doing until I was doing it and—"

"Sure *felt* like you knew what you were doing," he teased, his eyes sparkling mischievously.

Caroline could have belted him for making fun of her.

"Zach, cut it out and listen. I want you to understand that I'm not prepared to jump into bed with you as soon as we get to Vermont. I never intended my offer to keep you company as anything more than a friendly gesture. I guess I should have said something sooner, but I saw your reservations and it looked as if you'd already arranged for separate rooms, so I thought it would be okay."

"It's fine," he told her with a smile. "I'm just giving you a hard time. I hadn't intended on making you my love slave for the week."

"Oh," she said, wondering why she now, perversely, felt disappointed.

"Honest," he said, "this week will be a lot of fun. But it will be good, clean fun. No fooling around, I promise. I don't know about you," he said, "but I wasn't looking forward to spending Thanksgiving holed up by myself in a one-bedroom apartment."

"You're exactly right," she agreed. "This will be so much better."

But when they reached the Greenbriar Inne a few hours later, Caroline's nagging doubts returned. Their rooms were next to each other with pass-through doors conveniently joining them. Caroline unlocked hers and opened it a crack to see what was on the other side. Zach had already swung his wide, leaving it open, as if to let her know he was offering her free access to his room at anytime. She quickly closed hers and latched it securely. After a moment's consideration, she also moved an armchair in front of it.

Feeling better about the situation, Caroline turned and looked out the window. Although in Connecticut there had been only a brief dusting of snow, Vermont had already received its first old-fashioned blizzard. Almost a foot of the white stuff covered the hillside, sloping down to a stream outside her window. Lacy patterns of crystals decorated tree limbs, boulders and fence rails.

Caroline couldn't help smiling at the postcard perfection of the Vermont scene. She sighed, leaning against the window frame, feeling the tension drain away from inside her, as if it were a tepid liquid, seeping out from her pores. Zach was right. Just getting away for a week was what she needed.

Feeling suddenly energized Caroline launched herself at the desk in the corner of the room, pulling out a folder of assorted travel brochures. Several slick advertisements pictured trails at Killington, but other local resorts were represented, too—Mount Snow, Okemo and Stratton. There was another pamphlet describing local night spots, recommended restaurants, sight-seeing side trips and targets for shopping sprees. She felt her excitement mounting as she flipped through the material.

She hadn't expected to do much besides ski. But there seemed endless opportunities for fun—some aimed at families with children, other activities meant just for adults who wanted to remember what it was like to be a kid again. Growing up in New England,

Caroline recalled wonderful times playing in the snow with her brother and sister and their neighborhood friends. What a wonderfully carefree time of life. The only thing that cut short the fun was when their clothes finally wet through to the skin or Mom called them in for dinner.

Caroline sighed, smiling, feeling lighter at heart than she had in years.

"You done unpacking?" a voice called through her wall.

She cast a lazy glance toward her unopened suitcase on the bed.

"Haven't started!" she yelled. She hesitated only a minute before shoving aside the armchair barricade and unlatching the door to let Zach step through.

"What have you been doing?" he asked, laughing at her. "You haven't even taken off your jacket."

She shrugged. "I thought that was part of the reason for a vacation. No schedules to keep."

"Well, we have to eat." He glanced at the clock beside her bed. It was after 1:00 p.m. "I'm going to eat my ski boots if we don't find some real food."

"I can unpack later," she said. "Where do you want to have lunch?"

"Somewhere fast and easy, so we'll still have time to ski this afternoon."

"I was checking out a map of the area. Looks like there are plenty of fast-food joints on the way to the hill," she remarked helpfully.

"The hill?" He grinned at her. " I think you'll find Killington more than a hill."

"Whatever," she said, flipping a brochure at him. "Here's a list of nearby restaurants. It looks as if a lot of them are strung along the Killington Access Road, which seems to be the way from here to the—"

"Mountain," he supplied. "Fine, we'll bring it along with us and see what looks good." He folded the brochure and stuffed it into the pocket of his tightly molded ski pants. "If you're planning on trying to ski this afternoon, you'd better change into something warmer and layered, so you don't freeze out there."

"Good idea," she said cheerfully. "I'll meet you downstairs in the lounge by the fireplace."

* * *

Fifteen minutes later, Caroline felt far bulkier and less agile than she had when they'd arrived. She didn't own one of the stylish Thinsulate-lined ski suits, like those sported by models in the brochures. She'd made do with long underwear and a pair of blue jeans. To keep her top warm, she pulled on a turtleneck jersey, wool sweater and down-filled jacket with a hood. Doubling up her socks made her chunky leather boots pinch her toes.

"I don't see how Olympic skiers can look so graceful suited up like the Michelin man!" she exclaimed as she performed an exaggerated waddle into the lounge in the lower level of the inn.

Zach took one look at her and his eyes lit up with amusement. "Maybe you should spring for a real ski outfit."

"Not on your life," she retorted. "That would be a waste of money. I'd wear it this week, and it would probably hang in my closet for the rest of my life."

He put an arm around her and gave her a friendly squeeze. "You never know. You might catch the skiing bug and end up spending half of every winter on the slopes, snow bunny."

She shook her head, giggling. "I wouldn't bet on it, Mr. Dawson."

With Zach's skis clamped to the roof of the Accord, they drove up a winding road that climbed what Caroline now agreed could rightly be called a mountain. In fact, Killington, Zach explained, was a cluster of six majestic mountains, laced with over seventy-five miles of trails. Cable lines for lifts etched black threads across the white snow. Zigzagging tracks crisscrossed the mountainsides, as brightly garbed skiers snaked down the slopes. Some were graceful, others crashed repeatedly, and struggled out of snowbanks every hundred feet or so. Either way, it looked like great fun to Caroline.

The road was six lanes wide to accommodate the crush of skiers during the busiest times of the winter. But now, during the early season, there was little traffic. The Access Road was lined with fast-food shacks, T-shirt shops, skiing and snow-boarding equipment outlets, restaurants and bars and souvenir emporiums. Occasionally Caroline caught a glimpse of a cedar chalet or a bank of glass and wood condos between snow-covered evergreens, silver birch and the barren limbs of deciduous trees. It was a beautiful drive, and she hardly felt the passing miles.

At last, Zach pulled up in front of a place called the Telemark Deli and Pizza. They went inside and ordered a large pizza with everything on it, then sat down with their sodas to wait for their lunch to cook.

The luscious aroma of olive oil, garlic, oregano and fresh tomatoes aroused Caroline's appetite. She felt as if she could eat the entire pizza by herself, by the time their number was called.

"This is wonderful," she exclaimed, pulling from the pie a triangle of steaming dough topped with mozzarella, pepperoni, onions and green peppers. The hot cheese strung out in gooey threads. Laughing at the mess she was making, Zach broke the strands with his fingers and popped them into her mouth.

She licked his fingers automatically, and only then realized how familiar a gesture it had been. Feeling flushed, she put down the slice and wiggled out of her jacket. "It's getting hot in here," she mumbled.

"Mmm," he agreed around a bite of his own. But his eyes drifted away from hers, as if trying to distance himself by focusing on other parts of the dining room.

Caroline followed his gaze. A pretty blond college girl and two brunette girlfriends were dipping garlic bread sticks into tomato sauce and laughing over a story one had just finished telling.

"They're very pretty," Caroline commented. "I can hardly remember being that young."

Zach turned and looked at her, his eyes suddenly hard. "Trying to tell me they're too young for me?" There was a strange edge to his voice she didn't like.

"No, of course not. It's none of my business who you look at or why," she said, sitting up straighter. "I just remarked that they were pretty...in a young, immature kind of way..." Why was she digging this hole deeper for herself? She sounded jealous even to her own ears.

Zach studied her from beneath lowered lids. "You agreed we're here as friends."

"We are," she said, hesitating only slightly before adding, "isn't that what you want, too?"

"Of course," he said quickly. "And that should leave either of us open to spending time with other people, if the opportunity arises. Like if some guy shows interest in you, and he seems...well, right for you, then it would be okay for you to tell me to make myself scarce for a while."

Caroline nodded stiffly. "What you're really saying is, you expect me to do the same for you. You want to be free to pick up a woman if you feel inclined." Suddenly the pizza didn't taste nearly as great as it had.

"That's not what I'm saying at all," Zach growled. "I just want you to relax and have fun with anyone you choose. I don't want you to turn down any opportunities just because I'm here. I don't need a baby-sitter."

"I can see that," Caroline muttered under her breath.

She looked at him, still unsure what was going through his mind. Maybe Zach was simply continuing to encourage her to be open to meeting men, as he had from the start of their friendship. Or maybe the sight of a bouncy coed had suddenly changed his mind about who he wanted for company on his vacation.

She turned and observed the table of college girls. The blond was glancing coyly Zach's way, and Zach seemed quite aware of her interest.

Caroline dove into the pizza with renewed energy. "Come on and eat," she grumbled. "You said you wanted to get in some skiing this afternoon."

Chapter 12

For the life of him, Zach couldn't figure out what had gotten into Caroline. One minute she seemed relaxed and open to new adventures, content with their just being friends. The next she had jumped all over him for taking a casual interest in the girls seated across the restaurant from them.

He was utterly confused.

The thought of his being attracted to, or even worse, picking up one of the coeds at the Telemark seemed ludicrous—even if he had been alive and free to do that sort of thing. They must have been a dozen years younger than he was. To him, they looked more like daughters than prospective lovers. He wouldn't for a moment seriously consider going to bed with one of them.

But apparently Caroline believed that was a real possibility, and, he could tell, she was thinking about it as they ate. She chewed mechanically at the pizza, avoiding his eyes. Her movements were brittle, as if sharp bits of glass lay embedded beneath her skin, making every motion painful. She didn't talk, except to briefly answer questions from him about her skiing experiences.

The remainder of the ride to the base lodge, she sat silently in the passenger seat, glaring out the side window. He wanted to come right out and ask her what was really wrong, but he was afraid he'd only make the situation worse. If Caroline was feeling possessive, it could be for only one reason—she was falling in love with him, as Suzanne had claimed. And that was something he couldn't afford to have happen.

He parked the car as close to the lodge as possible. Zach unstrapped his skis from the roof, then opened the trunk to remove the rest of his equipment.

"Why don't you go on up to the lodge and wait for me inside while I unload," he suggested. "You'll be warmer there."

"I'm all right," she said stubbornly. But she wrapped her arms around herself, and soon, her lips were turning a translucent pink, verging on blue.

"Standing around in this cold won't do you any good," he grunted.

"So, what do you want me to do? Jumping jacks?"

He was losing his patience with her. "We're in a bit of a mood, aren't we?"

"My *mood* is none of your concern," she snapped.

Zach stopped in the middle of pulling his molded polymer Nordica ski boots out of the trunk and studied her expression. Her brown eyes, usually so warm and soft, were as cold and unyielding as the outcroppings of granite he could see higher up on the mountain behind her. But the way she clamped her lips together was revealing, as if she were trying to hold in erupting emotions, and she'd balled her fists inside her mittens and shoved them under her elbows, as though to keep herself from taking a swing at him.

He dropped the boots back into the trunk, slammed it closed and propped the skis against the side of the car.

"What are you doing?" she asked, her eyes growing wide with concern.

"We have to talk," he said abruptly. "Right now."

Caroline started to shake her head in denial, her expression suddenly worried as she stomped her feet and hugged herself harder to keep warm. He saw her right foot inch to one side, as if she were about to flee. Zach grasped her hand and pulled her back toward the passenger door.

"Get in," he said. "We have to get some things straight."

She obeyed but looked so frightened that his heart went out to her. Still, he couldn't risk blowing his mission because she decided to cut herself off from him emotionally. If she told him to get lost and took off on her own, how could he make sure she'd run into and connect with the right man to father her child and take her into his heart?

He'd already tried working invisibly. That had been a disaster. He had to be on the scene, making sure things went smoothly. If she no longer welcomed him as a friend, he'd be in an impossible situation.

Somehow, he had to pull her back into the circle of his influence. He had to encourage her to trust him. He had to show her how much he . . .

How much he what? How much he cared about her? How incredible she made him feel inside every time her soft brown eyes settled on him?

He swung open the driver's door and dropped into the seat, still at a loss for the right angle to approach her. Without spelling it out in so many words, Meher had let him understand that he was forbidden from telling her the truth about who he was and why he was forcing himself into her life. He could give her only so much information without crossing the boundaries of his heavenly mandate.

But what if Caroline guessed the rest? That might be okay, he reasoned. Or it might get him into even deeper water . . . All he really knew was, he had to regain her trust if he was to do his job.

Zach decided he would give Caroline all that he could. Then he would pray that his good intentions would be enough to satisfy the Archangel and he'd be allowed to continue his mission on Caroline's behalf.

Letting out a low groan and a muffled curse that Meher was undoubtedly frowning upon at that very minute, Zach turned toward Caroline on the leather seat. To his surprise, she was looking straight at him, as if she'd been watching him closely while he'd been debating with himself.

"I have to explain a few things to you," he stated.

"You don't owe me any explanations," she replied tersely.

He opened his mouth to object, but she plunged on.

"You've made it perfectly clear that you're never going to get serious about us, that you're not interested in developing more than a superficial relationship—"

"Shut up and listen for one minute!" he growled between clenched teeth.

Caroline lifted her chin and pointedly closed her lips. She observed him coldly, down the length of her pert nose, and he felt as if he were being reprimanded by his second-grade teacher, on whom he'd had a most painful crush.

"I'm sorry," he blurted out. "I don't know why you make me so angry sometimes."

"Perhaps because I remind you that you have a conscience buried somewhere beneath that amazing supply of testosterone you've confused with a brain?" She quirked one eyebrow at him.

"I'm all too aware of my conscience these days, thank you. And as to my hormones, I think I've kept a damn good hold on them, considering—" He broke off and rubbed his hand over his face in aggravation. "Listen, I told you I'd explain myself when I could. You said you understood, you'd be patient."

Caroline blinked at him, for the first time looking unsure of her ground. "I thought I could, but it's difficult to trust someone who works so hard at being mysterious."

He studied her honestly puzzled expression, weighing his options. "Okay," he said at last. "This is how things stand." He took a deep breath. "I can't tell you everything. I can't even tell you why I'm unable to explain myself. But if I give you an idea why I act the way I do, maybe you can accept the rest on faith."

She looked at him skeptically. "I feel as if I'm about to be the object of the most outrageous male pickup line in the history of civilization."

He shook his head emphatically. "No, Caroline. No, I'm not trying to do that to you. I genuinely care about you, and I don't want to hurt you. That's why we have to clear the air."

She flinched, almost imperceptibly, her hands drawing deeper into her lap. She'd removed her mittens. Her fingers looked white with cold, and he spontaneously reached out, cupping his palm over them, to warm them. She didn't pull away, but her cocoa-butter eyes lifted to meet his with a puzzled expression.

"It must seem to you that I don't know what I'm doing from one minute to the next," he began, almost in a whisper. "I give you signals that I want to be near you, that I'd like to make love with you again . . . then I turn and run."

She made a swallowing sound in her throat, but her expression didn't alter. "I guess that's pretty accurate."

"Well, you're right on all counts. I'm terribly attracted to you, Caroline. I can't tell you how difficult it is to be near you and not touch you."

"Then why don't you touch me?" she whispered, the words slipping smoothly between her lips, beckoning him to her.

"Because if we become lovers, it won't be in your best interest."

A flame suddenly flared in her eyes, turning them the color of burnt toast. *"Not in my best interest?"* she snapped. "Who are you, Zach Dawson, to decide what *is* or is *not* in my best interest? If I want to sleep with a man—whether it's you or someone else— I should damn well be able to do it without getting anyone's permission!"

He gripped her hands tightly in his, willing her to understand. Why wasn't she picking up on his thoughts the way she had before? Was it because she was too upset? Because he wasn't able to concentrate properly while his mind was in such turmoil and his heart was being torn in a dozen directions?

"Caroline, please believe me, I only want to do what's ultimately the best for you." She opened her mouth to protest again, but he didn't let her get out a word. "You have a future, *a very important future to fulfill.* It involves a man who will love you far beyond any self-love he might feel. He will cherish you, protect you . . . and your child."

He let the words sink in slowly, and knew they had when the last remaining tinges of color drained from her cheeks. "I have no child," she whispered dully.

"You *will* have a child, as I told you before, and he or she will be as beautiful in its own way as Jimmy was. You'll never forget your first baby, but this child will fill your heart with joy you can't now imagine." All of these things and more, he instinctively knew. But further explanation, he dared not give her. Already, Meher was sending warning arrows of pain that jabbed at the center of his chest. Zach stopped talking, and watched Caroline cautiously for a reaction to his words.

Her lips trembled. Her whole body seemed to quake with emotion, and for a moment he was sure she was going to weep. But she didn't.

"Zach, this is preposterous!" she cried. "You know it is. You're not a psychic—I wouldn't believe you if you claimed you were. Besides, you seem to be far too levelheaded a man to talk like this."

He searched desperately for the right words, the safe words. "I'm only telling you what I know. I can't tell you *how* I know it, it's just the way it is."

Her eyes narrowed as she peered deep into his eyes. Long moments passed. Outside, it began snowing again, the flakes drifting down and laying themselves thickly on the windshield of the car. The world was silent. They were cut off from everyone, everything, it seemed. Still, she studied the rugged contours of his face, considering his words.

"I don't understand any of this—it sounds insane," she murmured at last, "but something tells me I should believe you." Caroline shook her head and stared at him. "Zach, no one knows the future. You're just saying these things to make me feel better, aren't you? To make it easier for me to go on with my life."

He shook his head, his eyes holding hers reassuringly, begging for her trust.

Caroline looked down at their hands in her lap, her feathery, dark eyelashes shadowing her thoughts. For a while longer, neither of them spoke, but Zach felt beneath the levels of their silence, an intense flow of wordless communication rushing between them.

When she at last looked up at him, she said with renewed strength in her voice, "So if I'm supposed to end up with a man other than you, Zach Dawson...why do I feel the way I feel about you?"

"I don't know," he said truthfully. Just as valid a question was: Why did he feel so utterly lost at the thought of giving her up? "Maybe you need someone to be your friend, while you wait for Mr. Right?"

Caroline bit down on her lip and made the kind of face a little kid would if asked to eat brussels sprouts. "I don't feel about you the way I would feel about a friend, who was meant to be only that and no more," she murmured. One of her hands slipped out from beneath his and rose to carefully stroke Zach's cheek, as if it were something red-hot, and she was wary of burning herself. Reflexively he turned toward her touch, pressing the hard ridge of his jaw into the softness of her fingertips. He reached up and grasped her hand, brought it to his lips, reverently, and kissed her open palm.

"I find it very hard to think of you as only a friend, too," he managed to say, despite the warning signals shooting through his chest. "Caroline, believe me, if I had control of my own destiny, I'd want—" He couldn't go on. The pressure from within his ribs was almost crippling.

She let out a stiff, little laugh. "Zach, everyone has control of the direction of their own lives. It's called making choices."

"No," he said with a bitter laugh, "not everyone. Not always." Overcome by his own sense of loss and his inability to give her what she was asking for, he encircled her with his arms. Zach held her to his chest, praying for the strength and patience to battle his warring emotions, to learn to accept the things he had no hope of changing: his own death...and the loss of the only woman who'd ever meant a damn to him.

Had he fallen in love with Caroline? Maybe he had.

Or maybe he just missed life so much that he was clinging to the one mortal who made it possible for him to linger in the world of the living.

Was he using Caroline to deceive himself into believing he was alive again? No, he decided. He knew in the depths of his soul, he was dead. There was no going back to retrieve what had been crushed from his body that tragic August afternoon. But she made him *feel* alive, made him feel as if the best qualities in him had survived. By helping her, he felt he'd become a better person, the man he should have been in life.

Maybe maturing into manhood was a little like dying for every male. He had to give up the old, selfish ways to grow into a nurturing adult. He wished he'd known that sooner. Maybe things would have turned out differently.

Zach became aware of Caroline's subtle movements within his arms. She'd brought her hands up between their bodies and was softly moving them into the unzipped opening of his jacket. Her touch, although separated from his chest by layers of clothing, generated a pleasant heat within him. He should really release her, he told himself. He should break the connection right then, before it was too late.

"Tell me why you can't control your destiny," she whispered into his flannel shirtfront.

"I'll tell you what I can," Zach agreed after a moment's thought.

The pressure in his chest had lessened. But if he crossed another boundary, the Archangel would let him know. He'd just have to go slowly.

"I told you about my cousin, Zane—"

"The one who died in the construction accident." She finished the sentence for him.

"Yes. We were very close. In some ways, we were...almost one." He waited for Meher's reprimand, but it didn't come.

Caroline nodded. "After my brother and sister and I became adults, we seemed much less involved in each other's lives. But Suzanne has a brother, Andrew, who lives in Montana, and I think she sometimes feels as if a part of herself is missing, so long as he's that far away."

"I've known siblings like that," Zach said quietly.

"It's amazing, isn't it?" Caroline lifted her eyes and gazed distantly at the thickening blanket of snow over their windows. "Once, Suzanne was at the store with me, and suddenly she said she knew something terrible had happened to Andy. She felt a terrible pain in her right arm, and she thought she heard his voice calling her name, although he was clear across the country at the time, and she knew it." Caroline looked at Zach intently, as if curious to see his reaction to her story. "Suzanne telephoned Butte immediately, and Andy's wife said she'd just talked to him at work, and he was fine. But, later that night, the phone rang and when Suzanne answered, it was her sister-in-law, in tears. Andy had gone out to lunch with a business associate that day. The other man had driven, and the car had been hit on the passenger side, shearing off the door and nearly tearing off Andy's right arm as well. The surgeon wasn't sure he'd be able to save it, but he did."

Zach watched Caroline's lips moving as if she were under the spell of her own words. Before he'd died he'd have scoffed at such beliefs. Mumbo-jumbo, he'd have called her yarn. Telepathy, psychic awareness, near-death experiences. They were all a crock in his book.

Now he wasn't sure of anything. After all, if he could return to life as an angel—what other miracles might be happening all around him that the scientific world didn't understand or refused to acknowledge?

"Yes," he said, wanting her to come back into his embrace, for he sensed their holding each other was as comforting to her as it was for him. "There is a lot in the world we can't explain."

Caroline looked at him questioningly. "Were you aware of the moment when your cousin died?"

He thought for a second, then decided to follow his best instincts until Meher pulled him up short. "Yes," Zach said. "I guess I knew right away..." Hadn't he looked up and seen that awful shadow closing in on him? "I miss Zane a lot."

"Oh, Zach, I'm so very sorry."

"Me, too," he said. "I miss knowing that he'd have had a wonderful life...if he'd met someone like you. He'd have liked you a lot."

Caroline smiled. "That's a nice thing to say."

"It's true," he said. "I guess that's one reason why I'm so attracted to you. I almost feel as if, well, as if I'm sworn to look after you, to make sure your life gets back on track and you end up happy."

Her eyes sparkled prettily as she wiped the last traces of tears from them. "Sort of like my guardian angel?"

Zach drew in a sharp breath. She noticed and looked suddenly concerned. "Did I say something wrong?"

He concentrated on the spot in the center of his chest, deep within his heart where he'd feel the Archangel's warning jab, but nothing came. Apparently they were still treading on safe ground, as long as Caroline did the guessing and he avoided volunteering "classified" information.

"No, you didn't say anything wrong," he reassured her, giving in to the urge and enfolding her in his arms again. "If it makes you happy to think of me in that way, go for it."

She considered this new possibility. Looking up at him from close quarters, her mouth formed a pretty pout. "Actually there's something about that image that bothers me."

"Oh?"

"I have trouble imagining an angel, guardian or otherwise, making love the way we have. Aren't angels supposed to be sexless?" She quirked a brow at him playfully.

Zach flinched. She'd reminded him of feelings he'd been working hard to bury. "I wouldn't know about that," he said shakily.

"Angels." She shook her head as if to dismiss the idea. "Don't get me wrong, I do like how safe I feel when I'm around you, Zach." She pushed away from him just enough to take his hands in hers. "But there's also an awful lot of electricity zapping between us, and that has nothing to do with friends looking out for each other."

"I know," he admitted reluctantly.

She traced the outline of his right hand with her index finger. "So, how do we deal with this?" she asked softly.

"I don't have a clue," he admitted.

Caroline watched Zach's expression intently. He was such a complex man.

She sometimes thought she understood little sections of his personality, as if he were a jigsaw puzzle and she could make out the portion where the blues blended with the reds, or where one shape suddenly took on meaning. But the whole of him escaped her.

Perhaps it was his natural inclination to protect people he cared about. Sometimes that trait comforted her. Other times the result seemed almost comical, like his unsuccessful attempts to matchmake.

But there was more to him, she was sure. There was the passion he kept holding back. A man didn't look at a woman the way Zach looked at her, unless he ached to have her in his bed.

She could understand how the death of his cousin might have changed his life dramatically. Perhaps he'd been so shaken he felt he had to protect himself from intimacy. Then learning about her loss had drawn him to her, despite all that, and brought out his protective instincts. She could understand that, too.

"Zach," Caroline began softly, choosing her words with care, "may I tell you what I'd like to do?"

"I guess," he said warily.

"I don't know what makes you believe some mysterious man is going to appear out of the blue and give me another child. All I can tell you is, I feel *right* when I'm with you. Maybe what you're trying to tell me is true, and I'll fall in love with someone else a year or two, or five from now. Maybe you're helping me understand that I *could* love again." She touched her lips to his throat.

"Trust that feeling," he said, his voice low against the sound of the wind whistling outside the car.

"I want to, Zach. I really do want to hope again, but . . . but—"

"But what?"

"I can't ignore the feelings between us, now, right here while we're talking and touching like this."

He closed his eyes as if willing himself to be somewhere else. But when he opened them he looked straight at her, and their steady azure gaze nearly took her breath away.

"I can't take advantage of you," he said, his jaw tightening. "You trust me, and I don't want to lose that trust. It wouldn't be right for me to give in to my damn hormones and make love to you, every night, all night long . . . the way I want to . . . then give you nothing in return." His voice grated with emotion. "Because I can't promise you a tomorrow, Caroline. I wish I could explain why, but I can't."

Her heart thrummed in her ears and it took her a few minutes to catch her breath. At last she regained her composure enough to speak. "Zach, I never thought I'd say this to a man. It doesn't even sound like me talking," she admitted. "But something tells me we were meant to find comfort in each others' arms, at least for the few days we have together, up here in Vermont."

He stared at her as though his very life depended upon every syllable that passed between her lips. "Something tells you?" he repeated.

"Yes, it's a very strong feeling that's almost in words but not quite." She shook her head, feeling utterly confused. "I can't explain it, and you'd never understand, I'm sure. Credit it to women's intuition maybe?" She smiled dimly at him. "The point is, I know in my heart that what I need right now is for us to be as close as possible."

There, she'd said it. The urge to put her thoughts into words had gripped her with shocking strength. Wanting to be with Zach wasn't just a whim, or a sudden physical hunger for a man, any man. Zach was, for all his craziness, *the* man she was meant to be with. She would have staked her life on that.

Maybe it would take some convincing to help him understand. Maybe he would never see things as she did. But something told her he was falling in love with her just as swiftly as she was falling for him. And after all the horrible things that had happened in her life, she wasn't willing to walk away from this one chance at happiness.

Caroline pushed further back from Zach to get a better look at his face. His eyes held a glittering, dazed expression she'd seen in survivors of a natural disaster. "Zach, do you understand what I'm saying to you?"

He nodded stiffly. "Yeah. You would like for us to make love tonight."

"This afternoon . . . tonight . . . tomorrow . . . all week . . . I want to remember what it's like to be loved without limits by a truly good man, a man who can be strong for me and put me above his own pride."

Zach stared at her, a storm of emotions clouding his suntanned face. Among them was the barely contained desire she'd seen etched in his rugged features so often before. She could almost feel his longing, a need so strong she wondered why he hadn't already pulled her into his arms and kissed away her words. But there was also fear there, a bright, sharp fear that she couldn't explain away.

"I want to love you more than you know," Zach said, his fingers trailing gently through her hair, sending delicious chills up her spine. "Maybe . . . maybe that's why we're together this week. Maybe this is meant to be a healing process for both of us?"

He let the words hang in the air, as if waiting for a response, but not from her.

After a moment, the tension seemed to ease slightly from around his eyes and mouth, and he looked directly into her eyes. "So be it," he said, letting out a long sigh, as if everything had suddenly come into focus for him. "We'll be together for these seven days, and we'll be everything a man and woman can be for each other."

"And after that?" she whispered.

"You have to understand and accept that I'm not the man for the rest of your life, Caroline. I'm just not. But I can share with you these days in the snow. And if that's what you want, it's what I want to give you."

She felt an overwhelming but inexplicable surge of warmth for him. Somehow, she'd known he wouldn't promise her more. Strangely she didn't feel disappointed that she was right. Her heart felt suddenly lighter, ready to hum along at an easier rhythm now that she and Zach had promised themselves to each other for the little bit of time they had.

Then Zach pulled her into his sheltering, muscled arms again and they kissed tenderly in the snowbound car.

At last she looked into his eyes and smiled. "Let's try this skiing stuff," she whispered. "Then we'll—"

He touched one finger to her lips, sealing the words behind them. "Yes," he agreed. "Then, *we will.*"

Caroline signed up for a *Lose the Fear of Skiing Clinic* for beginners, while Zach paid for a group lesson for himself at an intermediate level. As she listened with only half of her attention to the woman instructor talking about the equipment they'd soon be renting, Caroline realized she felt exactly the same about her arrangement with Zach as she did about learning to ski—excited and scared to death.

Never in her wildest fantasies had she ever imagined "shacking up" with a man she'd known only a few weeks, for whom marriage wasn't an option. She considered herself conservative and cautious by nature. Although she and Rob hadn't been married the first time they'd made love, they had been engaged. He'd wanted sex even sooner, but she'd been firm that she intended to save herself for her husband, or at least for her husband-to-be. Rob had proposed the next night, and they'd made love before the little diamond chip had warmed on her finger. That was as wanton an act as she'd ever imagined for herself.

Now, she'd made a pact with Zach Dawson to be as intimate as any husband and wife, but without promises for the future. Her mother would be scandalized, her brother and sister would shake their heads and worry about her. Her father—God rest his soul—at least she didn't have to worry about what he might say to her on the subject of her lascivious behavior!

Caroline looked up at the slate gray sky, dancing with tiny white crystals that stung her nose and cheeks. *Sorry, Daddy. I didn't plan on life turning out this way.*

"Are you coming, Caroline?" A voice broke in on her thoughts.

She brought her glance back to eye level. The instructor, a brisk, square-bodied woman of about fifty years, looked as if she'd spent every one of them on skis. She beckoned for Caroline to follow the other five students to the equipment rental station.

"Count me in," she said, smiling.

Chapter 13

As Caroline stood in line with her class, waiting for her equipment, she watched the quad-chairs looping swiftly up and down the mountainside. Every once in a while, a novice skier would miss the chair seat on its upward swing from the base lodge and the lift operator would have to stop the cable, to the embarrassment of the poor soul who would have to pick himself up out of the snow, dust off and then awkwardly climb aboard while experienced skiers watched in amusement. Just as bad, Caroline could see herself losing her balance while trying to leave the chair at the top. She'd skid into a mammoth snowbank at the top of the mountain, then ungracefully plummet down the entire slope, her skis hopelessly entangled. If she were lucky, she'd survive with only a few broken bones to show for the experience.

The real tragedy would be, she thought wryly, she wouldn't be in any shape to tumble beneath the sheets with Zach that night—what with the casts, splints and pulleys supporting her in her hospital bed. Caroline giggled at the picture her mind had drawn, then she remembered the predatory gleam in Zach's eyes as he'd given her a goodbye kiss before they'd separated for the few hours their lessons would take. She decided, after all, he might not let *anything* get in his way.

Maria, her instructor, was wonderfully patient. The older woman took her time, helping each of her six students don their astronautlike boots and adjust the clamps for proper tension. Then they learned how to wedge the boot toe into the binding and stomp down hard with the heel to lock the boot into place on the ski.

Maria demonstrated how the binding would automatically release if they took a spill. Then they practiced falling down in the snow and getting up again by turning the blades of their skis across the slope of mountain. With the help of her ski poles, Caroline was able to lever herself up off the snow with a lot less struggle than she'd anticipated, recalling her earlier experiences. It was all great fun—adults playing in the snow as if they were children, forgetting the real world of mortgages, office politics and family pressures.

Next, they worked on gliding slowly on two skis on the flat. Then Maria showed them how to form a wedge with their skis and snowplow slowly down an incline. Caroline remembered this from her trips with Suzanne, when all they'd done was snowplow down the same shallow slope, over and over. But this time Maria was able to demonstrate how they could get up a little speed then slow down at will, whenever they felt they were going too fast.

Every once in a while, Caroline looked across toward the intermediate slope, hoping to spot Zach. But it seemed that scores of men wore similar black-and-purple ski jackets. As the two hours of her lesson wore on, she found her attention wandering from her skiing techniques as she anticipated returning to her room at the Greenbriar with Zach, and her heart raced and leapt with joy. She could have flung off her jacket and lain in the snow, right then, and she would have felt as warm as if she'd been sunning herself on a tropical beach.

Zach's class followed one of the trails marked with blue rectangles. There were over one hundred miles of skiable slopes on the cluster of six mountains that comprised the Killington resort, with seventy-seven different trails. Blue indicated intermediate difficulty. The Green Circle trails were for beginners. Black Diamonds were reserved for expert skiers. Double Black Diamonds were for Olympic level skiers or those bent on suicide.

He'd met the challenge of a few advanced trails in the past, and could handle most terrain fairly well. His natural agility and the muscles he'd built in his legs and thighs on construction sites, suited the sport. But he wasn't fool enough to risk breaking his neck without a refresher course, especially while thoughts of Caroline distracted him constantly during the afternoon. All he could think of was making love to her, in as many ways as his creativity allowed, and for as long as his stamina—or Meher—let him.

Zach worked at carving wide turns down the mountainside, shifting his weight to the forward-riding ski when making the cut to come back across the trail. The instructor was a young man named Chris, still in college, a downhill racer for Dartmouth's ski team. He could have made it down the entire fall line of the mountain in less time than it took for most skiers to boot up, but— Zach had to give him credit—the kid didn't succumb to the temptation to show off.

At Chris's age, Zach remembered, he'd been so full of himself his father was constantly after him to "straighten up and act responsibly."

It had taken him a long time to do either. In some ways, he supposed, he never had grown up. He initially chose construction over college because it allowed him to continue doing what he'd done all of his life—mess around with building stuff and tearing it down. Grown-up Lego!

Now, he wouldn't have the chance to grow up in a way that would have made his old man proud of him—by marrying a good woman and raising a family. But maybe, for his own sake, he could salvage his soul. He would do everything necessary to help Caroline get a grip on her life and start over with a new husband—even if it tore at his insides to let her go when the time came.

If showing her how a real man could love her was what she needed and what Meher expected from him, well, he guessed he'd have to do his duty.

Zach grinned, inhaling the freezing air. Not many men, dead or alive, could ever hope for such a pleasant job.

Zach looked around for Caroline on the snow-covered hillside. Six trails converged, ending in the beginners' training area. Three chair lifts, as well as an old-fashioned rope tow, took off from and returned there as well. It was close to four in the afternoon, and two bus loads of high school students had just descended on the area, adding to the crush of skiers. He worried about finding Caroline in the crowd.

At last he picked out her bright red, puffy jacket from the other skiers. She was hiking toward the rental shed, her skis balanced on her shoulder like a pro. Lowering his goggles over his eyes, he pushed off, gliding swiftly down the gentle slope, maneuvering around kids and seniors who were adjusting their bindings or stretching out muscles in preparation for their first run of the day.

With a bit of his old flair for impressing pretty girls, he swerved around Caroline at the last moment, sending a wall of snow flying as he skidded to a dramatic stop in front of her.

Caroline's mouth dropped open, and she looked as if she were about to deliver one of his father's lectures when she suddenly dissolved into laughter.

"Oh, it's you! I thought you were a show-off college kid."

"The college students around here seem a whole lot more responsible than I remember being," he admitted, flipping up his goggles. "How was your lesson? I lost track of you."

"It was great fun," she said, propping the heels of her skis in the snow alongside her poles. "I now know how to put on my equipment, glide in a straight line, *and*—" she raised one finger for dramatic emphasis "—fall down and get back up again."

He laughed at her. "What if you come face-to-face with one of those massive pine trees? Can you go around it?"

She considered that possibility for a second. "I figure I either go straight for it, and the better life form wins, or I make a crash landing in the nearest snowbank."

"I'd choose the latter, if I were you," he advised, laughing. "I'd hate to see what a faceful of bark would do for your lovely complexion." He brushed his mitten over her cheek, still pink with exertion. The snowflakes clinging to the fabric powdered her skin prettily. She shivered.

"Are you cold?" he asked.

"Not really. I was surprised by how warm I felt as long as I kept moving. But now that I've stopped, it's beginning to feel chilly out here."

"I was going to ask if you wanted to ski some more, but if you'd rather quit for the day..." He didn't want to appear overanxious to get back to the Greenbriar—even though being alone with Caroline in his room was all he could think about.

"I guess I'd like to go back to the inn now," she admitted, a quiet tension in her voice. Beneath their casual banter, he'd felt a hidden excitement building. It was as if neither of them dared dwell on what they'd promised each other would happen that night.

It wasn't as if he couldn't remember what making love to Caroline had felt like. For him, it had been a wonderful gift from the other side of the grave, a wondrous, soaring blend of emotions and sensations he'd believed he would never again experience.

The trusting, needful way Caroline had responded to his touch, was so different from anything he had known with other women. Like himself, the women he'd slept with sought the instant addictive jolt of random sex. Neither side had been particularly concerned with the tenderness or deeper meanings of the act. At times, he imagined they came to him much as an athlete consults a physical therapist or trainer—to work out the kinks, get the body in tune again, reassure him- or herself that the muscles and joints are all functioning as they should. Only in their case, they were working out with different parts of their bodies.

When he had made love with Caroline, he sensed that she wasn't simply repeating a learned action, or looking for instant gratification. Her needs had more to do with remembering what it was like to be alive, trying to feel what love could be like in its purest form. He didn't know if he'd been able to give her those things, but he was sure going to try during the course of this week.

"Let's go," he said, bundling her skis and poles with his own and hefting them easily to his shoulder. He started off toward the rental-return window.

Zach didn't have to turn to know that she was following him, or that her nervous anticipation of the evening was just as keen as his. Subtle waves of emotion whispered through the frigid air to him in the dying light of day.

Once they were in the car and on their way, it took all of his self-control to keep his foot firmly on the brake, controlling their descent on the mountain instead of hitting the gas and speeding to the bottom. As far as Zach was concerned, the faster they got back to the Greenbriar and settled in for the night, the better. But he forced himself to drive at the speed limit, even though his heart raced faster with every minute, then he parked quickly and threw himself out of the car. He nearly pulled the bindings off of his skis by failing to loosen the clamps holding them to the roof of the car before trying to remove them. Zach felt like running headlong for the room.

By contrast, Caroline barely rippled the air as she strolled down the hallway ahead of him. She seemed totally in control of her emotions as she let herself smoothly into her room and shut the door quietly, leaving him fumbling with his key then maneuvering skis, boots, poles and himself, like some clumsy slapstick comic, through the doorway.

Zach threw the equipment on the floor and stared up at the ceiling. "If I'm botching this job by sleeping with Caroline North, you'd better tell me now!" he shouted. "No fair messing around with subtle hints."

He waited for a heartbeat, then another. "Well?" he breathed out in exasperation.

By the time he'd counted to ten, twice, and no answer came, he figured he wasn't going to get an answer. He wondered if there was such a thing as a short circuit in the Heaven-to-Earth communication network. Maybe he'd wake up in bed the next morning with Caroline, and find a furious Meher standing over him, demanding an explanation.

Or worse.

He might not even get a hearing. The powers that be might well dump him directly into an eternal inferno for his sins. Zach sat down in a lump on the sofa and buried his face in his hands.

"Tell me what to do," he begged. "I want to touch her so badly my hands hurt. But if this is wrong—just say so, loud enough for me to hear you. Just say it's the worst thing I could do for her, and I'll walk away from her this very minute. I don't want to hurt her. I—"

A gentle singing sound filled the room. It was as if a thousand hummingbirds had swarmed around him. The reverberations of their tiny wings beat the air, creating an ethereal music unlike any he'd ever heard.

Zach lifted his head from his hands and looked around.

Nothing was there.

His skis, poles and the nylon bag containing his boots lay on the floor where he'd dropped them. The sliding glass door that led out to a deck was closed, and outside lay a smooth blanket of snow stretching down steps toward a break of birch trees. He walked over to the TV, flicked it on then off again. He checked the radio to be sure it was off. Neither seemed to be producing the sweet euphony that was filtering through his spirit like a timeless chorus.

"Is this a no or a yes?" he asked aloud.

The song lifted in pitch, curling inside of his soul, comforting and quieting his fears.

"It's a *yes*, isn't it?" he whispered. "This is what Caroline needs. You arranged this little trip from the moment Suzanne insisted on a vacation for her friend to this afternoon in the car—when we decided to... Meher, you're something, old pal."

The song immediately began to fade. Voices so perfect, ultimately pure, achingly haunting, drifted faintly away.

So, that's that, Zach thought.

The Archangel had determined that the job of his newest third-tier rookie was to comfort Caroline in a physical as well as spiritual way. Maybe the only means by which she could be reached was through the loving touch of a man? Maybe he, Zach, first had to teach her how it felt to be cherished, before she could completely heal and trust another man with her heart.

At least he'd been completely frank with her. She knew they could be together for only a brief time. She seemed to accept that limitation. He would carry out his mission now without feeling guilty. And what a sweet mission it was. He could think of nothing he'd rather do than hold Caroline in his arms and make love to her.

Then another thought occurred to him, chilling his enthusiasm. The question was, even if she could accept leaving him...could he accept leaving her?

He laughed bitterly. In his case, he really didn't have a choice.

Caroline shut the door to her room behind her and leaned heavily against it. Her heart was racing, her mouth felt so dry she could hardly swallow. Although she'd made up her mind to sleep with Zach, her body seemed to have not adjusted to the idea. Her stomach alternately flopped and tightened nervously.

Caroline crossed the carpet quickly to the bathroom and stared in dismay into the mirror over the sink. Her face was flushed bright red. Her hair had whipped into a tangled mass of dark curls, around eyes that resembled those of a startled night creature.

"You're a grown woman," she told her reflection. "You don't have to make excuses to anyone for your actions."

So why was her pulse crashing around inside her body? Why did she feel like tearing out of the room, into the snow, running as far away from Killington and Zach Dawson as she possibly could before she dropped from exhaustion?

Caroline drew three long, slow breaths, looked herself squarely in the eye, and started brushing out the snarls that framed her feverish face.

She was still standing in the bathroom, arguing with herself, sweating through her ski clothes, when a soft knock summoned her from her trance.

"Are you decent?" Zach called through the door separating their rooms.

"Do you care?" she called back, surprising herself with her boldness.

"Actually I'd prefer that you—" he stood with a hopeful look on his strong face as she swung open the door "—weren't. Oh shucks."

Caroline grinned. "Sorry to disappoint."

He stepped hesitantly into the room. "Are you having second thoughts?"

"No. Yes . . . maybe," she murmured, frustrated with her indecisiveness. She pulled off her jacket and sat down on the bed, balling up the down outer garment in her lap and hugging it like a familiar stuffed animal, for comfort. "I *do* want us to be together this week. I really do."

"But?" He walked over to the honor bar beside her TV set and crouched down to check out the selection.

"Until now, I've always thought people should save making love for the one special person they loved."

"And you don't love me," he stated, straightening up with two miniature bottles of wine in his hand. He held them out to her.

She shook her head. "I don't know how I feel about you just now, Zach," she said, although her heart immediately berated her for the lie. "I guess maybe it's different for a man. I've read so many times that men can have sex, or they can make love. It's two different functions to them."

He put the wine back in the refrigerator, shut its door and turned to look at her, his eyes darker than she'd ever seen them. "Are you trying to get me to say that I love you before we sleep together again?"

She didn't like the tension in his voice. "No, I'm not trying to make you do anything, Zach. I just wish we each knew what we wanted. *Really* knew. It would be so much simpler that way."

She rocked on the edge of the bed, clutching her jacket, and suddenly burst into tears. Hot, stinging, angry tears that she was helpless to stop.

Zach rushed forward, dropping down on one knee in front of her. "It's all right if you don't want to do this. It's your decision. It always has been. I'm not forcing you to—"

"Hush," she said, placing her palm over his lips. She gazed down at him, her tears drying on her cheeks, understanding without his having to say a word, how deeply he felt for her. It didn't matter that he couldn't put his feelings into words. Suddenly she knew her decision had been the right one. If she passed up the chance to give herself to Zach for that week, she knew she'd regret it for the rest of her life.

"It doesn't matter. Nothing matters. I want you to make love to me," she told him fervently.

"Right now?"

"Just give me ten minutes," she whispered.

Her knees felt so rubbery with emotion, she could barely stand. Caroline hobbled toward the bathroom. She didn't realize she was still clutching her jacket until she turned to close the door behind her and found her hands full.

Dropping the coat unceremoniously on the tile floor, she quickly stripped off layers of ski clothes. She was glad she'd had the presence of mind to insist upon showering after the afternoon's activity. She felt less than fresh and worried that she might smell a bit like a locker room if Zach took her straight to bed.

Moving with renewed urgency, she stepped into a stinging hot shower, lathered herself with a floral soap provided by the inn and rinsed off all traces of the day's perspiration. She decided against washing her hair, since she'd shampooed it early that same morning. It tended to dry out with daily washings. Besides, it would be faster if she didn't have to mess with blow-drying it now. She found herself unwilling to put off being with Zach a minute longer than was absolutely necessary.

After hastily running a towel over her skin, Caroline spritzed herself with her favorite vanilla-scented cologne, then looked around, only then realizing she'd brought no clothes in with her.

"Great," she muttered.

"What's wrong?" Zach called from her room.

"I forgot to bring anything to wear."

"I don't mind."

With a jealous sting, Caroline realized he must have played similar games of verbal foreplay with countless other women. He'd undoubtedly continue fine-tuning his flirtation techniques in the future. But she shook her head, willing bitter thoughts away. This was no time for having second thoughts. She'd made her decision, and she would stick to it, because being with Zach was what *she* wanted.

But one thing she couldn't do. She couldn't make herself walk through that door, into that room where Zach waited for her, buck naked.

Grabbing a large, dry towel from the rack, she wrapped it snugly around her and tucked it into place, then took just another minute to apply a touch of eyeliner and pale pink lip gloss. She definitely didn't need the blusher.

Gingerly she opened the door and stepped through. Caroline's eyes roamed the room. Her gaze drifted to Zach, lying on one hip on her bed, one arm bent to prop up his head on that hand. A small hand towel was draped loosely over his hips, hiding very little. The thought flashed past her that one quick tug from either of them would reveal the state of his arousal, and she drew in a sharp breath of pleasure.

"So you showered, too," she murmured, aware of the woodsy male scent that hadn't been in the room when she'd left it.

"Uh-huh."

His blond hair was still wet, combed casually back from his face, appearing darker for its dampness. She itched to run her fingers through its damp strands.

His smile still promised fun, but his eyes bored into her, steely and intent, as if she were the only woman he had ever wanted, would ever want...for all eternity. She knew it was a trick men were capable of pulling off when courting their woman-of-the-moment. Rob had done it, melting her insides when he'd wanted to...at first. After their first year together, he'd no longer bothered trying.

Maybe limiting every relationship to a short affair was the only way to avoid the heartbreak of watching that wonderful rapt expression disappear from a man's eyes. But oh, she thought, wouldn't it be lovely if every day, for the rest of her life, she could gaze into Zach's eyes and see his hunger for her? Just for her...just for her...

She shivered at the delightful thought, even though she sensed such a dream could never turn into reality. A man like Zach, whose lust could run blazing hot, had to cool down sooner or later.

"Come here," he said, holding out a long, muscled arm, beckoning her toward him.

She obeyed, feeling as if the moment was destined to be.

Walking to the side of the bed, she stood in front of Zach, her arms at her sides, the towel tucked under her armpits and across her breasts. With each intake for her breath, she became poignantly aware of the terry fabric stretching and loosening around her ribs. If she took in full lungfuls of air, she was sure the thing would come unwrapped and drop to her ankles. She tried to calm her breathing.

"Are you afraid?" Zach whispered.

"A little," she admitted. "It seems as if it's been so long...you know, since the last time. And everything feels so different, up here, in a strange setting."

His hand continued to reach toward her, but she stood still, not daring to move either forward and onto the bed, or backward and away from him. It was almost as if she feared any move on her part would break the spell that was weaving itself around them, shutting off all outside interruptions. The faint sizzle of snow tires on cars passing by the inn on the highway had become almost imperceptible now. The light from outside the sliding glass doors had dimmed to a faint purplish glow, cast across the snow by the setting sun.

Zach's fingers inched closer to her, and to her towel.

Caroline was mesmerized by the intricate web of muscles and tendons crisscrossing the back of his hand. Even now, when he was trying to be gentle, he exuded an aura of strength, fragilely reined in. She sucked a cool ribbon of air between her teeth as his fingertips touched the hem of her towel and she waited, her heart pounding in her ears . . . waited for him to bare her.

But he didn't.

Instead his hand slipped beneath the plush toweling, smoothing upward between her thighs. His palm was rough. Perversely she liked feeling its gentle scrape against her silky skin. He slid his hand around behind her thigh, cupping her bottom, then pulled her toward him until her knees bumped the edge of the mattress.

Zach's eyes locked with hers. He edged forward on the bed, nudging aside one corner of the towel with his head, just high enough to allow his lips to press against the tender flesh of her thigh. His hand, behind her, gently kneaded as his heated kisses trailed up her leg to her hip, then down and forward to the velvety hollow between her legs.

Suddenly Caroline lost all sense of balance. Reaching down with one hand, she steadied herself against his muscled shoulder. His blue eyes flashed up at her as he brushed his lips over her most intimate flesh, then burrowed into her.

"Oh, Zach," she moaned softly. "I can't stand . . . can't stand . . ."

"Can't stand what?" he asked.

"Up." And her legs buckled beneath her as she tumbled limply onto the bed beside him.

She felt him moving over her, realigning his body with hers, loosening the towel from around her. She was almost afraid to open her eyes and look into his again, terrified that she might not see mirrored in them the intensity of passion she was feeling. Lust, need, love, the desire to please . . . so many feelings rushed through her at once that it was impossible to sort them out, to determine which were valid, and which might only be phantoms of the moment.

Zach's hands smoothed over her. "You're trembling," he observed in a throaty voice. "Do you want me to stop?"

All it took was his question to clear her mind. "No, oh no, Zach. Please don't stop now." She reached up around his wide shoulders and pulled him down so that his chest pressed into her breasts, covering them with warmth and a suffusion of glorious tingles. "If you don't make love to me this very minute, I think I might just die."

She found herself laughing nervously, while tears of happiness clung to her lashes. It felt as if the shame and agony of Rob's rejection, following upon years of unadmitted frustration with his awkward lovemaking, was finally dropping away, leaving her. A dark cloud that had once blocked the sun from her life seemed to release her as she sank deeply into the crisp, white bed linens under the welcome weight of Zach's body.

A fire shone in his eyes that she gloried in as he quickly took care of protection before parting her long legs with his knee and shifting his hard body to press himself upward into the soft, ready folds of her femininity. He slipped effortlessly inside her, and she suddenly felt complete, as if he were the final piece of a puzzle that was meant to be all along. And a rush of fire blazed through her belly, shooting into her chest, stealing her breath away.

"Oh, Zach!" she gasped. "Love me!"

"I am . . . Heaven help me, I am, Caroline," he groaned.

Zach waited for the lightning bolt to strike. Literally.

Wasn't that the way it always happened in books and movies? As a little boy, conscientiously delivered to Sunday school each week, he'd firmly believed that stealing coins from his mother's penny jar would exact a quick and agonizing punishment from the heavens. His Sunday school teacher had related assorted, terrifying forms of retribution doled out to biblical characters for their sins—and assured Zach and his classmates that stealing, even a small amount, would be taken just as seriously as lying, disobeying one's parents, or—that most mysterious act—fornication.

And here he was having sex with the woman Heaven had entrusted to his care. What was wrong with this system? Weren't they paying attention up there? Was Meher on an extended coffee break?

As Zach had lain on Caroline's bed, waiting anxiously for her to finish her shower, he rationalized that he was being provided to Caroline as a kind of therapist, to help her cross from her pain-filled past to a healthy, happy relationship with a man who would fulfill her needs. But did she have to respond with such enthusiasm to his touch? Wasn't it going a little overboard for him to feel so involved in her spiraling climaxes?

With excruciating effort, he controlled his own mounting desire, holding himself back each time she clutched his shoulders and arms and shuddered with another wave of delight. He marveled at how free she was with her body and her responses to him . . . after having gone for so long without a man who could bring her the passion she deserved.

When, at last, she lay limp and sated, almost shyly smiling up at him from beneath her long, dark lashes—he thrust one last time then closed his eyes and contracted the muscles in his back and buttocks, and climaxed long and hard into her as she wrapped her silky legs around him, holding him captive within her blazing flesh.

It took Zach a good while to recover.

He rose slowly through layers of euphoria, like a swimmer returning to the surface after a deep dive into a tropical pool. There was a sensation that he had to hold his breath until he reached the top, where he'd at last be able to again breathe normally.

He gulped down air and stretched himself out over her. Her legs relaxed slightly but didn't drop from around his hips, and he was glad. He felt at home there, cocooned with her.

They slept lightly for a while, their bodies touching, fingers of one hand linked with another, as if they were both afraid to let go. He needed contact with her flesh just as his feet required solid earth to walk on, as urgently as his lungs needed oxygen to breathe or his stomach hungered for food. His very survival seemed to depend upon her.

It was at that moment, as he held her beneath the sheets, that Zach realized the depth of his sacrifice. He hadn't thought of making love to Caroline as anything but pure pleasure before this. But now he knew that he'd never be able to forget Caroline North, not in an eternity.

Leaving her, Zach knew, would surely destroy him.

Chapter 14

Caroline awoke, curled within the tight hollows and muscled mounds of Zach's chest and abdomen. His biceps and forearms wrapped around her, holding her close to him, as if to protect her from the uncertain gray light of dawn that seeped through the vertical blinds of her room at the Greenbriar. Holding very still, she took stock of the quiet messages her body was sending her.

Subtle tingles reminded her of the times Zach had softly coaxed her into consciousness then worked his magic on her, swiftly bringing her again to a hungry need for him, then satisfying her once more. The muscles the entire length of her legs were tight and vaguely sore, as if she'd run a great distance. With remarkable vividness she recalled tightening them possessively around Zach's hips and, one time, squeezing so hard they'd cramped. Laughing with embarrassment, she'd had to beg him to release her so that she could stretch out the ill-timed charley horse before coming back to bed.

And there was a reminiscent puffiness to her lips, where Zach had kissed her, again and again. The mere memory of his mouth closing over hers left her dizzy. There were also dozens of gently pulsing spots all over her body that spoke to her of the night, each recalling the tender or reckless touch of Zach's fingers, tongue, body as he took possession of every inch of her flesh. Caroline glanced down at her breast, pillowed against his arm. Just above the right nipple was a pale purplish shadow, a mark left by his mouth as he'd drawn her between his warm, wet lips . . . just a little harder, no doubt, than he'd intended. But it didn't hurt at all, and she smiled, enjoying the sensation the tiny bruise aroused in her.

A very primal feeling—branded, in a way, she thought wryly. Zach's woman. The woman who was meant to be his. Fate.

She didn't censor her thoughts this time. All of his assurances that they couldn't be together seemed irrelevant this morning. How could he claim that the explosion that had occurred between them was anything less than a joining of two souls, destined by the stars? But she wouldn't voice her thoughts to him. She sensed that one night together wouldn't be enough to chase away whatever deeply rooted belief convinced him they couldn't stay together. *Give us a week together,* Zach Dawson, she thought blissfully, *and you'll change your mind.*

He stirred beside her, pulling her bottom into the bend of his hips. She could feel warm curls of hair . . . the shape of his early-morning arousal tucked into her backside. She squirmed just enough to let him know she was awake.

"How did we both survive that night?" he asked drowsily.

"We must be in great physical condition." She giggled, feeling like a girl again. A girl who had just learned all over again what it was to be a woman.

"I think I could sleep until noon."

"And miss all that great skiing?" she teased, flipping herself over to face him. The sheets were warm and smelled evocatively of their own bodies. She ached to stay here, in them, with Zach wrapped around her.

But she sensed she needed to keep him busy to chase away any morning-after doubts he might have. "Come on, lazy bones, we both signed up for classes. They start at nine o'clock, don't they?"

He slipped his arms around her waist and brought her tighter into the hard length of his body. "We've got hours before then. It can't be any later than six o'clock."

"It's seven, and we need to shower, dress and have breakfast before—"

"Okay. Okay," he said, dramatically lifting his hands away and releasing her. "You win. We came here, so we said, to ski...so ski we shall."

They met in the hallway after washing up and dressing, then walked downstairs to the breakfast room. Caroline was famished. She couldn't remember ever having such an appetite. She ordered a breakfast platter of a three-egg omelet, sausage, a stack of pancakes served with Vermont maple syrup, spiced apples and wheat toast with coffee.

Zach finished his plate of steak and eggs and sat back to observe her with a look of amusement as she polished off her last pancake and started spooning marmalade on the first piece of toast.

"So, what are you thinking?" she asked through a mouthful of crumbs.

"I'm just wondering how a woman who devours food the way you do, doesn't weigh three hundred pounds."

"I don't normally eat this kind of breakfast," she objected. "It's usually a piece of fruit and a cup of decaf tea."

"Then it's a wonder you're around at all."

She shook her head. "I can't imagine why I'm doing this. I've never been a big breakfast person." She crunched away happily on her toast.

"If you don't stop soon, they'll be rolling you down the mountain."

"Then I'll be a very happy snowball." She grinned at him, and he smiled back. He sometimes seemed to be rationing his smiles, as if he had only so many left to give. She wished he could just let them come when he felt the urge.

At last, she sat back in her chair and stared with amazement at her empty plate. "I don't believe I ate all of that."

"I'm a witness. Think that will hold you until lunch?"

She shook her head. "Make that dinner...maybe even breakfast tomorrow morning."

Classes formed on the beginner slope, as before. The instructors, in their magenta-and-gray ski jackets, dotted the white hillside, gathering little flocks of students around them, like mother hens sorting out their chicks in a crowded barnyard.

Caroline left Zach with his group, and marched across the packed snow toward the rental shed to pick up her equipment. After a brief skirmish with her bindings, she was booted and snapped into her skis. She glided slowly over to her group.

Maria had mostly the same students as the day before. One of the men who'd been falling down a lot was absent, and Caroline guessed he'd probably been too embarrassed to show up for a second day. Poor guy, she thought.

He was replaced by another man, who seemed to have skied before. He also observed Caroline's progress with a good deal of interest.

"You're doing just fine," he said, positioning himself beside her when Maria instructed them to line up across the hill after they'd warmed up by practicing their gliding wedges.

"I'm feeling surprisingly steady today," she admitted. "Now if I can just stay on my feet on a real hill." She glanced apprehensively toward the intermediate slope, which ended a hundred feet to their right. Some of the skiers flew to the bottom, ending their runs with a dramatic spray of snow from their blades.

"You stick with me, I'll show you how that's done," the man promised, winking at her.

Caroline raised a brow at him. "I thought the instructors were the ones who did the demonstrating."

He slid closer to her, as if marking his territory. "Most of the pros here are pretty good," he allowed graciously, "but what you need to do is put in a lot of snow miles, and someone experienced to practice with."

"I have someone to practice with," she said succinctly, pointing toward Zach's group with one of her poles.

Zach must have been looking for her. He raised an arm and waved at her.

"Your husband?" her classmate asked, sounding disappointed.

Caroline nodded. She didn't owe him an explanation, and letting him believe she was a married woman seemed the simplest way to discourage him.

He looked momentarily deflated, then shrugged as if this sort of obstacle often presented itself. Almost immediately, his attention turned to the woman standing to his left.

Caroline stifled a laugh of astonishment. Having been out of the dating world for so long, she'd forgotten how quickly some men could shift gears.

"How are your gliding wedges feeling?"

She turned to face Maria, who'd been working her way down the line, coaching each of her students individually on form.

"Pretty good," Caroline admitted. "I feel a lot more stable on these glorified toothpicks today than I thought I ever would."

"Good. Show me your stuff. Ski down to that tree on the right, making at least three curving turns along the way. I'll be right behind you."

Caroline felt the muscles in her legs automatically tighten. "Behind me won't help if I lose control," she stated nervously.

Maria smiled. "Not *that* sure of yourself yet, huh? Okay. Remember to hold your wedge. I'll stay right in front of you all the way. The worst that can happen is you'll run over me, but I'm big enough a lump to make you stop."

"How reassuring," Caroline said, laughing at the image Maria had painted.

She was amazed to see the woman ski backward down the slope with perfect control, coaching her through the weight changes from one ski to the other on each turn. They came to a smooth stop a few feet short of the lofty pine tree.

"That was perfect," Maria said, beaming at Caroline.

Caroline caught a glimpse of the man who'd been flirting with her earlier. He'd apparently struck out with his second choice in the group and moved on to the last woman.

Maria followed her glance and chuckled to herself. "Dag never gives up."

"You know him?"

"Oh, let's just say he's a regular. He can ski as well as some of our instructors, when he wants to. But he always signs up for the beginners' classes so he can show off for the ladies, and—" she winked "—maybe get lucky."

Caroline shook her head in amazement. "You let him get away with that?"

Maria shrugged. "No rules state he can't take a lower level class. We discourage students from moving up too fast, but moving down doesn't pose a safety threat. All he has to do is say to the director that he feels a little insecure and would like to review his basic skills . . ." She flipped a hand as if to say that his playing Lothario was of no importance to her.

Caroline couldn't help wondering at how obvious some men could be about their intent. Zach certainly was the other extreme. He was so full of secrets. So wrapped up in whatever hidden fears had trapped him in his loneliness. She suddenly felt an overpowering warmth and a need to be with him.

After finishing her lesson, she found Zach near the snack bar.

"Are you hungry yet?" he asked.

"Not really," she admitted.

"How about we ski a little longer, since you have your equipment for the day. Have you learned how to get on and off a lift?"

"We practiced a few times," she said. "I managed to stay on my skis and not kill anyone."

"That's a good sign." He laughed at her and slung an arm around her waist. Then his face darkened, and she followed his glance.

He was watching Dag move across the trail in front of them.

"Isn't that a guy in your class?" he asked.

"Yeah."

"He seemed to be talking a lot with you. Looked interested in more than your skiing form."

Caroline felt a little thrill of satisfaction. "I think he had in mind to teach me some special techniques, without skis."

Zach grimaced.

She laughed. "Are we a little jealous?"

He coughed, and a puff of white fog clouded around his mouth. "Me? Jealous?"

"Yes, you. I wasn't aware you were watching me that closely."

"I was concerned you might fall and hurt yourself. You're just starting out," Zach explained unconvincingly.

"I see," she said.

"Besides, he looked as if he was bothering you."

Caroline pretended to study Dag with interest. "Actually he's rather good-looking, don't you think?"

Frowning, Zach spun around and glared at the man who had just stepped into line for the quad-chair lift.

"I mean, you're always after me to meet new men. Maybe he's Mr. Right?" she mused innocently. "Wouldn't it be lucky if I just happened to run into him here, on this trip?"

Zach raked his fingers through his hair and stared at her in undisguised exasperation. "Let me remind you where you were just a few hours ago, lady! You weren't thinking of *other men* then, were you?"

Caroline let a smile slip out. "No, I don't suppose I was. You were keeping me pretty well occupied, if I remember correctly."

But his anger reached a full, rolling boil, and his blue eyes flashed dangerously, as if he hadn't even noticed that she was laughing at him. "Soon as you're out of my bed, you're on the prowl for another man?" he growled.

He sounded so churlishly cavemanish, she couldn't help laughing out loud.

"What?" he roared. "What's so damn funny?"

"You," she said. "You're so gullible."

He stared at her, at a loss.

"The guy's name is Dag, if it's his real name at all," she said. "Our instructor told me he makes a practice of picking up women by taking the beginner course over and over again, even though he's been skiing for ages."

A dark twinkle shot through Zach's eyes. "You were pulling my leg."

"Of course," she said, feeling deliciously naughty. "Although, I might prefer another portion of your anatomy," she whispered in his ear before turning quickly away and pushing off toward the lift line.

She sneaked a peek over her shoulder and caught a look of astonishment on Zach's face. A second later, he'd recovered and, grinning, was chasing her down the slope.

The next five days were the happiest in Caroline's memory. She and Zach were inseparable, day and night. They flung open the connecting doors and used the two rooms as one. When they weren't skiing or picking out a different pub or restaurant to relax in after they were too cold or exhausted to ski any longer, they were ensconced in his bed or hers, intent on pleasing each other, or curled in each other's arms as they watched a movie on TV. Each day seemed a little miracle of its own, bringing her more joy than she could have ever imagined was possible.

On the day before Thanksgiving, they skied together all morning. Taking the Juggernaut Trail from Killington's peak, at over four thousand feet, they wound their way slowly through the fairytale landscape, aglitter with ice and snow, stopping to kiss or hold hands under an icicle-strung pine tree, looking out over a picturesque winter-world of tiny cottages, chalets and hotels that spread out at their feet.

When they reached the bottom, Caroline was happily out of breath. "My legs feel like rubber," she gasped, giddy with exhaustion.

"Then you should stop, at least for a while," Zach stated. "Your last run should be the one before you lose muscle control."

"You sound like a textbook," she commented good-naturedly, releasing her bindings and stepping out of her skis.

They split a chef's salad, since neither felt hungry enough for a big meal. Then they returned to the Greenbriar for a long soak in the bubbling hot tub, which had become a luxurious part of their après-ski routine, and often a prelude to making love.

Caroline eased down into the steamy water, feeling at peace with herself and the world, which seemed to have changed drastically since she'd come to Vermont with Zach. Her old existence, so full of pain, frustration and disappointment, hadn't simply disappeared. It felt as if it were scenes from another woman's life. She could believe in things she never thought she'd believe in again— love that lasted forever...a man who put her pleasure and well-being before his own. In the rosy glow of love, all things seemed possible.

Caroline soaked happily until Zach snaked an arm around her waist and whispered in her ear. "Let's go back to the room. I want to stoke up the fireplace and make love to you in front of the flames."

She smiled up at him. "Sounds wonderful."

After they'd made love, Caroline brought them each a glass of wine, and she sat in the V between Zach's long legs on the floor while they sipped their wine and snacked on slices of crisp McIntosh apples and sharp Vermont cheddar.

"I've just realized something," she confided to Zach in a whisper as he supported her, her back pressed against his wide chest.

"What's that?"

"During the last year, before I met you—I never once went to bed at night, looking forward to the next day."

He brushed his lips soothingly against her hair. "That's terrible."

"You must have felt that way when your cousin died," she said. "Being as close to him as you were."

"I suppose," he said, but his voice sounded distant and a subtle tension tightened the muscles in his arms, enclosing her. For the first time in days she was reminded of the invisible but unyielding line he'd drawn between them. He seemed able to give her just so much of himself, then he could go no further.

The warmth of the fire, the wine's cozy buzz through her veins, Zach's warm body wrapped around her, and the fatigue of a day's skiing—all left her limp, unwilling to feel anything but complacent with life at the moment. She chased away fleeting doubts and spoke from her heart. "Wouldn't it be wonderful if we could just stay in Vermont, forever? Just never go back."

She felt Zach's body tighten, and he eased himself back from her by an inch.

"It can't happen, Caroline. You have obligations, and so do I," he stated bluntly.

She turned and stared up at him. "Taking up permanent residency at the Greenbriar wasn't a serious proposal." She put down her wineglass and turned in his arms to look up into his eyes. "But now that you've brought it up, I don't know why some variation on our staying together wouldn't work."

Her heart thudded in her chest as the seconds ticked by, and Zach didn't reply.

"Zach, say something," she whispered urgently, moving further away from him to better study his expression as his arms dropped from around her. "Give me at least a hint that will help me make sense of what we've become. We're more than temporary lovers. I *know* we are."

He shook his head, his features as emotionless as if they had been carved from stone. "I told you I couldn't promise you anything beyond this week."

Caroline's throat tightened, closing off her breath for several seconds. "You can't or you don't want to?" she forced between her lips.

"Either, take your pick," he said abruptly, standing up. He walked into the bathroom and shut the door behind him. She could hear water running, splashing. She dropped her face into her hands and squeezed her eyes shut. Hearing his icy words was all the more painful after the love they'd shared in the past days. And it was love, wasn't it? She'd been so sure . . . so very sure.

When he came out he looked as if he'd scrubbed his face with a coarse washcloth, as if to make himself as alert as possible, or to drive away the last traces of the comfortable intimacy they'd established. "Maybe we should take some time out to calm down," he said stiffly, picking his jeans off the floor and pulling them on. "I'll be in my room if you need me." He turned toward the connecting door.

"Zach!" she shouted his name, and with it, out poured her heart. "I've fallen in love with you."

He froze midway through the door and stared morosely at his hands. "Please don't say that."

Caroline felt as if her entire body were suddenly empty, stripped of all emotion, all caring. Her eyes burned with tears she stubbornly held back.

"The hell with you," she rasped. Pushing herself to her feet, she strode toward Zach, shoved him the rest of the way through the door and slammed it behind him. Barely able to see what she was doing through the flow of tears, she fumbled for the lock and found it.

She'd be damned if she'd lay her heart at any man's feet then wait around while he stomped on it. If he didn't feel the same way about her, fine. Let this be the end of it. Apparently she was no more to Zach at that moment than what she'd started out being when they'd planned the trip—a skiing buddy and dinner companion. All they'd added to the equation was unlimited sex. No commitment, no emotional attachment . . . at least from his side.

Disgusted with herself for letting him get to her heart, she wiped away her tears and looked around the room, trying to decide what to do next—murder Zach or simply walk away from him, forever.

One thing was clear to Caroline—she had to move on with her life. Nothing Zach could say to her now would change her mind.

Her eyes rested at last on the telephone. Picking it up, Caroline dialed the front desk and informed the clerk she'd be leaving a day early. What next? There was no way she could ride back to Connecticut in a car with Zach. She telephoned the airlines, not very hopeful that she'd find a seat on a flight the day before Thanksgiving, but a small, local airline promised they could get her from nearby Rutland to Groton.

When she hung up, Caroline felt satisfied that she was at least taking steps to move her physically away from Zach. There was a soft knock on the connecting door.

She ignored it and went to the closet to retrieve her suitcase. With a sudden surge of energy, she heaved the soft-sided bag across the room and onto the bed. After quickly dressing herself in jeans and a sweater, she pulled underwear, jerseys, sweaters and panty hose out of drawers and tossed them in the general direction of the bed.

The second knock was louder.

She refused to answer.

"Caroline, I'm sorry you're angry with me. You have every right to be."

"Darn right!" she shouted.

"Please open the door. I want to talk to you."

"I'm busy now."

"Come on, please, open up." His words vibrated against the door, as if his lips were pressed against it.

"You can talk all you want," she sang out over her shoulder as she continued packing. "Can't guarantee I'll be listening very hard."

There was a pause, then Zach's voice came to her, lower, denser, tougher than she'd ever heard it. *"Open the damn door, Caroline!"*

"No."

It made her feel noble and justified to refuse him. She felt in control. She felt she had made the first in a long string of necessary decisions. When she was back in Mystic, she would make it clear to Suzanne, Ralph and anyone else likely to try to change her mind, that she would have nothing to do with Zach Dawson from this day forth.

She was also finished with taking advice on dating from any-one. She would find her own men, if she wanted any. She didn't plan on playing the role of a recluse, as she had before Zach came along. She had to give him credit for jarring her out of that rut, but it was all she'd thank him for, *if* she ever again bothered speaking with him.

Moving on to the closet, Caroline tore dresses and jeans off hangers.

A sudden thud from the direction of the connecting door made her jump and turn toward it. The wooden panel shuddered, but remained firmly shut.

She smiled. Fat chance Zach had of breaking through a door as sturdy as that one appeared.

The door thudded again, and groaned. Caroline stood still, her arms full of clothes, scowling warily at the way the wooden panel bowed under Zach's assault. She swallowed, her eyes growing wide as she watched the wooden panel shiver and buckle inward under another assault.

"If you break down that door, Zach Dawson, *you're* paying for the damage, not me!"

She didn't really believe he could smash his way through to her room. That sort of macho show of force was harder to accom-plish than most people realized. She'd watched her brother at-tempt to knock down a door when he'd locked himself out of his house. The result had been a dislocated shoulder and a phone call from a neighbor's house to a locksmith.

Holding her breath, she listened hard. After a full minute of si-lence, Caroline decided Zach must have given up. She smiled with gratification. *Serves him right,* she thought. *He's probably gotten himself a nice bruised ego along with a sore shoulder for his ef-fort.*

Then she heard carpet-muffled running steps, growing louder.

In the next instant, everything happened so fast she could hardly absorb each motion. The central panel of the door buckling in-ward, the wooden jamb cracking then tearing loose from the wall, the knob jerking then exploding out of its socket in the wooden door... and all of it falling toward her in a blizzard of splinters.

Caroline dropped her armload of clothing, screamed and leapt out of the path of flying rubble. The accompanying crunch and crash sounded as if a bulldozer had plowed through the wall.

Zach bounded into the room, his eyes flashing with anger, and didn't stop until he'd pinned her against the far wall.

"Now, we *are* going to talk," he growled dangerously, inches from her face.

She'd seen him frustrated to the point of snapping, holding back his anger, rigid with unexplained tension. But never had she witnessed him, or any other man, possessed by such rage.

"Someone will be here any minute!" she gasped. "The other guests, they'll have heard the noise and reported it to the desk."

"Your point?" His eyes blazed at her, hot as the blue-white centers of flames.

"The police."

"That's supposed to make me not strangle you where you stand?"

She nodded hopefully, her entire body trembling.

Zach grasped her shoulders and shook her once, hard—then immediately released her. "Got the picture? I may *feel* like throttling you within an inch of your pretty life, Caroline, but I'm not going to. You're too important to me . . . and to others."

She gaped at him. "What the hell is that supposed to mean?"

Striding away from her across the room, as if to put distance between them and restore his sanity, Zach smoothed back his mussed blond hair and swore under his breath. Abruptly he spun around and glared at her.

"You are the most maddening woman I've ever met."

"You've said that before," she snapped, feeling safe enough for a well-chosen retort but not brave enough to come any closer to him.

"It's still true." He groaned, lifting his eyes to the ceiling as if he were about to address someone hanging from the lighting fixture. "Why can't you make this any easier on me?"

"You're not exactly making it easy on me, either," she retorted crisply. "I guess expecting you to tell me the truth was asking too much. All I wanted was an honest reason why we couldn't be together for more than a few days. That's all, Zach." She drew a deep breath. "I didn't ask for a commitment that involved living together, and I certainly didn't demand marriage. Just tell me there's another woman, or you were married before and your first wife died or dumped you or cheated with your best friend. Tell me what's haunting you and keeping us apart."

"If I told you the absolute truth," he said heavily, sinking onto the bed, "I would disappear from your life before you could blink an eye."

Caroline stared at him, shaking her head. "You mean you'll feel that you can no longer face me? That I'll be ashamed of you for something you did? I still don't understand, Zach." She started toward him, but he held up a hand.

"No. Stay where you are, and listen. *Just listen.*" His eyes scanned the room nervously, before focusing on her at last. "Remember, you called me your guardian angel?"

"Right."

"If there were such a thing . . . if we had spirits or other people or even pets who made it their business to watch over and protect us, then there would be certain restrictions, don't you think?"

"Restrictions?" She blinked at him. He'd gone from not talking at all to talking gibberish. She didn't know which was worse.

"Like a guardian—" he seemed extremely cautious of picking the right words "—couldn't *knowingly* do anything to harm the person he or she was protecting."

"I suppose that makes sense, *if* there were such a being. Zach, what's all this about—"

He held up a hand. The muscles supporting his neck grew taut. The color of his eyes faded to a dull, lusterless hue, drained of hope. "The thing is—" he lowered his voice to a whisper "—if an angel tried to help a person get back on her feet and make a new life . . . then that angel couldn't use the trust he'd been given to do something harmful to that person. Right?"

"If you're talking about our having sex, you weren't exactly raping me all those times, you know!" she snapped. "I had a lot to say about what was going on, Zach Dawson."

"I wasn't referring to that," he said wearily.

He had the look of a man who had given up everything that was dear to him. Suddenly his lack of willingness to continue the fight frightened her. "Zach, I've tried to be patient, tried to understand."

"I know you have. I know," he said sadly. "But I told you before…about your future… I'm not part of it, Caroline. I can *never* be part of it. Maybe I was fooling myself by letting this week happen the way it has. But I know that I—" he gazed off across the room as though seeing none of it, focusing, instead, on something beyond its walls "—let's just say I could never make you happy in the way you deserve. I can't give you what waits for you."

She swallowed, then swallowed a second time before she could speak. Her anger and pain formed the words her mind couldn't conceive. "At least be a man, Zach, and say what you really mean. It's not that you can't stay with me…you simply *won't* stay. You've made a choice."

"We can be friends . . . still," he said lamely.

If she hadn't been so hurt, his little boy appeal would have won her over in a second. "No, Zach. Not friends. Not anything." She turned toward the bed, scooped up her scattered clothing and stuffed it into the open suitcase. "You might as well stay the last day and enjoy the skiing. I've arranged for a flight home."

She slammed the case shut and took one last look around the room that had seemed so perfect and full of love only hours before. Now her eyes roamed it coldly, wishing she could extinguish every memory of it and what had happened there.

She seized her suitcase and slung her purse over one shoulder. "Goodbye, Zach."

Chapter 15

Caroline's words wounded Zach more deeply than any physical injury he'd endured during his mortal years. Desperately he wanted her to trust him, to believe, totally and without reservation, that he'd done all he possibly could to make her happy.

But he understood how difficult it must be for her, to accept him on faith. He could offer her no further explanation for his behavior. Meher's warning had been dangerously clear and unbending. As soon as Zach had attempted to suggest to Caroline anything about his role as an angel, the ominous tingling began in his heart, intensifying, threatening to remove him instantly from his Earthly mission. He'd had no choice but to give up and let Caroline walk away from him, still convinced that he was stringing her along like some jerk who didn't value her as the most wonderful, cherished gift a man could have.

As Zach turned from her room, stepping over splintery boards, he heard her speaking in a taut voice to someone in the hallway. "I'm afraid there was an accident. You'll need to send someone up to assess the damage and—"

He shut the remaining, undamaged door behind him, cutting off the silky voice that had cast a spell over him time and again, bringing him helplessly into her arms.

How had he let things get so out of hand? He'd honestly tried to follow Meher's mandate. But the Archangel hadn't given him nearly enough ammunition to use against a woman as strong-willed, or as beautiful and so full of love as Caroline North. If he'd been more detached, less attracted to her, maybe he'd have been able to concentrate on his job.

He'd always been able to take charge of his relationships with women. Paul had been right on target when he'd described Zane, his former self. He'd rarely exceeded a third date with the same woman because three dates could be friendly, no strings attached. After that, a woman started expecting things. So he never telephoned after #3. And if she called him, he found it easy enough to discourage her. Give her the cold shoulder for a week or two, mention other pressing engagements, let one of his neighbor's wives leave the greeting on his answering machine for a week or two... It never took his dates long to figure out he was ready to move on.

But none of those other women had done to his head and his heart what Caroline North had done. Somewhere along the way, they'd become friends, which was unheard of for him. Then they'd become lovers. And, slowly, the two relationships had blended, combining the best of both in a bond so strong he'd been unable to extricate himself from its silken web.

If only he'd been alive, everything might have worked out. It seemed ironic that the one time he'd fallen completely for a woman, he was helpless to keep her.

Zach sighed. Even worse, now he'd botched things so badly he couldn't even hover around the edges of her life in his mortal form and keep an eye on her. She wouldn't allow it. Yet somewhere, there was a man whom Caroline was supposed to marry... and it was still his duty to find the guy for her.

Zach crossed to the sliding glass window and looked across the glistening expanse of freshly fallen snow. The moon cast a pale glow across softly undulating drifts. "Meher," he whispered, "you've got to bring me back. I need a replacement, you must see that by now."

There was no answer. First Caroline, now an Archangel giving him the silent treatment.

"Come on, guy, it's pretty obvious this isn't working. I've blown it. I give up. You must have someone better qualified for this job!"

A twinge of pain in his chest chastised him. Zach held his hand to his breastbone and winced, feeling short of breath. "Okay, so I deserved that for being smart mouthed. Now bring me home."

"Have you earned the privilege of coming home?" a familiar voice rumbled close to his ear.

Zach swung around, but Meher wasn't there. "Earned it?" That must be part of the bargain. He had to do his job before he could reenter Heaven. "Give me another job. It doesn't have to be easier, just more up my alley. I'm real good with kids—older ones, that is. Babies scare the living daylights out of me. But give me a troubled teenager, some kid mixed up with the wrong crowd, drugs, crime . . . I'll straighten him out. Try me," he pleaded.

"No."

"No?" Was this it? Was he doomed to an existence wandering somewhere between life and death, never knowing peace?

"You know your duty," Meher stated. "Protect Caroline North from her own despair and find her the man who will love her beyond all others and father her child. And one other thing, Zachariah . . ."

"Yes?" Although he couldn't see how the situation could get any worse, he sensed Meher wasn't about to deliver good news.

"You are running out of time."

Zach frowned, as a wave of panic washed over him with as fierce an impact as the monster wave he'd created at Eastern Point. "I am?"

"Most certainly."

"Well, listen, if I do run out of time . . . what happens to me?" Then a worse thought struck him. "What happens to *Caroline?* I mean, she'll be okay, won't she? Nothing terrible will happen to her, will it?" He was angry suddenly. He wanted answers. "Dammit, she's suffered enough pain to last a lifetime. Can't you leave her alone? Stop meddling in her future. She's coming out of her depression. She's stronger than she was, I can tell. She'll make it on her own, if you just give her time."

Zach sensed that Meher had broken the link and left him before he'd finished speaking. He pressed his forehead against the cold glass of the door and shut his eyes, willing away the gnawing fear in his belly. He thought of Caroline.

What would happen to her, now that he had failed her? What would happen to the child she would never bear...to the world that would never benefit from the gifts that child had been destined to bring to humanity?

Anger is good, Caroline thought as she sat on the Allegheny Airline flight from Rutland, Vermont, to Groton, Connecticut. *It's damn good. A great deal healthier than curling up in a ball and shutting out the rest of the world, hoping painful memories will someday fade.*

In fact, after dealing with Zach, she felt ready to take on anyone and anything. The greater the challenge, the better she'd like it. Zach was, she decided as she glared at a passing cloud bank through the bleary square of glass beside her seat, an impossible man—no, not just impossible, he was a man with severe emotional problems, who undoubtedly needed professional help. She had neither the expertise nor the patience to wean him from his juvenile behavior patterns or his past. If he wasn't able to accept the possibility of a future with her, there was nothing she could do to force the issue.

So, that was that.

But no matter how hard she tried to dismiss him from her thoughts, Caroline continued a running monologue in her head on the exasperating thick-headedness and selfishness of men, in general, and Zach Dawson, in particular. As the plane bumped down the runway at Groton Municipal Airport, she congratulated herself on having rid herself of him. Riding Interstate 95 in the taxi, heading for Mystic, she amused herself by thinking up gruesome forms of torture for men like Zach, who used women, then tossed them away rather than commit to a serious relationship.

Just a few miles before her exit, the steady flow of traffic on the Interstate jammed up. Caroline sat, impatiently drumming her nails on the cracked vinyl seat cushion as the taxi edged forward a few feet at a time, and forced herself to think about something other than Zach. Her first thought was how harried Suzanne must have been all week, working some of the busiest shopping days of the year with only temporary help. All so that Caroline could relax and have a romantic vacation. Now, Suzanne's good intentions had been for nothing.

Caroline decided, when the cab finally reached the exit ramp, to go straight to the Silver Whale, since there seemed little point in stopping by the apartment. All she could do there was unpack, throw in a load of laundry, think about Vermont...and Zach. She didn't want to dwell any longer on her disappointment. *Some things in life, you can change,* she thought absently, *other things are beyond your control.*

From a distant corner of her soul, a tiny bell seemed to be ringing persistently, bringing her attention back to her own words. Change. Control. Some things, beyond...beyond... beyond...Little Jimmy, her darling baby...

The tragic direction of her thoughts brought her up short, and Caroline found herself breathing hard and fast. Her head spun. She cradled it in her palms, trying to grasp a truth her heart had understood but her brain had never fully accepted, until that moment.

The cab slowed, pulling onto the local road that followed the river and led past the seaport. Caroline sat, rigid on the seat, poking her finger into the jagged break in the vinyl beside her hip. She forced herself to take slower breaths, counted to fifty, concentrated on stuffing dirty clumps of upholstery back into the split cushion—until her pulse felt as if were almost back to normal.

Yes, that was the thing, wasn't it? *Life happens.* You can control certain details, sometimes only the smallest, most insignificant. But all your fine intentions and best efforts can't, ultimately, change what is meant to be. The best a person can do is deal as effectively as possible with the inevitabilities of life.

Just as she had to learn to deal with Jimmy's death.

Her baby had died. There was no going back. No second-guessing whether she could have been more cautious about his sleeping position. No wondering if she'd checked on him just one more time during the night, might she have found him at the very second his little heart faltered? Then, just by picking him up and rousing him at that fateful instant...might she have saved her child?

Caroline pressed her head harder into her palms. "Oh, Jimmy...I miss you so much," she whispered so low the cabby couldn't have heard above the rumble of the engine. And she wept silent tears, letting go of the blame she'd heaped on herself for more than twelve long months.

When the last tear had trickled down her cheek, she felt emotionally spent but strangely renewed. Caroline looked out the cab's side window at the passing houses, people bundled in warm coats and scarves against the cold, a school bus dropping off a bevy of squealing children. The world seemed clearer to her, strangely brighter, as if a dark veil had been drawn away from her eyes.

Five minutes later, the taxi pulled up in front of the row of pretty shops on Water Street—decorated in pine boughs and brilliant red velvet bows for the holidays. For a fleeting moment, Zach's handsome face swam before her. Did she have him, by some twisted logic, to thank for finally seeing the light at the end of her nightmare? No, she decided immediately, he was too self-involved to be thinking of her feelings. Too busy protecting his own secret wounds, whatever they might be.

"Here we are, miss," said the driver.

Caroline paid him, still lost in thoughts of Zach as she dragged her luggage out onto the sidewalk. He would remain a lonely man, sheltering himself from hurt by never allowing anyone to get too close to him. She should pity him, instead of harboring a grudge.

Taking a deep breath, Caroline hefted her bags and strode into the Silver Whale.

"Now," she told her reflection, as they passed each other, going through the glass door, "it's time to get on with life."

"I wish you'd come to the house and have Thanksgiving dinner with Ralph and me," Suzanne said for what seemed like the tenth time that day.

They'd planned to keep the Silver Whale open late, the day before Thanksgiving, although other years Caroline and Suzanne had closed early to go home to start their families' holiday cooking. This year, Suzanne and her husband were breaking with tradition and wouldn't be traveling to spend the day with his brother in Massachusetts, so there would be just the two of them to feed, at home. And Caroline was on her own for the first time in as long as she could remember. So there seemed no reason to shut the doors on eager shoppers.

"I think I'll pass on dinner," Caroline said. "Really. I'll be fine. You two don't have to entertain me."

Instead of offering yet another argument, Suzanne pressed her hand to her stomach and grimaced.

"What's wrong?" Caroline asked.

"Nothing. I haven't been feeling too well this week. Must be that Asian flu that's been going around." She waved off Caroline's concerns as they worked together all afternoon and into the evening.

Ralph telephoned at 6:30 p.m., to try to talk his wife into closing up early since she still was feeling sick, but Suzanne wouldn't hear of it. "With the business we're doing today?" she said into the receiver. "It would be like throwing money out the window. We'll need every cent."

Caroline thought about that one-sided conversation for the next few hours as she waited on customers. At 9:00 p.m., when they finally closed the doors and turned out the lights, she sacrificed tact to ask Suzanne about her comment.

"I wasn't aware that you and Ralph were having financial problems," she remarked as they pulled on their coats.

Suzanne frowned at her. "What are you talking about?"

"You told Ralph on the phone, you needed money."

"Oh?" Suzanne's face momentarily brightened, then a shadow passed over her eyes and she looked away from Caroline. "It's nothing. You know how I exaggerate."

Caroline quickly stepped toward her and touched her on the arm. "Come on, what's up? Does this have something to do with me?"

"No," Suzanne insisted, then let out a short dry laugh. "Far from it, actually."

"Then what's up?"

Suzanne sighed, picking up a lace doily from a pile of hand-crocheted items on an oak buffet. "I hadn't planned on telling you yet, not with all you've had to work out for yourself."

A sudden panic seized Caroline, twisting her insides. "What's wrong? You've been sick—it isn't anything more serious than the flu, is it?"

Suzanne lifted her soft, amber eyes to Caroline's. Her lips twitched in a shy smile. "No, not at all. I'm . . . I'm going to have a baby, Caroline. I'm pregnant."

The words seemed to float in the air, detached from all reality for several minutes. Then Caroline's mind slowly plucked them, one at a time, like ripe fruit in a fragrant orchard, and held them carefully in her heart. Six months ago, if Suzanne had come to her with this news, Caroline knew she'd have been devastated. To learn that her best friend was soon to hold the joy of new life in her body and in her arms, when that gift had been so cruelly torn from her, would have destroyed her.

But now...now things seemed inexplicably different. She felt the sting of her own disappointment, but it was made lighter, less painful in the light of her friend's joy.

"That's wonderful," she murmured, then on impulse reached out and hugged Suzanne fiercely to her. "I'm so happy for the two of you."

Suzanne hugged her back, then pressed her away and looked hard into her eyes. "You're sure you're okay about this? I mean, I really wanted to wait until after Christmas to tell you. I thought it would be much too hard to get used to the idea, with the holidays and all..."

"I'm fine," Caroline assured her. "I fully expect to be this baby's godmother, though. There will be hell to pay if you choose anyone else."

Suzanne grinned and squeezed her hand. "I wouldn't have it any other way. As long as you come for Thanksgiving..."

"That's outright blackmail!" Caroline cried.

"Yup."

Caroline smiled, blinking back tears of happiness. "Guess I'll just have to eat your old turkey."

That night, Caroline went home to her apartment. She unpacked her travel bags, loaded dirty clothes into the washer, threw in soap powder and started it up. She busied herself tidying up the apartment, more to burn nervous energy than to do any heavy cleaning. At last, she fixed herself a light snack to make up for the dinner she'd been too busy to eat at the shop. When she sat down at the kitchen table with the plate of sliced apples, cheddar cheese and crackers, she looked at the clock. It was 12:17 in the morning, and she knew she'd be awake for hours, too wound up with the day's happenings and Suzanne's news to be able to sleep.

She thought about Suzanne and Ralph, and wished them happiness. She thought about six days of making love and playing in the snow with Zach, and surprised herself by not feeling desperately sad. She thought about Jimmy... with a tender smile on her face.

Life goes on.

All we can do is put one foot in front of the other as fast as possible and hope we can keep pace, she thought philosophically. A sense of absolute peace closed around Caroline, as if strong arms had enveloped her—warming and comforting her. She let out a sigh and closed her eyes, enjoying the sensation without questioning its source.

With the night stretching out endlessly before her, Caroline broke out one of her rarely used cookbooks and began flipping pages, searching for traditional Thanksgiving fare. She took her time choosing from among the recipes. An old-fashioned pumpkin pie, decorated with crust cut outs of miniature turkeys. A fragrant loaf of cranberry-orange bread. Sugar cookies with a pecan half pressed into the center of each, just as her grandmother had baked for her as a child. Sweet potatoes candied in a maple-syrup glaze. Any of the recipes would add a festive touch to Suzanne's table, and she couldn't very well go empty-handed.

She decided to make all of them.

"Now, what are the odds I'll have the ingredients?" she muttered to herself.

At least she'd had the foresight, a couple of weeks earlier, to stock up on staples—flour, sugar, eggs, milk. And when cranberries had gone on sale, she'd bought a couple of bags and tossed them into her freezer, on the off chance she'd use them.

All she lacked was orange peel and brown sugar. She'd have to borrow them from a neighbor, she thought, and was outside her door in the hallway before she remembered the time. With a groan of exasperation, Caroline spun back around and was about to give up on the bread and sweet potatoes, when she noticed that Zach's door was slightly ajar.

A thin stream of light outlined the opening. Perhaps a stray orange lurked in Zach's fridge? But what was the chance a bachelor would keep brown sugar on hand?

She bit down on her lower lip, studying the crack between door and frame. She had been sure Zach would stay in Vermont for the remainder of their reservation. He had no reason to come back and waste a day of skiing he'd already paid for. Unless . . .

Caroline glanced toward the small window located at the end of the hallway, overlooking the parking lot. Racing down the hall, she peered through the frosty pane, into the night. Illuminated by the blue-white light of the parking lamps, she could make out her own car and some of her neighbors'. Zach's car wasn't among them. So, he *had* stayed in Vermont. Stayed and found someone else to share his fun in the snow . . . perhaps in his bed, too.

A quick shiver of regret was all she allowed herself, then she spun around and launched herself through his door. She wasn't about to look a gift horse in the mouth.

The apartment had the distinct feeling of deserted space. The only light came from the overhead globe in the foyer. Caroline closed the door behind her and walked in, looking around as she turned on other lights.

She'd only been in Zach's apartment a few times. They always seemed to end up somewhere in public together, or at her place. Now she took time to soak up his Spartan decor. The only furniture seemed to be the sort that was absolutely necessary. One couch placed opposite a television set, which was centered on a low, square table. A cheap dinette set of simple glass and wood construction. Four chairs with neutral upholstery, around the table. In the bedroom was a standard double bed, draped with a navy blue cord spread. The bathroom cabinet held toothpaste, deodorant, a comb, a package of disposable razors . . . nothing more.

It was as if Zach's entire life were temporary, arranged to accommodate an unanticipated departure. The thought made her incredibly sad, to think anyone could live like that, with absolutely no roots.

Shaking off her grim thoughts, she crossed quickly to the kitchen and opened the refrigerator. An opened carton of milk, the date expired, sat on the top shelf. There was a bottle of store-brand ketchup and jar of spicy brown mustard in the door rack. The only two other items sat in the middle of the center shelf. A box of brown sugar and a plastic bag containing two oranges.

She stared in amazement. What were the odds?

* * *

Zach hadn't taken long to make up his mind what he'd have to do. As soon as he saw the Killington courtesy bus pick up Caroline in front of the Greenbriar, he packed his gear, paid the manager for the damaged door and their stay and rushed out to the parking lot. Only then did it occur to him that he didn't have to take the conventional mode of transportation.

Besides, he felt that it was crucial he stay as close to Caroline as possible. There was no telling what her emotional state might be after their fight.

He stepped out of his mortal form as if he were mentally shedding his skin. The process seemed to be as simple as letting the idea of returning to his disembodied form cross his mind. Suddenly he was on an airplane, listening to Caroline's brain take vicious swipes at his character.

When she was in the cab on the last leg of her journey, driving up the highway from Groton to Mystic, he finally made his move. Gently, pervasively, he inserted his own thoughts between the shafts of her bitterness and disappointment. He eased her out of her rage and helped her remember the most painful moments of her life, in a new light.

Zach wondered why he hadn't been able to do this for her earlier, but decided it must have something to do with her own readiness to leave behind the guilt she'd been carrying around.

By the time the cab pulled up in front of the Silver Whale, she was calmer. The only thing he hadn't been able to do was make her see *him* in a positive light. She'd ended up pitying him, and that hurt... hurt deeply. But, he reasoned, how she felt about him was unimportant, as long as she reclaimed her own life and was able to open herself to the man in her future.

When she decided to bake that night, he unlatched his door and planted the missing ingredients for her. When she nearly forgot to pull the first batch of cookies out of the oven and they were on the verge of burning, he whispered in her ear and she immediately shot a glance at the clock over the oven and gasped, "They should be done!" When the pie was nearly ready to bake and he realized she'd forgotten the half teaspoon of ginger, he knocked the little canister off the kitchen counter. After picking it up she rechecked the recipe and blended in the right amount with a sigh of relief.

"Just wouldn't have tasted right without it," she murmured to herself with satisfaction.

He yearned to tenderly touch her again, from his mortal form. To feel her in his arms, one more time. But the most he dared was to hold her for a quick moment while she sat in her kitchen, letting her feel loved and comforted, anonymously. For he knew she'd never welcome him into her heart or her body again. Ever. And that regret, as much as any of his life, broke his heart.

Thanksgiving Day, Zach urgently wished he could shut himself away in the dark, empty apartment across the hall from Caroline's. But his duty was clear, and he had to make sure he didn't miss an opportunity to shepherd her toward her destiny.

Caroline baked and cooked through the night. At 6:30 a.m., Thanksgiving morning, she phoned Suzanne. "What time do you want me to come over?" she asked.

"Anytime after noon," Suzanne said, "and don't bother bringing anything."

"Too late." Caroline rattled off her contributions to the menu.

"Whoa! It's been a long time since you spent more than twenty minutes in a kitchen."

"I haven't had a reason for a long time," Caroline admitted. "I'll be over before one o'clock with the goodies."

She napped from seven to eleven, then rose to shower and dress in tartan-plaid wool slacks and a bright red sweater. She looked very Christmasy, Zach thought fondly, as if she were already looking forward to the next holiday.

He never let her out of his sight, not because he felt he had to protect her every step she took, but because something inside him warned that he'd be given only so many more opportunities to be with her, to watch the graceful way she drew a brush through her hair, to smile at her casually sexy, swinging walk . . . to hear her shriek, then laugh at herself when she nearly dropped a pie while loading the car with deliciously fragrant treats.

He longed to be the one who would spend every holiday with her, sharing her joy and laboring over the preparations, side by side with her. With every breath, he ached to hold her. He mourned her loss as surely as if she herself were soon to cross through death's door. He wondered if being together in an afterlife would be the best he could hope for, then immediately snatched back his silent wish to be reunited with her.

No, he wouldn't rob her of her future, even if it were the only way to keep her for himself.

"I can't believe you made all of this last night!" Ralph Godfrey exclaimed as he carried the loaf of cranberry-orange bread and an enormous tin of cookies into their house from Caroline's car.

She set the pumpkin pie on Suzanne's kitchen table. "I guess I just got carried away with the spirit of the season," she admitted, grinning at him.

He was a wonderful man—quite ordinary to look at. Not Suzanne's usual style of boyfriend. But Ralph had quietly and persistently wooed her away from her other, flashier admirers. He'd visited the Silver Whale almost every day, to browse or purchase a small item—usually a package of gourmet tea bags or one of the blank greeting cards. He invited her to summer evening concerts on the lawn at Connecticut College, or took her sailing on the Sound, or drove her into the country for a lazy picnic of wine, cheese and fruit. And they'd turned out to be the perfect match for each other.

Now they will raise a family together, Caroline thought, and once again felt a warm wave of appreciation for the steadfast man Suzanne had married. She looked across the living room at Suzanne, who wore a comfy-looking beige corduroy jumper over a turtleneck jersey dotted whimsically with tiny turkeys.

"Come on," Suzanne said. "I need help finishing up the vegetables, although heaven only knows how we're going to eat them with everything else we have here."

"You can survive on leftovers for the next week," Caroline said cheerfully. "You won't have to do any cooking."

When all the food was at last assembled on the table, they sat down and joined hands, and Ralph said a few words of thanks. They began eating, with very little conversation. After a while, Suzanne spoke hesitantly about their baby, asking Caroline's advice about making over the guest room into a nursery, as she ladled more gravy over her mashed potatoes.

At first, Caroline felt a twinge of sorrow, but she encouraged Suzanne and Ralph to talk about plans for their family. The bitterness and grief she'd suffered for so long were overshadowed by their joy. She was honestly thrilled for them.

But other feelings seemed to be working on her, and she had more trouble sorting these out. Throughout the meal, Caroline felt a warm presence hovering in the room, as if she weren't the only guest sharing the table with her friends. When Ralph had said grace, she'd automatically reached across the white linen table-cloth toward the fourth, empty chair.

She couldn't imagine what she'd been thinking—certainly not that she missed Rob, who had sat with them at this same table for other meals. But as her hand stretched across the corner of crisp white linen, she could almost... *almost* feel a hand close around hers. And later, when she tuned out Suzanne's happy chatter, she thought she could hear a deep voice repeating, "It's all right now. You're going to be fine." And she believed it.

Outside, the sky grew gray. It began to rain, then turned to sleet. They ate and chatted until they all proclaimed they'd have no room for pie if they consumed one more bite. Ralph turned on the football games while they all three cleared the table, covered leftovers for the refrigerator, and loaded up the dishwasher. Suzanne brought the pumpkin pie out to the dining room. Ralph carried in dessert plates and forks. Caroline was in the kitchen, getting the whipped cream out of the refrigerator when there was a knock on the front door.

"You should have told your other guests to come on time!" she shouted toward the dining room. "They've missed the main course!"

Suzanne and Ralph laughed from the other room, then she heard the front door creak open.

"Probably just some kids selling Christmas cards," Caroline muttered to herself as she squirted a dollop of whipped cream onto her fingertip and licked it off. "Smart. Folks are home today and—"

Her ears pricked up at the sound of Ralph's voice, rising in irritation. Then Suzanne said something muffled, urgent.

Caroline froze and listened harder. There was a third voice—a man's.

Good Lord, please don't let it be Zach! she thought frantically.

She didn't want to see him, couldn't bear the thought of having to face him. Her carefree mood ruined, she slammed the can of whipped cream down on the counter and waited, praying Ralph would have the good sense to turn Zach away. If he didn't . . . She looked around the kitchen, realizing she was cornered. The only door led into the dining room, which opened straight to the foyer.

"Hey, listen," Ralph called out, no longer muffling his words, "she won't want to see you." Heavy footsteps scuffed across the parquet flooring of the foyer, and Caroline tensed as Ralph shouted. "Can't you do this through your lawyer? Give her a break."

Caroline backed up two steps, her hips bumping against the countertop, and gripped the molded edge so hard her knuckles ached. Her mouth went dry, and she sucked in an audible breath. The instant before the kitchen door swung open, she knew it wasn't Zach who'd crashed their Thanksgiving.

Robert Erik North stood in front of her, his hands on his hips, a quizzical expression on his face as he observed her.

Rob wore a suit, as if he'd just come from work or was on his way to church—although neither was probably true. He rarely donned anything as casual as Dockers; she'd never seen him in a pair of jeans. He was, she realized, somewhat shorter than she'd remembered him, and wider in a plumpish, nonmuscular sort of way. She wondered why she'd pictured him in the months after he'd left her as towering over her—a threatening figure accusing her of unwittingly killing their son. He was, in actuality, only three inches taller than she. His face was a mild expanse, centered by two dark eyes that sometimes seemed a muddy brown but were nearly black with frustration now. He'd grown a thin mustache. She thought he looked ridiculous in it.

Caroline felt something like a large, warm hand settle on her left shoulder. She could actually feel the reassuring weight of it, and the gentle indentations made by each of the fingers. She turned to see who it was before it dawned on her that she was still backed up against the countertop, and there was no room for anyone to stand behind her, and no one could have come into the kitchen without her seeing him, since she was facing the only door.

My imagination's run amok, she thought vaguely. It must have been the shock of seeing Rob after such a long time.

Rob looked at her, and frowned. "I thought from the reception I got at the door, I'd find you schlepping around in your bathrobe and curlers, or something." He chuckled, and she remembered how that tight, critical cackle of his had always made her feel small and unimportant.

A voice whispered from somewhere inside her, *You can do this. He's no longer part of your life. Tell him to go away.*

"No, I generally get dressed and run a comb through my hair before visiting friends for the holidays." She tipped her nose up at him, observing him a good deal more coolly than she'd imagined she ever would be able to do. "Rob, I don't know why you came here today, but I think you should leave. Suzanne, Ralph, and I are having a nice day together. It's rude to burst in like this on them."

As if they'd been listening at the door, Suzanne and her husband stepped into the kitchen.

"You heard her," Ralph said, flashing Rob a warning look that left no room for interpretation. "You'd better leave."

"You've got a lot of nerve showing up like this, after a year," Suzanne added stiffly.

But Rob didn't seem to be listening. He was staring at Caroline, his eyes slowly narrowing by fractions of an inch, as if he couldn't figure out what was different about her. "You have a tan," he said at last.

Caroline blinked in surprise. She supposed she did, after skiing for a week with a brilliant sun reflecting off the snow. "So?"

He shifted from one wing-tipped oxford to the other. "You must have flown south for a while. Florida, was it? Or did you book one of those island-hopping cruises?" He peered at her cagily. "Go alone, did you?"

A blur of beige corduroy rushed at Rob and, at first, Caroline didn't realize his attacker was her normally reserved partner. Suzanne pushed her face into Rob's then shoved him with both hands in the chest, knocking him off his heels. "What right do you have poking your nose into her private life—after what you did to her? Go away and leave her alone!"

Ralph was quickly at his wife's side, trying to slip a restraining arm around her.

Suzanne shoved Rob away and punctuated her sentences by jabbing her finger repeatedly at him. "Caroline can *do* whatever she *likes,* Robert. She *doesn't* have to answer to *you.*"

Caroline started to speak, but Suzanne held up a silencing hand.

An evil gleam lit her pretty amber eyes. "But since you're so curious, *I* can tell you she's just come back from a skiing week with a total hunk. And, if I were you, I wouldn't bet on their spending *all* of their time on the trails!"

"Enough, Suzy," Ralph warned. "Let them work it out. Come on, you'll just get yourself upset. It's not good for you or the baby." He turned toward Rob as he forcibly maneuvered his wife out of the kitchen. "Five minutes, North. Then you're out of here. I mean it," he added darkly.

Rob stared after the couple as if they were inmates in an asylum. When they were gone, he let out an amused chortle. "Talk about overreacting. What got into them?"

Caroline glared levelly at him. "They're my friends. They don't want to see me hurt again."

"Hurt?" Rob shook his head. "You sure seem to have sprung back—shacking up with some guy in the mountains, huh? Not the way a wife should be acting, if you ask me."

Caroline's mouth dropped open. "Wife?"

"Well, sure—we're still married, aren't we?"

She squinted at him. "Only technically. It seems to me you ended that episode of our lives when you walked out on me."

It had happened suddenly, but not unexpectedly. Rob came home one day, took two suitcases out of the closet and threw in his clothes, announcing he couldn't tolerate living with her after what she'd done to their lives. She hadn't heard a word from him for two weeks, then he left a message on her answering machine, saying he would come by one day while she was at the shop and pick up his TV and VCR. She could keep the furniture.

A month later, one of her regular customers mentioned she'd seen him in Norwich, a town about thirty miles north of Mystic, and thought he'd taken an apartment there. Since then, she'd heard nothing from him or about him.

And now, here he stood.

She'd often wondered what her reaction would be to running into him again. Now she knew. Every bone in her body vibrated with loathing for him. She itched to walk out of the room, end the conversation right then. But he must have had a reason for coming, and that made her curious.

"So," she said in a controlled tone, "what really brought you here, Rob? Not the hope of turkey and cranberry sauce, I'd guess."

He touched one side of his mustache in a self-conscious gesture and took a legal-size envelope out of his overcoat pocket. Holding it toward her, he stated coolly, "I've brought the papers for our divorce. They're all ready for you to sign. Knowing how you are, I thought you'd be pretty emotional about this sort of thing, so I didn't want to bring them to the shop."

You arrogant jerk! she thought. *Knowing how I am . . .* Had he ever really known her? Or cared to understand her feelings?

Nevertheless, his announcement took her breath away, if only for an instant. Then she was left with an overwhelming sense of relief—because a part of her life, a very painful part, was about to end . . . with the signing of those papers in his hand.

"Well, that's really thoughtful of you," Caroline said dryly. She reached out to take the envelope. "I'll read them tonight. If everything looks okay, I'll sign the agreement and get it back to you within two days. Fair enough?"

Rob studied her expression, as if wary of a trap. Slowly he pulled back his hand, still holding the manila rectangle. "There's something really different about you," he muttered, looking worried.

"Maybe it has something to do with my not letting you walk all over me anymore."

"Now, Caroline, you make me sound like a beast. I was just as hurt by Jimmy's—"

"Don't you *dare* mention our son!" she roared, lurching toward him, her fists clenched in front of her like a prize fighter's. "He's not going to be used as a bargaining chip. You wanted a divorce a year ago and you walked out on me. You made your wishes very clear. Well, I've gone on with my life—"

As soon as the words came out of her mouth, she was shocked to discover they were true. Only a few months earlier, she'd never have been able to say that to him or anyone else. But Zach had forced her to come out of the past and look toward the future, with his silly insistence on setting her up with men and looking at life through different eyes. He'd told her she had a wonderful future to look forward to, while others advised in pitying tones that she'd forget, in time. But she knew she never would forget Jimmy or the pain of losing him and seeing her marriage, however mediocre it had been, crumble in the days following her son's death. Zach had comforted her, accepted her grief as something she'd always carry with her, then firmly pointed her in the direction of the future. It had been the right thing to do for her, she now realized.

"All right, all right," Rob said with exaggerated reasonableness. "I just want you to admit, there are two sides to every argument."

"It was far more than an argument that broke us up, Rob. But I doubt you'll ever understand that." Caroline's skin prickled with anger, but the sensation felt wonderful to her, empowering her. She could say anything she wished, and there was nothing Rob could do about it. He no longer had any control over her. None. "You left me because you wanted to, Rob," she stated flatly. "Jimmy was just a convenient excuse."

He ducked his head and studied the envelope, turning it over and over in his fingers. "Look, maybe now isn't a good time for us to do this. I thought I'd just have you sign this and leave, but you're hysterical, you obviously can't handle this now." He quickly pocketed the envelope.

Caroline glared at him. "I'm not *hysterical*. I'm as rational as I've ever been. And if you think there's any chance of us getting back together, you're dead wrong."

His black-brown eyes drifted up over her, beneath slightly lowered lids, and she thought in horror, *My God, I know that look. He's turned on. He's excited because I'm standing up for myself.*

"Maybe you're right," he murmured, granting her a lopsided smile. "But we shouldn't do anything rash. Why don't we give ourselves a few days to cool down, then we can talk."

"No." She bit off the word. "Nothing's going to change."

He licked his lips and rolled his eyes around the room, as if searching for the magic words. "If we were back together, we could have another bab—"

Her fiery glare choked off the word before he could finish it.

"Well, like I said—we'll talk later." He turned as if to leave.

Caroline stepped forward, feeling strong, resolved, and even more intensely than earlier that day that she wasn't alone. "Wait, Rob."

He turned at the sound of his name, a hopeful look in his muddy eyes. "Yeah, Carrie?"

Cringing at his unwelcome familiarity, she forced herself to finish her speech. "If I don't receive the divorce papers within two days, I'll have my own lawyer draw up the necessary documents. I guarantee, they won't be as favorable to you as whatever you have in your pocket."

Chapter 16

The four and a half weeks between Thanksgiving and Christmas rushed past Caroline. She felt as if she were in the middle of an Impressionist painting—the colors of her life running together, suggesting real images but never quite succeeding in creating believable surroundings. Monet would have loved her days and nights.

She worked nearly round-the-clock at the Silver Whale. Business had never been better, and for that she was grateful. But there were days when Suzanne seemed capable of little more than throwing up between customers, and Caroline felt guilty for not being able to handle the shop entirely on her own, so that she could send her business partner home for desperately needed bed rest.

Rob called Caroline one night, at the apartment, hinting that he'd like to come over for a drink. "Before either of us signs anything we might regret, I think we should talk," he told her in his most rational voice. "I can bring over some Chinese tonight. We could just relax and talk things through."

How had he forgotten, she wondered, that some things couldn't be worked out? Such as the loss of their son, or the fact he himself had destroyed their marriage by blaming her for Jimmy's death?

"We've had a year to work things out, if either of us had wanted to," she reminded him quietly. "Quite frankly, Rob, I don't believe I ever considered reconciling with you."

"No?"

"No. Perhaps you did both of us a favor when you left. It left no question as to the limits of our relationship."

"We're still married," he said, sounding wounded. "You have no right sleeping with other men."

She hung up on him. There had never been a way to win an argument with Rob. He'd always been able to turn a situation around, lay the blame at her feet. The rules of the game hadn't changed, at least in his mind.

But experience had taught her that Rob often had a hidden agenda. So, when a mutual friend dropped in on her at the shop a few days after his call and told her she knew that Rob had been living with a woman in Norwich for at least six months, but she'd recently left him, then Rob's sudden attempts at reconciliation made at least some sense.

Meanwhile, Caroline was true to her word. She asked her lawyer to draw up the divorce papers and sent them off to Rob to sign.

She also kept an eye on Zach's apartment for any sign of his return. Although no one new moved in and his furniture remained—or, at least, she didn't see it being hauled away by a moving company—there was no sign of Zach.

During the few slack minutes of the day at the shop, she'd think of him then kick herself for allowing herself to daydream. Invariably her memories wandered tenderly across the moments they'd spent together. Sometimes Suzanne caught her in the act.

"I can always tell when you're thinking about him," she said, draping an arm around her shoulders. "You get that distant look in your eyes. Where are you? Back up in Vermont?"

"Sometimes," Caroline admitted. "Other times I just remember how much fun he was, doing ordinary things. Like shopping for my dress or playing tennis."

"You're still in love with him," Suzanne stated, as confidently as if she were pointing out that the sky was blue and the earth was round.

"I suppose I am," Caroline admitted with a wistful sigh. "But a one-sided love doesn't work."

Suzanne looked at her, then her eyes drifted for a moment, as if she were listening to distant music, trying to pick out the melody. "I—I don't know how I could know this," she said slowly, "but something tells me, Zach cared more for you than he could tell you."

Caroline stared at her. "That doesn't sound like you at all."

"I know," Suzanne admitted with a shrug, "I'm not what you'd call a blazing romantic. But it's what I felt inside me, when you said your love was one-sided. Maybe Zach loved you as much as you loved him."

"Well, he's gone now," Caroline whispered.

But, somehow, Zach's absence didn't feel total. At night, when Caroline dragged herself home, exhausted from the mad assault of holiday shoppers on her little shop, she made herself a carafe of hot herb tea. She'd set the bright red thermal jug beside her while she flicked cable channels, searching for any amusing program to take her mind off the day's craziness. There, in the quiet familiarity of her own apartment, a steaming, fragrant mug cupped in her hands, the TV providing a wall of background noise, she was most conscious of Zach's memory . . . which seemed so real it was almost a presence.

At first, his intrusion into the privacy of her life was irritating, keeping her from being able to totally relax. But gradually, night after night, Caroline found that if she didn't fight the sensation of his nearness, thinking about him soothed her.

Sometimes when she closed her eyes and imagined Zach in the room with her, she felt as though his strong fingers were kneading the stress from knotted muscles of her shoulders and the back of her neck, or massaging the aching soles of her feet.

He was there—in her body and in her soul. And she didn't know how one man had so indelibly left his mark on her. Even when she desperately needed to hate him for not wanting to keep her with him forever, she couldn't feel anything but thankful that he'd stepped into her life for the short while he'd been there.

It was while cherishing that thought she usually dropped off to sleep each night. Sometimes she was already in her bed, her head resting on one pillow, the other tucked into her chest and stomach, where Zach had lain, his long, muscled back pressed into her. Sometimes, she was lying on the couch with the TV still on. On a few mornings, she awoke, unsure where she was until her eyes adjusted to the early-morning light and revealed the rosebuds on her bedroom wallpaper. She couldn't remember having walked from the living room to the bedroom, although she must have. Then the feeling that she was wrapped in strong arms slowly left her and she launched herself into another day of dealing with holiday shoppers.

Zach realized he was stalling. In the weeks following their trip to Killington, he had stayed close to Caroline, telling himself that he was working on a new strategy to get her together with the man she would marry. Finally, one night, not long before Christmas, he faced the fact that he really must settle down to business.

Zach watched Caroline prop a bed pillow behind her head, lifting her soft, brown hair away from her neck and across the pillowcase. She cracked open a novel she'd brought home from the library, and settled comfortably in her nest of sheets and blankets that smelled of her perfume and, intoxicatingly, of her flesh. He felt the need within him rise again, as it did every night. He knew he wouldn't rest, even in his disembodied state, until he'd folded himself around her, giving to her the warmth of his love—although he could ask nothing in return. He came closer to her and spent long minutes soaking in her feminine essence. Her eyes focused on the book, and occasionally she turned a page, but her glance often wandered, and he wondered if she actually felt him standing there, watching her.

"You have nothing to worry about," he told her, as he often did in the quiet hours of the night. "You will have another child, and this time your husband will love you deeply, and stand by you."

She blinked then smiled softly, as if she'd heard him and understood.

At first, she'd stubbornly blocked out his messages, refusing to let him into her heart. But she'd grown more receptive each time he'd sent her his thoughts.

Sometimes he knelt on the carpet beside the couch as she stretched out on it. Gently, so gently, he'd run invisible hands over her body, until he felt individual muscles relinquish their hold on her. When she lay limp, totally relaxed, she'd close her eyes and smile, looking so beautiful his insides would melt.

Often, when she shut her eyes, he'd wait for her breathing to even out, signaling she'd drifted off to sleep. Then he'd lie down beside her on the cushions and allow himself to recall the places and ways he'd touched her as they'd made love...the sparks in her eyes when they reached their climaxes together...the kittenish sounds of contentment that issued from low in her throat when she curled up, satisfied in his arms, after they'd made love. And his heart would ache, because he knew that soon, very soon, he'd not even be able to touch her through his spirit fingers. Once his job was finished, Meher wouldn't allow him to visit her or follow the ups and downs of her life. Zach knew he'd never see her child, never watch her cradle it tenderly in her arms or witness the joy in her eyes.

That night, he waited until she was sound asleep on the couch, then he lowered himself over her, pressing his spirit form above her like a warm blanket. She stirred beneath him, smiled dreamily and whispered, "Za-a-a-ch."

"Yes," he replied. "It's me."

He wasn't sure she'd heard him, but she stirred slightly, and gracefully lifted her arms, as if to embrace him. Her arms lapped over and through him, coming to rest on her own chest.

"More than anything in the world," he whispered into the sweet curve of her ear, "I want to make love to you one more time. One more time to last for an eternity."

She murmured something unintelligible and lengthened her body as if she were responding to his words.

"I promise," he said, looking up at the ceiling, half expecting Meher to be glaring down at him with grim disapproval. "Tomorrow I'll bring her a man I know she'll like. But I believe with all of my heart that we *both* need this. If I'm wrong, stop me. Stop me now.''

He waited, fear clutching at him. But nothing happened.

He took Meher's lack of response as his blessing, and hoped he was right.

Moving away from Caroline, Zach willed himself to take on his physical form. It took the blink of an eye, no more. He looked down at himself, naked. Of course. He wouldn't have imagined himself clothed at a moment like this.

If Caroline woke up, he wondered what she might say or do. But she was deeply asleep, so tired from weeks of hard work and too little rest, nothing short of an earthquake would likely interrupt her slumber.

Zach effortlessly lifted her and carried her from the living room, down the short hallway and into her bedroom. She hadn't made up the bed that morning. He laid her, still sleeping, in the nest of mussed sheets then took his time—breathing soft words of love into her ear as he moved aside the terry-cloth lapel of her robe to kiss the velvety mounds of her breasts, working his way downward with tender dedication as he pressed his lips to her navel, the firm flesh over her belly . . . then lower, to her most intimate self . . . until she moaned with pleasure. He watched her face for any sign of awakening, but her eyes remained closed. If she was conscious, it was only half so, yet she reacted completely and intensely each time he touched her.

Zach gave her time to build toward and sink away from her climaxes, then build again. When he knew she was ready, he pressed himself into her and felt her shudders of delight even as he released himself within her for what he knew must be the last time.

Caroline awoke the next morning feeling as if she'd had the most marvelous dream. She could remember no details, only a sense that whatever had happened during her unconscious moments, she felt perfectly at one with herself and cherished. She floated through her early routine of showering and dressing for the shop. Her body was bursting with energy she hadn't possessed in weeks.

"How is Mother Suzanne feeling today?" Caroline asked when she arrived at the Silver Whale.

"About as lively as the burnt toast that was all I could keep down this morning," Suzanne groaned. She shook her head. "I know this morning sickness will have been worth it when the baby comes, but I'd rather just skip to the chase."

"You still have a long way to go." Caroline patted her on the back compassionately.

"Now that's a cheery thought," Suzanne sighed.

"Hey, once the morning sickness phase passes, you'll feel a lot better."

"Good." Suzanne squinted at her. "You sure look on top of the world today. Has the Christmas spirit finally gotten to you?"

"For some reason, I slept especially well last night." But she suspected it was more than that.

The dream, whatever it had been about, had been tauntingly impossible to recall in detail. But as the day wore on, delicious snatches drifted back to her.

A sensation of being lifted and carried...of a man's strong arms protecting her, his hands on her body, all over her body...arousing her...satisfying her deeply...

She shivered at the memory, then caught Suzanne staring at her across the counter. "It's chilly in here today," Caroline said, and put on a sweater to cover for her strange reaction.

There was no doubt in her mind that Zach had been the man in her dream. But how real his touch had seemed! Had it been just the sheets, the pillows, maybe even her own touch against her flesh that had driven her to ecstasy in her sleep?

She couldn't make herself believe that. Yet what other explanation could there be? And why, even after other details came to her, didn't she remember walking from the couch to her bed? Had fatigue taken so great a toll on her?

They worked steadily throughout the day, neither of them taking time out for lunch. At 5:00 p.m., Caroline finally sent Suzanne home. "You shouldn't push yourself so hard while you're trying to adjust to carrying a baby," she told her. "I can handle the last few hours with our temps."

It was almost closing time when the bell over the shop's door tinkled prettily and she looked up from the mail order she'd been wrapping to see a tall man wearing a leather jacket and a smart wool cap step through the door.

"May I help you?" she asked.

"I—I'm not sure," he said. "I was walking down the street, on the way to the bakery to buy my sister some rolls and a pie for tomorrow's dinner, when I stopped in front of your shop."

"And?"

"And something told me I had to come in."

He looked so handsomely dazed she couldn't help smiling at him. If she hadn't known better, she'd have guessed Zach was at work again, trying to set her up. But she hadn't seen Zach since she left him in Killington, and Christmas was just around the corner.

"Why don't you look around and see if there's anything that appeals to you," she suggested.

"I already see something that appeals," the man said, then looked as if he regretted being so outspoken. "But I'm darn sure she's not for sale," he added quickly. "Listen, I'm sorry to bother you. I can see you're very busy. I'll leave you to your paying customers."

Touching the brim of his cap, he turned to leave.

"Wait!" Caroline shouted, then felt herself blush. "I'm going to be closing up in twenty minutes. If your sister doesn't mind you showing up a little late for dinner, maybe we could have a drink."

His smile broadened. "I think I'll call her and cancel."

Zach thumped a fist on the sales counter, just missing a display of crystal unicorns. He shut his eyes, blocking out the scene in front of him. Ray Symons was a good man, a lonely man who was ready to marry and be a good father and husband. He wasn't rich, but he was financially stable. Zach knew he'd be attracted to Caroline, and she'd like him.

All the basic equations worked, so Zach had steered Ray through the door of her shop and let nature take its course.

He should have been happy when they instantly hit it off, should have been thankful that he was finally nearing the end of his mission. He could feel encouraging vibrations between the two of them as they flirted casually.

"Now let me come home," he begged Meher. "I've done what you asked. Ray's the one, right? He'll take care of her. Don't make me hang around and watch him court her. Please!"

But Meher didn't answer, and Zach was still Earthbound.

Zach paced the wooden planks of the Silver Whale, trying to tune out Caroline's and Ray's friendly banter. He couldn't believe that anything this stranger might feel for Caroline could be a fraction of what he felt for her. But maybe that was how he'd view any man who was attracted to Caroline. None of them would be good enough for her.

Why should he be so possessive of her? Was it simple male ego? The pride inside that told him no other man could make Caroline as happy as he'd been able to make her?

But that was ludicrous. He was dead. And she had a long life to live.

Zach watched them cross the street and enter the pub on the other side. He stayed outside, and it started to rain. He waited, unwilling to witness them warming up to each other. The pain of losing her was deep and dark, a reflection of the night, which was blowing into a hearty Nor'easter.

Curtains of gray rain sluiced the streets. Even though he was without a body and impervious to weather, Zach moved closer to the pub and, out of habit, stood under the awning. Caroline and Ray sat near the window, a candle on their table, talking easily. If Zach had wanted to, he could have listened in on their conversation. But he couldn't force himself to take more punishment. His heart was breaking, and he asked again that Meher allow him to return to Heaven and give him another assignment. Mercifully one that would wipe away every sweet memory of Caroline so that the pain would stop.

But nothing happened, and he waited and waited, torn between keeping Caroline in sight to be sure she was safe with Ray, and slinking back to his apartment, alone again with his misery.

At last they came out.

"I can't believe I fell for that old one," Caroline gasped, tears in her eyes she was laughing so hard.

"Oh great," Zach muttered. "He not only looks like a *GQ* model, he tells great jokes."

Ray held the door open for Caroline then clicked open his umbrella and raised it over her head. The wind rocked them both, and Ray put an arm around Caroline's waist to steady her as they moved onto the sidewalk, toward the street. They were laughing and shouting over the gusts, paying more attention to each other than to anything around them.

Although the wind whipped and whistled up the narrow street, Zach heard the unmistakable rumble of a car engine. He looked up to see an older model sedan moving haltingly down the street, as if the driver was having trouble seeing through the rain.

As the vehicle came closer, Zach could make out a white-haired woman in the driver's seat, peering through the windshield. The top of her head was barely visible above the steering wheel.

Caroline and Ray stepped off the curb, into the marked crosswalk, but the woman didn't slow down. Intuitively, Zach knew what was going to happen.

Don't let her hit them! he thought. But the car seemed to speed up rather than brake.

Making himself visible, he leapt directly in front of the vehicle. The bumper shot forward, striking him in the knees, tossing him up onto the hood of the car. His body smashed into the windshield, and he felt as if every bone in him had shattered.

Through his pain, Zach could hear screeching tires, Caroline's scream, and Ray shouting, "Watch out!"

The car swerved to a stop, and he fell off the side of the hood and lay on the ground. He lifted his head just enough to see that Caroline had reached the opposite sidewalk safely and Ray was shielding her view by putting himself between her and the accident scene.

Only then did Zach think himself back to his invisible state. The pain miraculously stopped, and he stepped away from the car to watch what would happen next, wanting to make certain everyone was all right.

"Are you okay?" Ray asked Caroline.

She nodded. "You?"

"Fine." He scratched his head. "Must have awful good brakes. It was almost as if that car hit a wall, the way it stopped so suddenly. It missed us by no more than six feet."

"Felt more like six inches," Caroline gasped. She looked around. "Was anyone hurt?"

Zach waited nervously as the elderly driver was helped from her car by two passersby. She looked around with a horrified expression as a crowd gathered around her in the rain. She began sobbing and wailing incoherently.

Caroline was watching her, concern growing on her face. She reached out and stopped a man who'd just walked past the car. "What is she talking about? We're okay."

He shook his head. "She says she hit a man. She ran into him and he smashed into her windshield. She was sure she'd killed him."

Caroline looked up at Ray. "Did you see a man get hit?"

He shook his head, then scanned the street around them. "No, and there's no sign of anyone having been hurt. Poor old thing, she's in a state of shock, probably hallucinating."

Caroline nodded and smiled faintly up at Ray. Her eyes sparkled in the rain, and Zach thought she looked as beautiful at that moment as he'd ever seen her. "Someone once told me about guardian angels," she murmured. "I feel as if mine must have been pretty close by tonight."

Christmas came and left, and it was a happier time than Caroline had expected it could ever be. Ray was attentive and brought her gifts on Christmas Eve and again on Christmas day. Suzanne and Ralph glowed with the anticipation that the following year they would be three for Christmas. The shop was doing wonderful business. And although Caroline decided against spending the holiday with her mother, brother, or sister, they talked on the telephone, and the news that year was all happy.

But as January began, Caroline began to feel uneasy about the way her relationship with Ray was developing. In the beginning he'd seemed almost too perfect—great looking, polite, intelligent but with a charming sense of humor, never objecting to anything she said or did, always trying to please her. But as time went on he began finding small ways to control her. She suggested they go skiing at a local resort, and he said the sport was much too dangerous. She expressed an interest in taking a cruise, but he felt cruises were overrated and overpriced, and besides several lines had recently failed health department inspections. She took up jogging to counteract the extra calories she was consuming since they were dining out so often, but he warned her against winter runs when glare-ice might take her by surprise.

"I know he means well," she told Suzanne, "but he's smothering me!"

"Why don't you just tell him how you feel."

"I should. I know," Caroline admitted. She sighed. "It's strange, but in a way I feel more lonely now, with a boyfriend, than I felt while I was alone and Zach lived across the hall."

Suzanne shook her head. "You haven't forgotten him, have you?"

"No, I guess not. There are days when I feel as if all I'd have to do is call his name, and he'd be there."

"Go talk to Ray. Better yet, the two of you should make love all night long. That will chase away the Zach memories."

Caroline laughed self-consciously. "Maybe we'll do that."

She hadn't told Suzanne that she and Ray had never made love. Maybe, Caroline thought, that was the real cause of the friction she felt building between them. The problem was, no matter how often Ray had expressed an interest in sleeping with her, she had never felt right about being intimate with him. He was a nice man and fun to be with. But she didn't long for him the way she'd longed for Zach since she left him at Killington.

A week later, Caroline broke up with Ray.

"I knew it was coming," he told her, sounding only a little sad. "We just never got past the point of being friends."

"Being friends is the best way to start," she agreed, diplomatically. She didn't feel it necessary to tell him that he hadn't, in her estimation, even crossed the friendship hurdle.

"But you're looking for something more," he said, hugging her goodbye. "I understand."

Actually her reason for breaking up with Ray had nothing to do with wanting someone different in her life. She'd intentionally distanced herself from dating several weeks earlier when her body started sending her warning signals that something was amiss.

On the morning of Superbowl Sunday, Caroline cornered Suzanne while they were preparing snack trays for the party Ralph and Suzanne were throwing later that day.

"My period's late," she said as soon as Ralph left the kitchen.

Suzanne stared at her. "Ray?"

"No, that's impossible."

"Then who?"

"Zach. It can only be him."

Suzanne's mouth opened and closed several times before it formed distinguishable words. "Then you must be at least two months along."

Caroline sighed. "I'm not sure. December was so hectic. I was sure I had my period, but I didn't mark it on my calendar as I usually do."

"But it must have happened when you were in Vermont, because you haven't seen him since. Right?"

"Right."

"That's two months by my figuring. You'd better get yourself to your gyn."

"I'm going to take a home test tonight," Caroline assured her. "If it's positive, then I'll call for an appointment."

That night, Caroline stopped by the drugstore and bought a pregnancy test, even though she kept telling herself she must be wrong. Zach knew how afraid she was of getting pregnant, and he'd been conscientious about protecting her. Condoms rarely failed, she knew, but if they did it was usually because they tore or slipped off at an inopportune moment. Nothing like that had happened, so she couldn't see how he could have impregnated her.

Besides, the timing was all wrong. The more Caroline thought about her situation, the surer she was that she'd had her December period. She remembered feeling out of sorts for a couple of days, recalled taking a very hot shower one night, letting steaming water run down her back. Hadn't that been to relieve cramps?

So how in heaven's name had she gotten pregnant? she asked herself as she waited for the results of her test.

* * *

Zach waited outside the bathroom, pacing while Caroline ran the home pregnancy test. He wanted to be in there with her, to prove to himself immediately that she was wrong. But he was pretty sure that, if she sensed he was watching her, she would feel self-conscious, so he allowed her her privacy.

Five minutes later, she rushed out of the bathroom, her cheeks colorless, her eyes glazed. He rushed in and peered at the little strip of paper she'd discarded in the trash basket. Pink. He picked up the box and read the directions.

"Pink," he muttered, "positive reading."

She was pregnant. Lord help him. She was pregnant. And he didn't have to ask her to know that there was only one possible father. Him.

Chapter 17

Caroline observed Dr. Maggie Mason across the obstetrician's desk. "I don't understand," she said finally.

"To put it another way, I'd be very surprised if you were sixty days along. More than likely you're just a month into your pregnancy—but there's no doubt, you are pregnant."

"That's impossible," Caroline objected. "Just a month?"

Dr. Mason shrugged her slim shoulders. She chose brightly colored dresses for her days in the office over the traditional antiseptic-white smock. Maggie had delivered Jimmy, and stood beside her three months later in the same hospital on the darkest day of her life. They had been friends ever since.

"I've been wrong before, Caroline. I'm just giving you my professional opinion." Maggie leaned toward her, over the cluttered desk. "You must have suspected, since you came to me. Have you given any thought to what you want to do?"

Caroline stared blankly at her for a fistful of rapid heartbeats before it occurred to her that Maggie was asking if she intended to keep the baby.

"Oh...well, I—" She lowered her head and blinked. Now wasn't the time for tears, or for feeling sorry for herself. She had decisions to make; a clear head was a must. "I have to give this some thought," she said softly. "Some very careful thought."

Caroline drove slowly back to the shop on Water Street, parked in the alley and let herself in the rear door. She made herself a cup of tea—a new flavor they'd just received: maple-vanilla. A few minutes later, Suzanne stepped through the curtain into the back room and found her sitting at the little worktable littered with packaging materials, glitter and reels of satin ribbon—fingering a spool of gold twine.

She crossed the room quickly and pulled a chair up to face Caroline's. "So the doctor verified it—you're pregnant," she stated, having read the verdict in her eyes.

Caroline nodded twice before silently mouthing the word, *Yes*.

"My gosh, when it rains it pours," Suzanne said, patting her own stomach. Then her smile faded. "I wasn't trying to make light of your situation...oh, hell, yes, I was. I want you to be happy, Caroline. I don't know what you intend to do, but...have you even considered that this might be the very best thing that could have happened to you?"

Caroline shook her head. "I don't know what to think," she said numbly. "I swore I wouldn't have another child. If I carry a baby for nine months and give birth to him or her...and something happens again—" She drew in a sharp breath and forcibly blew it out, but the motion didn't lessen the aching tension that tied her insides in knots.

"Did your doctor say anything more about your chances of having another SIDS baby?"

"Maggie told me the same thing she's been saying all along—no guarantees one way or the other."

Suzanne nodded. "Is there any possibility that you and...well, that you and Zach might get together and—"

"I think it's pretty obvious Zach won't be around for this child!" Caroline snapped, flicking the delicate gold cord away from her. "He fought getting involved with me from the beginning. I don't know why I held out hope for so long. I was so sure we were right for each other." But it hadn't been all her, she reminded herself. She remembered Zach breaking down the door at the Greenbriar to get to her, to try to talk her into staying with him. And she recalled the heart-melting gaze of total devotion that shone in his eyes whenever he'd made love to her.

Caroline shook her head. Nothing made sense anymore. But she couldn't hate him, no matter how she tried. "I ordered Zach out of my life," she murmured between stiff lips. "I hurt him deeply, Suzanne. Now he's gone. I doubt very much I'll ever see him again."

Her friend nodded sadly. "Don't you think it's at least fair to tell him about this? I mean, he might surprise you. He might—"

"No!" Caroline cut her off. "I wouldn't want to use my being pregnant to force him to come back to me." She shrugged. "I'd tell him if I knew where he was, though. You're right, it's only fair."

"Paul? His friend from New Haven?"

"I telephoned him from the medical center. The only address he has for Zach is the apartment in my building. He hasn't seen him in months." She hesitated, worrying at her lower lip with her teeth. "Know what?"

"What?"

"I was married to Rob for seven years. *Seven years,* and I never, for even a moment, loved him in the way I loved Zach in the weeks we knew each other. Isn't that incredible? I *loved* that man with all my soul... and now I'm carrying his baby, and he's gone... gone..."

Suzanne squeezed her hands. "I'm so sorry, hon. Sorry it didn't work out... and you've got such a difficult decision to make. Do you want to take some time off? Go somewhere to think?"

Caroline hadn't considered leaving town as an option, but now it sounded like a wise idea. Somehow, she had to clear her head, consider the many implications of her situation... make sure she was doing the right thing—for herself, and for the fragile life she was carrying within her.

Zach stood in the back room of the Silver Whale, stunned by the words he was hearing. Although he'd been right beside Caroline in the obstetrician's office an hour earlier and heard the news first-hand, it hadn't immediately sunk in.

Now it did. Like a demolition ball crashing through a brick wall.

When he'd made love to Caroline in her apartment as she lay half asleep, he didn't use any protection because it simply hadn't occurred to him that an angel was capable of impregnating a woman. The other times they'd been intimate, he'd worn a condom, but that had been only for Caroline's peace of mind—or so he'd thought. Now she was carrying his child and there was no arguing with fact.

Zach stared at Caroline's worry-creased brow, her liquid brown eyes, in horror. He had broken his trust with Heaven. Meher had given him an important job—to protect Caroline North and find for her the ideal husband. Her life mate. The father of her child. With a heavy heart, Zach realized he'd now made that virtually impossible. He had destroyed what little faith Caroline had regained in the male gender, and given her the responsibility of a child she wasn't ready for.

As if destroying her life wasn't bad enough, Zach thought now as he towered over the two women in the back room of the Silver Whale, he had foiled the course of history. Obviously, now that Caroline wasn't carrying the child Meher had intended, her son or daughter couldn't prevent a war, discover a cure, or do any of the miraculous things Meher had hinted at.

And it was *all his fault!* Due to Zachariah Zach Zane Dawson's raging lust for a woman he should never have let into his life—or death—the world would be a poorer place.

Still invisible to the two women, Zach raised his eyes to the open beams of the ceiling, hung with dried herbs. Every muscle in his body grew rigid, every nerve vibrated as he imagined the cool, white mists of Heaven. "Let me come home now," he pleaded fervently. "You can see what a mess I've made of things. Please, take me away from here."

Instead of feeling the gentle breeze of a forest glade against his nonexistent skin, he winced at the frigid, disapproving blast that swept down on him. Was this to be Meher's only answer?

"Come on," he said impatiently. "If you don't replace me now, Caroline is the one who will suffer. I'm already dead, for God's sake!"

Still there was no answer.

Caroline and Suzanne seemed to be unaware of the one-sided argument taking place only a few feet away from the table where they sat, still talking solemnly, quietly.

"Punish *me,* not her!" Zach shouted.

At last, he sensed the familiar rumblings of Meher's voice, which soon grew to a painful roar in his ears. Zach clamped his hands over his ears, as a penetrating chill stole across his soul, dragging him into its icy clutches and tugging him away from the cozy, raftered room behind the little gift shop.

"You will not be welcome until you return to her and make right what you have done!" Meher clearly wasn't pleased with him.

Zach was astounded. "I—I can't do that! Don't you understand? I slept with the woman. I made love to her without any regrets. And you know why? Because I *love* her! I love her more than I thought I could love any living thing on this Earth. But I put my own feelings and desires above what was best for her." Zach drew a ragged breath. "I may not have been a religious man, but I know what I did was wrong. And I can't make her *un*pregnant. So, do with my soul what you will, but I'm begging you to give her a chance. Help her out, Meher!"

"That is *your* job," the Archangel rumbled.

Zach shook his head in dismay. "Then tell me what to do. I don't have a clue."

"Find her," Meher instructed. "Reassure her of your love. Tell her that everything will be well with her. Tell her . . . tell her . . . tell her . . ."

"Tell her what? How is *talking* to her going to help anything?" he demanded.

But the Archangel's words had faded to an absolute, endless silence.

Zach looked around at the little storage room, sensing that something was different . . . wrong. Caroline and Suzanne were no longer at the table. He rushed over to the desk where Suzanne kept a calendar on which she marked deliveries and orders. The last date crossed off was January 24. Three days had passed since Caroline's visit to her doctor. He'd been gone for three whole days . . .

What might have happened during the time he'd lost?

Terrified that Caroline might have already made her decision, Zach envisioned himself in his mortal form and immediately rushed into the showroom of the Silver Whale. Caroline was nowhere in sight. Suzanne was talking with a customer. Zach waited in the back corner for a few minutes, but when the two women didn't seem any closer to ending their conversation, he walked over to them.

"Suzanne, where's Caroline?"

She swung around to face him, a startled expression on her face. "Excuse me," she told the woman. "I'll be right with you."

Grabbing Zach by the arm, she steered him to the far side of the room. "Caroline won't want to see you, Zach."

"She may not want to see me, but I need to talk to her. It's important."

Suzanne chewed her bottom lip, looking torn. Finally she shook her head. "No. She's gone away for a while. And I'm sure she wouldn't want me to tell you where she is. Something important has happened to her and—"

"I *know* about her being pregnant," he declared impatiently. "I know that I'm the father and—"

"*How* do you know?" Suzanne broke in, her eyes narrowing suspiciously. "You couldn't. No one knows except Caroline, me and my husband, Ralph. And he's got enough sense to keep news like that to himself."

"It doesn't matter how I found out. I have to know if she's all right. If the baby—" His heart felt as if it had stopped beating, stopped pumping blood through his body—which only seemed right, since he wasn't really alive anymore. Urgently he grabbed Suzanne's arm. "She hasn't . . . didn't . . ." He couldn't even voice the terrible fear eating its way through him.

"No, she's still pregnant." Suzanne glanced anxiously at her customer, who was beginning to move toward the door, then back to him. "Although, from the things she's told me, I don't know why that would matter to you."

Frustration and anger boiled up inside Zach. Everyone thought the worst of him. But could he blame them? If he'd had a chance during his life to meet Caroline, maybe things would have been different. Maybe he'd have been a better man, seen the value in families, children, the honest and strong love of a woman. But as things stood . . .

"You have to tell me where she is," he growled.

"Sorry, Zach."

He closed his eyes tightly and concentrated. *I want to be with her, Meher. Put me wherever she is.*

Zach opened his eyes, but he was still in the Mystic gift shop.

Suzanne was looking at him, confusion mirrored in her amber eyes. "Listen, Zach," she said hesitantly. "If you hang around long enough for me to telephone her and ask if it's all right . . ."

"She'll never agree to letting me come to her," he said.

"Maybe not." She sighed. "But it's the best I can offer."

Caroline sat in the Jacuzzi, her eyes drifting lightly closed as she let the warm, bubbling water work its magic on her body. After two days at the Greenbriar, she had finally begun to see things clearly. Then Suzanne had called, telling her that Zach was looking for her.

She wished she knew why Zach had tracked her down. He'd refused to explain over the phone. She wasn't foolish enough to believe he'd had a change of heart and intended to surprise her with a marriage proposal. She refused to set herself up for that ultimate disappointment.

Yet Suzanne had said he knew about the baby. And that puzzled her. Did he also know *how* she'd become pregnant, when she couldn't recall their making love without protection? She was curious.

But, Caroline admitted to herself, she also wanted to see Zach again, because there were things she had to say to him that couldn't be expressed in a letter or over the telephone. By confronting him in person, sharing with him her feelings, she sensed she could clear a path for herself to the future . . . one that wouldn't include him, sadly, but one she believed she could handle.

When Suzanne had called her that morning, and Caroline had given her permission to put him on the line, he said he would catch the first local flight to Rutland. She figured that the earliest he could get to Killington was midafternoon. But when she lazily opened her eyes, squinting against the sun's brilliant glare through the windows encircling the Jacuzzi, Zach was standing over her, holding her terry-cloth robe.

"It's been less than two hours since Suzanne telephoned!" she gasped. "How did you—"

"Connections," he said, his voice gruff with an emotion she found impossible to read. His eyes glittered darkly—no longer blue, rather a color she couldn't define. "Do you want to go back to your room to talk, or should we go somewhere for lunch?" he asked.

She stared at him, unprepared for how intensely his presence affected her. Her breath was short, flickers of electricity tingled down low in her body. "Maybe we should just go for a walk," she suggested shakily.

She stood up out of the water, and his glance took in her bathing suit as the warm water sluiced off her flesh. His eyes lingered on her for the few seconds it took her to slip into the robe and wrap it securely around her. "Wait for me in the lobby," she said over her shoulder as she strode quickly out of the spa, hoping her trembling shoulders wouldn't show through the thick robe.

Back in her room, Caroline dressed warmly and tugged a knit cap over her still-damp hair. She didn't particularly care how she looked, didn't bother with makeup. All she wanted from Zach, she reminded herself, was an explanation for what had happened that had gotten her pregnant, then she'd share with him her decision about the baby. After that, she suspected he'd leave, wanting nothing more to do with her. That would fit his usual behavior pattern.

As she locked the room behind her and walked down the floating stairs to the lobby, she braced herself for his farewell speech, knowing that any excuse he offered for not staying with her would be inadequate.

She found him in the downstairs lobby, standing in front of a wide expanse of glass, overlooking the snow-covered, wooded hillside. Vermont had had a record snowfall that winter; a solid three feet covered the flat areas, mounding over five feet in the drifts, creating breathtakingly beautiful scenery.

But it was Zach she couldn't stop staring at. A lock of his caramel blond hair tumbled over his forehead, giving him a lost-little-boy look. His wide shoulders were slumped inside his ski jacket, and he'd dejectedly jammed his hands into his pockets.

"Let's go," she said abruptly, banishing all tenderness from her voice. If she once let her guard down, Caroline knew she'd only fall in love with him all over again. She couldn't afford to let that happen.

Zach gave a short nod and followed her through the door, into the cold. She'd dressed sensibly in her down-filled ski jacket, long underwear beneath her jeans, gloves and hat. He had apparently come prepared, and wore similar gear to shield himself against the cold. They moved in the tidy silence created by a world blanketed in white crystals. Only the packed snow on the partially shoveled path crunching beneath their feet, the whisking sounds of their jacket sleeves against their jackets, and the soft puff of their own breathing broke the muffled silence.

When they were a few hundred feet from the Greenbriar, moving into a wall of silver birch, Zach put out his gloved hand and gently touched her arm. "This is far enough. I have something to tell you."

"Good," she said briskly. "I have questions that need answering."

"I'm not sure I'll be able to answer all of them." His gaze locked with hers, and she found she was unable to break the connection "Maybe I'd better just say what I have to," he whispered, "and hope it's good enough."

She watched him blow a frosty trail from his full lips. As angry as she was with him, she ached to feel his mouth on hers. But she determinedly banished the image from her mind and concentrated on what he was about to say.

"Caroline, I—"

She had been ready for a long-winded confession from him—a typically male dodge like, "I'm just not ready to settle down and raise a family." He might offer her money to help support the baby if she chose to keep it. Or, he might try to force her to get an abortion, to make "the problem" go away. He did the one thing she hadn't been prepared for.

With a groan of surrender, Zach pulled her into his arms, pressing her to his chest with such ferocity, her breath rushed from her lungs.

"Just listen to me. Don't ask questions," he growled, his lips brushing the cold rim of her ear.

She said nothing, wasn't sure she could have gotten in a word if she'd tried, because the words spilled out of him so quickly.

"I can't explain why things have been happening between us, the way they have. All I can say is . . . I love you, Caroline. I love you as I've never loved another woman. If there were any way Heaven could allow us to be together, I would be with you. I would stay with you, and share the happiness of raising the beautiful child we've made, and *I* would be the one to make you happy every day of your life. But there are circumstances I'm helpless to explain, which make our being together impossible."

She started to open her mouth to protest, but he pressed his lips to hers, silencing them.

"No," he gasped, sounding as if the wind had been knocked from him, like a football player who's just been tackled. He pressed a fist to his chest, and his face turned so white she wondered if he was in pain. "Just listen, please. I'm sorry for the way I've messed up your life, and I'll detest myself throughout eternity for hurting you. But I honestly can't say that I regret having loved you, because without knowing you as I've done, looking back on my life would have been a pretty bleak view." He tenderly stroked her cheek with one callused finger. "You are a miracle . . . your baby is a miracle . . . and I love you both, will always love you both. Please consider those truths when you make your decision."

Caroline stared up at him. A glow of selfless love suffused his rugged features. "Zach." She choked out his name, tears brimming over her long eyelashes. "I'd already decided before you called."

The muscle in his jaw throbbed, and her heart went out to him. "And?" he prompted.

"I'm keeping our baby."

Zach's heart soared. Maybe Meher's plans hadn't worked out exactly as the Archangel had planned, but Caroline looked as if she was happy with her decision and, as far as he was concerned, that was all that counted.

"Are you sure?" he asked.

"Absolutely," she whispered against his cheek. "I'm not at all sorry that we met, or that we made love, or that I'm carrying your baby. I've learned I'm strong enough to handle whatever life dishes out. If this child was meant to be born to me, I will do whatever I can to keep it safe. But if, for reasons I can't understand, it's taken from me, like my first baby, I'll have to accept that, too. I certainly can't deny our child a chance to live."

Zach wrapped his arms even more tightly around her. He wanted to hold her there, with him, forever. "Caroline," he whispered hoarsely, "you must believe me—if there were any way I could stay with you, I would. No man could possibly love you more than I do, or take better care of you and your baby." He choked with emotion on the words that were his own, yet sounded so familiar... an echo of those spoken by someone else.

Before he could figure out where or when he'd heard them before, Zach felt himself wrenched out of Caroline's arms. He let out a cry of agony that echoed throughout eternity. If anything had ever felt right to him, it was being with Caroline. Why had Fate so cruelly deceived him? Making him fall in love with her, allowing their union then snatching him from her?

To his surprise, Zach found himself standing on a busy construction site. He looked around, at a loss for an explanation. This certainly wasn't Heaven—might it be the alternative?

Then he knew where he was—Hartford... the Madison Commercial Towers, where he had died in the accident. A lot of things appeared to be different, though. The soaring central tower was no longer a steel skeleton; it was nearly finished, even the tinted windows had been set in place. And there were new faces among the crew. Zach heard Matt Trainer's curt voice from close up, and turned to find his foreman standing within two feet of him.

"Can't thank you enough, Zane, for giving my Chris a job, second summer in a row. It's made a big difference in the boy. He's earned himself a mountain of self-respect working with the crew. Don't even talk to that old crowd of his."

What is going on? Zach wondered frantically. It was as if he'd never died, and another year seemed to have passed. Meher, or his own overactive mind, must be playing tricks on him—allowing him a glimpse of what his life might have been like if he hadn't gotten flattened by a falling generator?

Zach pressed the heels of his hands into his eye sockets. *Stop this insanity,* he thought. *Help me make sense of this!* In the same instant, two images flashed through his mind—Caroline . . . and an enormous black shape hovering over him. Zach looked up.

As if in slow motion, he watched as several links in the chain supporting the generator stretched, strained, then snapped. "Heads up!" Zach bellowed, shoving Matt in the chest and out of harm's way, while he dove in the opposite direction.

An explosive crash shook the ground when the generator landed, digging itself six inches into the packed dirt. Zach looked up from where he'd sprawled in the dirt. There was a moment of stunned silence, then men were rushing across the site, checking on each other, some running toward the crane, others toward Zach.

The operator's face was gray as he scrambled down from his seat and shouted across the yard. "Hey, boss, I'm sorry. I thought— hell, we used that same hitch a dozen times with no problem. I thought she was solid!"

"It's okay," Zach assured him. He looked around to find Matt dusting himself off. "Everyone seems to have made it."

"Man, that was a close one, huh?" Matt muttered, favoring one hip as he moved back toward Zach. "Swear I saw my life pass before me."

"I know what you mean," Zach said.

"Hey, Zane!" one of his men shouted at him. "I thought you were in a rush to leave."

"Leave?" He frowned, looking at his watch. There was no hurry. It was a weekday, only 4:00 p.m.

Then it struck him. The guy had called him *Zane!* So had Matt. Did that mean he was a mortal again? A flash of joy blazed in his heart, before he remembered Caroline again. Had she ever existed? Was she only a dream? Or a test of some kind that he'd had to pass to win back his life?

"Yeah, leave. Boy, are you ever in bad shape." Matt was shaking his gray head at him, chuckling. "You know, for the hospital. Didn't you just get a call from the wife telling you she'd gone into labor?" Matt slapped him on the back, while several men nearby grinned at him sympathetically. "Caroline will never let you forget it if you don't make it to the delivery room in time to welcome your firstborn into the world!"

Zane's mouth gaped open as he stared at the old man. It seemed to take forever for his brain to absorb the full implication of Matt's words. His love for Caroline and the time they'd shared had been real!

He found his work vehicle, a vintage Toyota pickup truck on the construction lot, jumped in and sped across town. As he ran a red light, and squealed around a corner, narrowly avoiding a taxi pulling away from the curb, a sudden, wonderful realization struck him. The man Meher had been seeking for Caroline had been him all along. He, Zane, was the perfect man for her—and it was *their* child who had been destined to be born and grow up to help make a difference in the world—his son or daughter, he thought proudly.

But the Archangel had a real challenge getting them together, since Zach was dead set against marriage and, in the bargain, had died, and Caroline refused to consider giving herself to another man. Zane grinned. Darned if the clever fellow hadn't pulled it off, against all odds.

As for Caroline, he sensed she'd probably never know how they'd come to be together. Not that it mattered now...

Zane pulled into the first parking space he found, not bothering to read signs to determine if it was reserved for the handicapped or physicians. Leaping out of the truck, he crossed the parking lot in long strides and ran through the electric doors straight to the information desk.

"Maternity!" he gasped. "Which way?" He was smiling so hard his face hurt.

"Second floor, all the way to the end of the corridor," the young man behind the desk directed.

Zach bolted up the stairs, not wanting to wait for the elevator. He held out his hands to stop himself from crashing into the nurses' station. "Caroline North!" he shouted, gripping the smooth wooden rail in front of him.

"North?" The woman seated behind the high countertop frowned as she ran a finger down a clipboard of names.

"Dawson! Try Mrs. Dawson." His heart was pounding so hard he thought for sure it would break through his ribs. He thought he must sound like a lunatic.

"You must be Mr. Dawson." The nurse smiled tolerantly at him. "Yes, here she is…in 218, that's the labor and delivery suite right over there." She pointed, but Zane was already bounding across the hall. He flung open the door and jerked to a halt in front of a bedlike contraption that had been cranked into sitting position.

Caroline was propped up in it, and she turned her head and smiled so sweetly at him, his heart warmed inside his chest. Her hair was the same soft brown, but it was longer, smoothing over the narrow shoulders of her pale green hospital gown. "Hello, darling," she murmured. "I see you made it."

"Yeah…yeah, I did." He took two shaky steps toward her and grasped one of her hands in his.

"The contractions are every three minutes now. It may not be long. The doctor will be right back."

"Good," he said. "Good."

Her fingers felt small and moist as they curled trustingly around his, squeezing harder as she puffed rhythmically to ease the pain and rode the wave of a contraction. He gazed at her with awe.

"I have to tell you something…something *very* important," he sputtered, touching his lips to her fingertips. "I love you, Caroline. I love you very, very much."

"I know, darling," she whispered, "I know. And I love you, too. But we have work to do now. Will you tell me again later?"

"Yes," he promised, stroking a wisp of hair out of her shining eyes, "every day of your life."

* * * * *

COMING NEXT MONTH

Take 4 bestselling love stories FREE

Plus get a FREE surprise gift!

Bestselling Author

MAGGIE SHAYNE

Continues the twelve-book series—FORTUNE'S CHILDREN—
in **January 1997** with Book Seven

A HUSBAND IN TIME

Jane Fortune was wary of the stranger with amnesia who
came to her—seemingly out of nowhere. She couldn't deny
the passion between them, but there was something
mysterious—almost dangerous—about this compelling
man…and Jane knew she'd better watch her step….

MEET THE FORTUNES—a family whose legacy is greater than
riches. Because where there's a will…there's a *wedding!*

Look us up on-line at: http://www.romance.net   FC-7

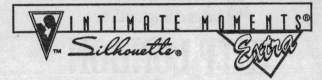

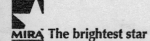

You're About to Become a *Privileged Woman*

Reap the rewards of fabulous free gifts and benefits with proofs-of-purchase from Silhouette and Harlequin books

Pages & Privileges™

It's our way of thanking you for buying our books at your favorite retail stores.

PROOF OF PURCHASE
Offer expires March 31, 1997
SIM-PP21

Harlequin and Silhouette— the most privileged readers in the world!

For more information about Harlequin and Silhouette's PAGES & PRIVILEGES program call the Pages & Privileges Benefits Desk: 1-503-794-2499

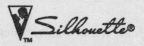

SIM-PP21